DRAGON CLASS

RIDERS OF JADE & FIRE BOOK 1

MELANIE ANSLEY

WRITING ROOSTER MEDIA

For my parents.

CHAPTER 1

If she had known what she was about to steal, she would have cut off her right arm before going through with it.

But Wang Kway Jin thought she was simply targeting a carriage full of unimaginable riches. She and the Red Crows had staked the inn at the crossroads for days now, in case their quarry came early. But, no, as Jin and Lu had overheard during their last job, the Dragon Class convoy landed at the remote inn on the fourth day, only one day after schedule.

Jin had watched the six riders descend with their dragons, the three largest beasts carrying transport carriages with doors on either side. The riders dismounted, bantering with each other as they unstrapped the safety harnesses that held the carriages to the massive bronze dragons.

Jin knew precious little of dragons, except that they

had keen hearing, sight, and, of course, dangerous jaws that breathed fire. So she watched, amazed, as the bronze ones shrank before her eyes to the size of the other three. She had never been this close to the beasts —besides that night at the viceroy's mansion.

Her jaw tightened, remembering. Since then, she had gone over her actions one by one, thinking ruefully about how she could have diverted the fates multiple times if only she had changed one small decision. If she and her partner Lu had not stolen a pipe they knew their archrival gang, the Iron Hawks, had been targeting, if only they hadn't run into the same Iron Hawks on the way home and killed one of them in self-defense, then they wouldn't have sparked a deadly clan war. And she wouldn't now be here, trying to redeem herself with her clan boss, Haitao.

Tonight, the Red Crows would steal this priceless treasure and frame the Iron Hawks so the empire would destroy them. If tonight succeeded, then the Red Crows would be the dominant thief clan in Gaozho. Haitao would give Lu his freedom as promised and would forgive Jin for starting a clan war. Depending on what they stole, perhaps he'd even make her his right-hand thief.

One of the transport carriage's doors opened, interrupting her thoughts, and three men emerged. She couldn't see their faces well, but one seemed tall and commanding in well-tailored trousers and vests, and another shorter but broad as an ox, with graying hair.

The third wore rich purple robes from head to foot, a hood obscuring his face.

A mage.

Though she had heard the inn's kitchen staff speak of magic being used to keep the dragons in check overnight, the knot of anxiety in her tightened. Jin preferred tangible obstacles to intangible ones.

Another carriage's door opened, and half a dozen soldiers in royal guard uniforms emerged, all armed. Riders began unsaddling their dragons, grumbling about the weather and the paltry food in these parts.

She scanned the surrounding trees. As she nestled in the crook of an ancient camphor, her black and brown pants along with her green cloak made her nearly invisible in the foliage. Her hood kept her light brown *huren*, or foreign, hair covered, and a scarf roped around her neck would hide her features if she pulled it over her nose. Hopefully none of the dragonriders would notice her round, distinctly huren eyes, but if they did, they'd probably think her one of the many mixed-race mercenaries or local thieves. Three of her Red Crow companions had planted themselves in the fir trees around her. The fourth and youngest, Mukang, had managed to work his way into the inn's kitchens days before.

She watched the grooms lead the dragons away from the stables, the mage following. The dragons would be kept in the pasture on the opposite side of the inn, where the innkeeper had already cleared all livestock and locked them away in secure stone pens to keep them safe from the large-winged guests.

But that didn't mean death didn't come for the animals anyway. At least twelve pigs had been slaughtered, and the ignorant traveler would have assumed this was for a large feast, for the guesthouse had been booked out a day in advance, with anyone needing to stay the night politely turned away. But the slaughter was to feed six dragons who had traveled far and carried something priceless.

The riders folded away the safety straps, and the tall man reached in and removed an oblong metal box with a handle. There were no locks on the carriage doors, which gave Jin pause. Valuables would not be kept in unlocked carriages. The riders flanked the first three men who had dismounted, while the soldiers began unloading traveling trunks from the other carriage. Inn servants rushed forward to help, hauling the trunks by their handles. One servant reached for the tall man's box but was clearly rebuffed.

The innkeeper came hurrying out to greet the guests, his robes of silk and red cotton flapping behind him. He bowed deeply to the thickset man and his tall, regal companion while clearly trying to keep his distance from the mage. The innkeeper gestured toward the inn, his words floating up on the late summer breeze but still incomprehensible from where Jin sat. She watched the soldiers pull out two long poles stored in slots beneath each carriage floor, then slide them through a row of metal rungs along either side of the vehicles. The dozen servants shouldered the poles and hefted the carriages to the stables as the riders headed for the inn door.

Were they going to leave the carriages unguarded? Haitao, the head of the Red Crows, had tried every informant he had, but no one could discover exactly what the precious cargo was.

A laugh sounded from near the inn. She looked to see the thickset man and his companion, still holding the box, disappear inside.

The box.

That must be the cargo. Inn servants had moved all the other trunks, but the man let no one touch his metal box. The treasure was much smaller than they had anticipated, and therefore instead of being guarded in the carriage as they had predicted, the item would be kept in the inn.

She was glad she had insisted she and Lu pose as guests to scout the interior beforehand, for now they'd have to break in to reach their prize.

The mage stood before the dragons, arms outstretched, chanting. The creatures paid him little mind, focused instead on snapping amongst themselves for the choicest spots to bed down. The hooded figure abruptly stopped, then turned and headed back toward the lodgings. Jin had learned from the inn's kitchen gossip the last few days that magic would keep the beasts from wandering the grounds and attacking livestock. At least she and her team could lift the treasure without having to deal with dragons.

She looked to where Lu was positioned on the far side of the pasture. The man was seven years her senior and the leader of tonight's expedition. He was the closest thing to a brother she had, and she wanted this to succeed—for both their sakes.

Jin could see no sign of Little Mole. The forty-odd-year-old man, nicknamed for the goji-sized mole at the base of his nose, had two crates of oranges ready near the pastures to distract the dragons if needed—for the beasts apparently found the fruits irresistible.

Night deepened, and servants emerged to hang lanterns in the cool air. Autumn would come early this year, judging by how quickly the day chilled with the sun's disappearance. The assigned night guards appeared, lighting pipes that glowed in the dusk. Jin watched as they made themselves comfortable at the entrance.

A few moments later, the inn door opened, and a young, wiry boy of fifteen came out bearing pastries. There were the customary polite refusals before each guard accepted and took appreciative bites. The boy retreated into the inn.

Well done, Mukang.

The dragons snorted and growled as they bedded down in the pasture. Their feeding had clearly made them drowsy. Likewise, the music and shouts of laughter from the inn were slowly fading.

When the sound of crickets overwhelmed the sound of chatter from inside the inn, Jin scanned the surrounding trees. She waited, expectant. At last, there came the short call of a nighthawk. Then two more. Everyone was ready. And Lu had, like her, realized that their objective was inside the inn.

She slid down her tree, her felt-booted feet finding the limbs easily. She dropped to the ground like a cat and listened, waiting for signs that the dragons had awoken or had caught her scent.

Hearing nothing, she looked toward the guards. One of them was already slouched unconscious against the wall, and the other was struggling against the poppy milk Mukang had folded into the pastry.

She paused behind a tree and saw Lu's bulky frame, also descended from his perch. She stole a look around the trunk. Both guards were now asleep.

The inn door opened to reveal the boy Mukang. At his signal, both Lu and Jin hurried over, slipping past the door. Inside, the reception room was shuttered and dark but for one lantern hanging on a hook from the ceiling.

Mukang closed the door behind them and dropped a wooden key into Jin's hand. He pointed at the ceiling, then held up eight fingers, followed by one. Eighth room. One guard on patrol.

Lu gave Mukang's hair a brotherly tousle, then followed Jin to the staircase. The inn had twenty-two rooms, with the eighth room upstairs being the largest.

They mounted the stairs, careful to avoid the ones they knew groaned.

On the second-floor landing, they waited for the single patrolling guard to turn a corner. They then hastened down the inky corridor until they reached the eighth door.

Jin slid the key in, careful to make as little noise as possible. They had instructed Mukang to oil all the guest room hinges the day before, and now she and Lu slid into the room and shut the door behind them without a sound.

A canopied bed loomed to her right, while a dresser and washstand occupied the left. Carpet silenced their footfalls as they walked forward, and the open shutters on the far end allowed enough light for Jin to spot the oblong box.

It sat nestled in an open trunk of clothes. Jin looked toward the bed, but the shadowy occupant didn't stir.

She stole forward and lifted the box, surprised at how light it was, given it was the length of her forearm and made of metal. A padlock held the lid closed. Lu rummaged through the trunk of robes to make sure they hadn't been decoyed, but Jin elbowed him. This box held whatever was so precious to the empire. She was sure of it.

"Put that down."

Both of them froze at the quiet, aristocratic voice. The two thieves turned.

The tall man from the carriage, wearing only his

inner robes, stood blocking the door, a long sword held ready in one hand. Shadows obscured his face, but his stance was sure, and Jin had to admire his silence.

Lu grabbed the wooden wash basin and hurled it. Jin tried to use the diversion to slip around the man to the door, but he was one step ahead of her. He blocked the basin with one arm so it crashed to the floor, then timed an expert kick that sent Jin stumbling.

The man grabbed her on her fall, but his hand slipped as she twisted, hitting her breast instead. He hesitated for half a breath, seemingly stunned at battling a woman. She took the opportunity to drive her fist into his chin. He staggered back with a surprised curse, but already, shouts and cries of alarm were spreading. They'd soon be outnumbered.

"Jump!" Lu shouted. The man launched himself at Lu, but Lu dove for the box. He lifted it, then ran and heaved it with both hands out the open window.

"No!" the man shouted, rushing them.

Lu pulled Jin with him, and before she understood his plan, they were flying out the window as well. Just before her feet hit the hard surface, Jin remembered this wall faced onto the inn's garden shed. They landed with a clatter of tiles on the shed roof, then scrabbled over its edge and onto the ground, where the box lay intact, its padlock unharmed.

"You could have broken it!" Jin cried, scrambling to her feet.

"I didn't have many options!"

Jin grabbed the box handle and ran, Lu following. The sound of a crash made her glance back. The man from the room had pursued them onto the shed roof, then the ground, and was now giving chase.

They rounded the corner to the front of the inn and the crossroads, where the welcome sight of a two-horse carriage greeted them. Fox held the reins while, next to him, Little Mole motioned for them to hurry.

Jin and Lu put in a burst of speed as the inn doors flew open and dragonriders spilled out.

They had nearly reached the carriage when the surrounding air seemed to crackle and a stream of fire slammed into the back of the carriage like some giant fist. The wood paneling popped as the flames billowed through the windows and the terrified horses ripped the reins from Fox's grasp and bolted. Jin spied the dragons, now all very much awake, one of them open jawed, smoke seeping from between its teeth.

The flaming carriage disappeared around the bend in the road, Fox and Mole with it. The mage's spell had kept the dragons from wandering but clearly didn't stop them from breathing flame. And Little Mole's oranges had clearly run out.

"The stables!" Jin cried. She couldn't afford to worry about Little Mole and Fox now. "There'll be other horses!"

She and Lu sprinted back the way they had come, toward the stables. The tall man spotted them and shouted for the soldiers. Jin and Lu reached the stables and bolted the doors just as riders arrived and began trying to break it down.

The stables had a meager collection of a dozen horses, and Jin and Lu had come too far to leave empty-handed or get caught. She began pulling a bridle over an ash-colored stallion while Lu did the same on a tan mare.

"You've trapped yourselves!" a voice boomed from outside. "Might as well surrender now!"

They paused, listening. This was not the tall man. The stocky one? Jin and Lu worked even faster on the buckles.

"The mages have unleashed the dragons!" the same voice shouted. "We'll burn the stables down if we have to. Out!"

Jin yanked the last strap on the horse and saw Lu's grim expression.

"They're bluffing," he whispered. "Did you see that man's face when I threw the box? They don't want that thing harmed."

She nodded, thinking hard. "Lu," she hissed, "if they have the dragons unleashed, we can free the other horses and escape with them. But we have to split their attention. You go north, I'll go west."

He nodded. "Meet at the caves. Remember the fall-back plan."

They cut all the ropes holding the other horses in place, the animals already panicked at the sound of dragons and the stench of fire.

"Ready?" Lu asked, one hand on the stable door and the other holding his mare's bridle.

Jin swung herself onto the stallion's back, hugging the box to her with one arm and holding the reins with the other. She nodded.

Lu shoved the doors open, letting go and slapping Jin's stallion on the flank before mounting his own. The horses bolted forward into the moonlight. Surprised shouts erupted as the soldiers tried to find the thieves amongst the horses, and the riders tried to keep their dragons from snapping up the fleeing animals. Lu broke out of the mass and headed north as agreed, drawing several soldiers and riders with him.

Jin steered her stallion toward the trees to the west, the box balanced in front of her and the thunder of hooves and flame behind her.

The trees would now be her only protection against fire-breathing dragons. She needed to reach the forest's cover. And stay alive.

CHAPTER 2

It was only when dawn broke that Jin allowed the frothing horse to slow to a canter, and then a walk, the box still pinned in Jin's stiff arm. They were in the forest paths, where no dragon could find them. Though mounted soldiers could.

She mulled over her conversation with Lu when they had been out late in the streets of Gaozho, on one of their patrols to ensure the Iron Hawks were not trespassing. The mood between the two clans had reached fire-hot levels in the hours after she'd killed the Iron Hawk man in self-defense, and it would have taken little more than a dragon's belch to ignite a war.

"You know this can go wrong, right?" Lu had said.

"That's usually what *I* tell *you*, not the other way around, big brother."

He had nodded, seeming distracted. "If it goes wrong, and we need to cut ties with Haitao, then meet me at the caves due west of the inn. I'll go there to find you."

"But it won't go wrong," Jin had insisted. "You've been careful, haven't you?"

Lu nodded. "But only fools and gods have no back-up plans. As the master of war says, when the enemy has option one and option two, plan on them choosing option three."

They hadn't spoken of it after that, and Jin had hoped that they wouldn't have to go to option three. But here she was, aching and exhausted, climbing the rugged track through wild bamboo and shrub to the caves.

They knew of these caves from their early training days, for Haitao brought his student thieves here to get them accustomed to deprivation. He had left Jin in one of the lower caves with no food or water, to see if she could survive three days until he returned for her. For three days, Jin trapped snakes and rodents for food. She had earned Haitao's respect, if one could call it that.

She dropped the box to the ground, then dismounted from the horse. In the dawn light, she saw a mark on the beast's flank. Where Lu had slapped the horse was a bright red handprint.

Blood.

Jin didn't need to check herself to realize it wasn't hers. She would have noticed an injury by now, even in her shock. Her throat tightened. Was it Lu's blood? He may have been injured in the roof leap and not informed her.

She picked up the box with her other arm and frowned. Was she imagining it? The box seemed heavier than it did the night before. She blamed this on her exhaustion and tugged at the horse's bridle, more determined than ever to reach the caves. He would be there. He simply had to be.

But when she arrived, there was no sign of him. The box was most definitely growing heavier by the minute, which made no sense. She gratefully put the box down and brought the exhausted horse in to tether his reins around a heavy rock. She needn't have worried, however, as the stallion was so tired that he could barely run if he tried. He was favoring a foreleg, and when she inspected the hoof, she found an acorn wedged there. She pried it out with much soothing of the horse and let the beast limp away from her. She was now foot bound, at least until the horse recovered.

Jin looked over at the box, and a sudden rage at the contents gripped her. She might never see Lu, Mukang, or anyone else from her thief clan again because of this. She was glad she had only taken a small team to the heist and hoped that some of them had escaped. Fox and Mole might have abandoned the carriage and escaped. Perhaps no one else in the clan would be implicated.

Jin tried to move the box further into the cave, but now found it so heavy she could barely lift it off the floor. Was it magic? She eyed the lock on it, deliberating. Making up her mind, she found a nearby rock and began smashing the sharpest edge against the latch. It took several goes, but the metal gave way, and she tossed the broken lock to one side, then lifted the lid.

She stared in confusion. She wasn't sure what she was expecting, but this was not it.

The box was padded in thick silk, and nestled in it was what looked like a rock, pale gray and speckled with white. Veins of light jade ran through it, which suggested precious material. But otherwise, it was an oval rock. A lumpy, oval rock that clearly hadn't come under any stone smith's tools yet.

She touched it and pulled back, alarmed. It was warm. This was no rock. She reached out again, her heart thudding in dread, and let her fingers run over the rough surface.

No, that was not rock. It was shell.

Which meant this was an egg.

She sat, dumbfounded. They had stolen an egg. And an egg this size could only be a dragon's. She rubbed her temples, mind racing. This was not just bad, this was terrible. They had robbed the imperial army of a dragon, something more priceless than any jewel or diamond. She stood, hope sinking. They couldn't sell a dragon's egg. Selling a dragon's egg was the quickest way to land in the tea rooms with the police, for no one but Empress Wu and her Dragon Class could own dragons, or their eggs. This thing was priceless yet worthless.

She paced the cave, her insides in a knot. Where was Lu? She walked to the mouth of the cave, hoping he would magically come in, uninjured, boasting about all the soldiers he'd defeated. But there was no sign of him. Nor were there sounds of anything else but the wind in the bamboo and the caws of birds nearby.

Jin turned back to the egg as if it would poison her by sight alone. She put a hand to it again. Was it just her, or did it feel hotter? Was there a way to tell if an egg was about to hatch? Cursed if she knew. She wanted to give Lu time to appear, but she didn't want to be anywhere near a newborn dragon.

Her heart squeezed, but she had to act. In the coming days, she could return and check to see if Lu showed, but she couldn't stay here—especially as the box had become too heavy to move.

She cut the horse free from its bridle. With its white coat and lame leg, she couldn't afford to have it with her. She'd be better off on foot, and the horse would likely find his own way home.

She stepped outside.

Stay.

She wasn't sure whether she simply imagined the word in her head, but something made her pause at the entry.

She turned. The egg still sat there in its box, its surface unmarred. She started out of the cave again, but something pulled at her, making her turn around. She stared into the shadows, wary.

"Who's there?"

There was no answer, and she berated herself for her foolishness. The cave was empty but for the box and the rock-like egg.

Something drew her to it. She stood, contemplating the thing. Despite her better judgment, she rested a hand on the top of the shell, feeling its warmth.

"Good luck, beast," she murmured, then turned to leave.

And that's when she heard it: soft, like the snap of a twig underfoot, but distinct.

Warily, she knelt by the egg and heard tapping from inside. A long sliver worked its way down the egg's surface. Something like a pulse pushed at the crack, and then tiny claws grasped the opening, pulling the shell inward. A slimy snout wedged its way out, followed by a scaled head.

She watched, mesmerized, as the thing emerged, covered in birth webbing and skeins of blood. It was pale green flecked with white, and a line of ridges ran along its back. It mewled, and two eyelids swept open, revealing deep yolk-colored eyes that shone even in the cave's dark.

Jin instinctively reached toward it, helping it slither on wet legs up and over the box edge, its tail whipping to dislodge the last of the shell. It was the size of a large domestic cat, even with its long tail, and small wings unfolded like ungainly stumps from its side. A muted humming began in her head, and she squirmed, alarmed.

Calm. Be calm.

She took a breath, and soon the humming was everywhere around her, almost exploratory, as the dragon looked her over and then opened its mouth again and gave a throaty chirp.

Rayshan.

Or at least she thought it said it, for she couldn't hear anything aloud. It seemed to be in her head, coming from a distance.

I am Rayshan, it said, more forcefully this time, and Jin somehow intuited the dragon was male. *Your name. I want to learn your name.*

"Jin," she managed to say. "Wang Kway Jin."

The dragon cocked his head and pressed a snout into her hand. *Jin. Gold. Kway . . . precious.*

"Yes," she whispered, surprised the dragon knew the meaning of her name. Then, experimentally, she said in her mind, *Can you hear me even if I don't speak?*

The dragon inhaled, nostrils flared, then hooked his tail around her ankle, like a cat.

Of course. We are bonded.

Her thoughts stuttered to a halt.

Bonded? She did not know what that meant, except that it sounded very permanent. Yet before she could think about what she was doing, she had slid a palm around the dragon's neck and wiped away the remaining birth slime. Rayshan hummed contentedly, placing his claws upon her lap. And though the claws hurt, she didn't mind.

"Are you hungry?" she asked. Why did the dragon's well-being seem of utmost importance to her? She should be gone, not here wishing she had meat, or at least the means to bring down a hare.

The dragon rumbled, turning around in the cave and sniffing the air. *Famished. . . . I can smell food. All types. From outside.*

She'd find food, then deal with the rest later, she told herself. "I'll find some. You must stay here, Rayshan. Do you promise?"

The dragon arched his back, stretching his wings experimentally. *I will wait.*

She nodded, still worried. Despite his claws and the row of sharp teeth lining his gums, she worried he was fragile and helpless. But it doesn't matter. You can't take care of it, she reminded herself. Find food, then leave.

The humming sounded worried. *You want to leave me here?*

"No, I won't." She'd forgotten he could seemingly read her thoughts. "I'll return soon."

He gave a soft, worried whine.

"I promise."

This seemed to calm him. She went to exit the cave but stopped. Something was wrong. She smelled smoke, which wasn't right, for she hadn't lit a fire, and the dragon smelled of blood and birth fluid. Which could only mean—

A blast of wind knocked her back against the wall, beating the air from her lungs. She coughed as she scrambled to her feet, and the newly hatched dragon leapt in front of her, teeth bared in an admirable act of ferocity. Its head ridges stood in a display of bone that made it seem twice its size.

Two dragons, one gold and one bronze, landed on the ledge of the cave, the bronze bearing a transport carriage. Half a dozen men swarmed in, swords drawn and bows nocked. They all bore the imperial insignia on their vests, and her gut twisted. The empire had found her, which meant she was as good as dead.

CHAPTER 3

The men fanned into a semi-circle, making escape impossible.

Two passengers emerged from the carriage. The first was the older, stocky man from the inn, who limped in one leg. Seeing him clearly, Jin couldn't suppress a shudder. He was a huren, but at first glance she thought him half statue, half man. The left side of his face was a marbled white, extending past his collar to unknown parts of his body, and his left eye was a cream-colored orb with no pupil. He wore black gloves, and a thick necklace bearing the Dragon Class seal hung around his neck.

The tall man she and Lu had fought stepped down after him, a darkening bruise marring an otherwise handsome face. He was now in fine-cut leathers, his thick black hair knotted in a warrior's bun on the top of his head. He had an aura of dignity despite the discolored jaw.

The huren with the white skin shifted his gaze from the snarling dragon to Jin and back. She couldn't tell if his afflicted eye could see.

"Mother of Buddha, it's a—"

The huren held up a hand, and the soldier who had spoken fell silent.

"I believe you have something of ours," the huren said. The white side of his face seemed atrophied, resulting in slurred speech.

Tell him I won't go, Rayshan said to Jin. At her hesitation, he insisted, *Just say it.*

"He says he won't go," Jin said, voice soft.

The man with the bruise frowned. "Who says?"

"The dragon." At their silence, she added, "His name is Rayshan."

Bruise stole a glance at the dragon while the huren snapped, "Who do you work for?"

Jin tensed. She would not rat out her clan, she had that much in her. She steeled herself, and as if sensing her distress, the dragon hissed at them all before backing against Jin, his ridges raised.

"It's bonded to her, Master Emar." Bruise stepped forward, his expression more surprised than hostile, given she had punched him the night before. "And she hadn't any idea what she was stealing." He gestured toward the broken lock. "Unless she's an idiot, she wouldn't be fool enough to open this if she knew what was inside."

Jin bristled at the insult but stayed quiet. He wasn't wrong.

The huren with the skin affliction, Master Emar, ignored his companion and asked again. "She might have decided to steal from her own employer. Who do you work for, girl? Tell me now and I will show leniency."

Still, she stayed silent.

Emar stepped forward, but paused as Rayshan snapped his jaws. Despite being less than an hour old, the dragon could still harm, if not kill, the man.

The huren drew his blade with his right hand. "I'm giving you a last chance. Who do you work for?"

"No one," she said. That wasn't a lie. Now that she had fled and the operation at the inn had failed, she could never return to Haitao. The realization hit her for the first time. She was adrift, untethered, which left her with cold fear. There was nothing to hold on to.

You have me, Rayshan said.

The words buoyed her momentarily.

"If she has bonded to the dragon, then the empress must know," Bruise said, examining her with a frown.

"You seriously believe a dragon has bonded to a girl, Your Highness?" the one named Emar asked incredulously.

Your Highness? That meant royalty, at the very least a cousin or nephew of the empress. Bruise was a royal.

Jin had struck a royal. Her throat closed at what punishment this would bring.

"How else do you explain that she still has both her hands?" the royal countered. "A Jade is too precious to lose, Master Emar. We'll take them both back and let the empress decide."

Master Emar seemed sorely torn but then gave an impatient snort. "Very well. No one speaks of this to anyone outside this group. Keep them under close guard. We will journey back to the imperial city tonight."

Before she could defend herself, the royal said to her, "I advise you not to fight. You will only get both of you killed, and despite everything you've done, I think none of us wants that. Besides, the dragon needs to eat, and we have food."

That, more than anything else, decided Jin's actions. Jin cautiously rose out of her defensive crouch and came forward. A soldier went to grab her, but a snarl from Rayshan stopped him. They watched her, swords still drawn, as she stepped out of the cave and took in all the soldiers surrounding them.

"We will need a cage for the dragon, and the girl shall ride with us back to the other group," the royal said to Emar, who had re-sheathed his sword.

Emar rubbed at the white patch near his hairline, pensive. "We'd best leave now."

While two soldiers hurried to obey, another trussed Jin's hands together. At her glare, he muttered, "You're lucky you're alive. I wouldn't complain."

They brought a bamboo crate and prodded Rayshan into it, then led her to the transport carriage strapped to the bronze dragon. The beast towered over them, and the ridges on its head flexed upward as it sniffed at her and the baby dragon. Though Rayshan snapped from his cage, this only elicited a grunt from the elder one, who promptly knocked Rayshan off his feet with one blast of air from his nostrils.

She climbed into the carriage, holding Rayshan's cage with her bound hands. Two rows of cushioned seats lined the inside, with enough room to seat twelve people at a squeeze. She warily sat down opposite Emar and the royal. The dragon's wings spread out, and then they were airborne, in a burst of speed that left Jin's stomach lurching.

She clutched Rayshan's crate to her and tried to ignore her fear, noticing that Bruise—the royal—was studying her intently.

"What's your name?"

"Jin," she said.

"Jin, Your Highness," Emar growled.

"Jin, Your Highness," she amended. Rayshan turned around, trying to get comfortable in the small cage on her lap.

"Well, I did not expect to be fighting a woman last night, Jin," His Highness said. "You're not of Han stock. What's your background?"

"I don't know." At Emar's look, she hastily added, "Your Highness."

The younger man gauged her, as if judging whether she was lying.

"I grew up on the streets and never met my parents. Your Highness."

"This just gets better," Emar grunted. "My name's Emar Kul. I oversee all Dragon Class recruits and our dragons. This is His Highness Prince Tai. If you want to live, then do as I say and when I say it. Understood?"

She said nothing, still digesting the knowledge that she had struck a prince, and he barked, "Understood?"

"Understood," she said. She debated whether to ask if Prince Tai was from the empress's own family or merely a distant relative with the title of prince, but just then the carriage landed with a jolt. Tai opened the door and leapt out immediately while Emar motioned for Jin to follow.

She gripped Rayshan's cage, examining him.

I am fine, he reassured her. *And one day I will soar like this dragon.*

They landed in a rocky clearing at the base of the caves where the other four dragons and remaining soldiers awaited. There were greetings and explanations, shouted orders as the men hurried to prepare for departure. Jin watched the prince and Emar board their carriage. Then she, Rayshan, and three of the burlier soldiers were ushered to another that had been cleared to make room for them.

They flew through the night, and Jin fell asleep against the side of the vehicle out of sheer exhaustion, waking when dawn bloomed through the latticed windows. Jin pulled herself up and looked at the countryside passing below. She wished she could share the excitement radiating from Rayshan, who was already awake and making tight circles in his cage. Now that she thought about it, she realized there was a tendril of excitement winding through her, and yet it wasn't hers. She looked down at Rayshan, who lolled his tongue at her.

Peace upon your morning, he greeted her.

I can sense your emotions, she said. How was this possible?

And I can sense yours.

She let the excitement in and immediately understood every grain of his elation. The freedom up here, with the sound of the dragon's wings beating above them, the view of the lands below, were all unlike anything she had experienced before. Through the carriage's windows, Jin saw dragons flying in a wedge around them, with two in front and three behind. They regularly swapped places in some drill only they understood, so that another dragon took the lead and another fell behind. Like birds, Jin thought.

Great fire-breathing birds, Rayshan snorted through their connection.

The dragon carrying them banked, then swooped, and Jin couldn't help but give a shout of alarm. The rider's laughter drifted down to her, and she craned her neck but could not see him. He shouted something, but the words were lost in the rush of wings and wind.

They flew for most of the day, stopping once for food and drink. Jin and Rayshan were let out for the briefest of times to stretch their legs, in a field she didn't recognize. She wondered if they had already left the province she knew. Having never traveled anywhere else in the empire, she now gazed out, curious, at her surroundings. The mountains here grew gentler, lusher, and the crops had become richer and heavier. She had heard that crops in the South grew unbidden, without being coaxed.

Jin and Rayshan were forced to sit chained, but at least he had respite from the cage. She kept an eye out for a means of escape. But the guards kept her hands bound even during meals, and the soldiers accompanying her stayed within arms' length at all times. Even when she asked to relieve herself, one of them held a chain attached to her ankle, looking away only when she threatened to hold it in and soil the carriage seats on their next flight.

She couldn't predict what would happen to her and Rayshan in the capital, but she saw no point in troubling the dragon, so she tried to talk about something else.

Jade dragons are rare, I take it.

Rayshan's tail whipped back and forth. *Very.*

Is it just your color that makes you different?

No. All dragons have a specific power.

Jin thought of the bronze dragons carrying them. *Like how those bronzes can grow and shrink?*

Yes.

Before Jin could ask further, one of the soldiers shoved a serving of food toward her: balls of rice and dried vegetables, some mutton jerky to be wrapped in flatbread. As they ate, Jin studied the dragonrider who flew their bronze. He was thick-boned, with coarse hair and small eyes that always followed his dragon. Some distance away, she noticed Emar talking heatedly with Prince Tai.

Catching her look, the bronze dragonrider transporting Jin grinned, but it wasn't friendly. "You robbed the wrong people, street rat."

She stiffened but said nothing. Most people dropped information when left to prattle on.

"This dragon was meant to be bonded to the king of Khitan, you know." The rider looked at Rayshan, who was tearing into a chunk of mutton. The other dragons were ranged around, similarly occupied with the goats the riders had bought from the surrounding farmers, who were obliged to relinquish livestock as needed. "And now there will be hell to pay."

"My companions will find me and come for me." Jin wanted to see if the rider would hint at any survivors or prisoners who were not with them. *Please, give me hope that Lu escaped.*

The rider gave her an incredulous look. "Even if any

were alive, they would be fools to come for you. You, girl, are on the short path to death if you're lucky."

"And if I'm not?"

The rider smirked. "Then it's the salt mines."

Dread rippled through her, and Rayshan hummed, anxious. Not wanting to distress the dragon further, Jin decided not to dwell on the prospect of slavery in the notorious salt mines. She spied the mage stepping out of the carriage that Emar rode, bearing a wooden box. Almost all mages were educated in the capital, she knew, and expensive to hire. Some provincial nobles kept one or two in their employ, but common folk had little dealings with them.

"Never seen a mage, eh, peasant?" The rider made a bemused noise.

Jin watched as Emar sat down stiffly on a rock while the mage moved his hands over Emar's white skin, chanting in a guttural monotone.

"What's wrong with that man's skin? And eye?" Jin asked.

A mixture of pity and fear flickered across the rider's face. "It's the white death."

"The what?"

"When a dragon dies, his rider starts dying too. Eventually the white death takes all of him." The rider stood abruptly, clearly unwilling to elaborate, and began gathering his things.

Jin looked over at Rayshan, busy cleaning his scales in the dirt, the realization sinking in.

If he dies, I die a slow death, like Emar. The thought made her lose interest in her food, but it didn't matter, for the soldiers escorting her instructed her to finish up. As she did, she was unnerved to catch the prince watching her, thoughtful.

"Let's fly," Emar shouted, raising his right fist in the air. The dragonriders finished the last of their food and hurried to ready saddles and tack. Jin's captors from her carriage motioned for her and Rayshan to board. They flew on for four days, passing over fields and rivers, gorges, and valleys terraced into steps ready for the rice harvest.

Jin took in every detail about the other dragonriders around them when she could. She noticed they used hand signals and colored flags at their armbands to communicate, as up here sounds were drowned out by distance and wind.

Can each rider only hear his own dragon? Jin asked.

Yes. We can only speak with those we bond with, Rayshan replied. *And we dislike anyone but our riders speaking to us. It's rude.*

She looked over toward the prince's carriage flying alongside. What was he doing without a dragon of his own? Emar's dragon had died, but she would have expected a prince with the convoy to have a dragon. Were there rules against princes bonding with dragons? She didn't know, but she had more pressing issues to think of—like her life being at stake.

CHAPTER 4

Jin's breath caught as she spied her first glimpse of Changan. The air above the empire's capital was cloudy with the smoke and steam of over a million people—the biggest city in the empire, if not the world. This was the city of emperors and slaves, of gods and demons. This was the beating heart of the Middle Kingdom.

Changan spread out in a grid, as organized as a checkerboard. Wide canals choked with boats and barges of all kinds cut through the city, two running east to west and another two running north to south, connecting with grand canals that Jin had heard of but never seen. These canals ran grain, tribute, and other goods to every corner of the empire. Haitao had shared stories of his early days, when he used to work the waterways stealing gold and goods from the barges, until police had clamped down and he had moved inland to easier targets.

The dragons flew over buildings gleaming in red and black roof tiles, streets teeming with people and camels and horses. Ornate palanquins bore the rich to various destinations, while mules and hired rickshaws transported lesser mortals. At the north of the city shone the blinding gold of the imperial palace, laid out in concentric squares, that by itself was the size of a city. Vermillion walls surrounded the palace proper, each ring protecting the royal family within. Every eave had stone animals to ward against evil spirits, and other protective animals keeping watch, and at all four corners of the palace stood tall gleaming pagodas, like sentinels.

The dragons banked as one, their wings tilting just enough to send them in an elegant spiral down to the outer ring of the palace. They landed in a courtyard, and immediately, dragon grooms rushed out to greet them.

Jin stepped from the carriage with Rayshan as soon as her dragonrider unlocked it. The dragon pushed his head against her palm through the cage, having grown even in the past four days.

"With me." Emar had materialized by her side and motioned with his hand for her to follow. She clutched Rayshan to her. "And the dragon cannot come."

Rayshan bared his teeth at this, but Emar wasn't moved. He motioned to a groom. "Take this dragon and be extra cautious. He's a Jade." He turned back to Jin. "I swear to you, you will come back alive to see him." Emar paused. "For today anyway."

Jin looked to Rayshan and nodded, handing the cage to the groom. *I shall find you later.*

Emar cut her bonds. She rubbed her wrists, wondering why he let her free now, but then realized: she wouldn't try to escape if she didn't have Rayshan, for his death would mean her own.

Jin followed Emar through courtyards of the richest décor. Or at least she thought they were of the richest décor until they entered the inner palace. And then she realized that any previous concept she had of rich was laughable now. They passed elaborate gardens and man-made ponds where multi-colored koi the length of her arm nibbled the lotus fronds. Manicured trees and pavilions tiled in the finest gold ceramic were arranged in a neat formation, following some pattern Jin couldn't fathom.

Emar led her into a long teak-and-rosewood corridor with marble floors and a gold-filigreed door at the end. Emar, despite his limp, kept a good gait, and Jin maintained a respectful two paces behind. They passed various personages of the court: nobles in silks and headscarves, ladies in bright linen gowns bearing baskets of candles, soaps, and other items for the household. At one point they passed a dozen mages in purple robes, their hoods pushed back from their heads as they transported a bamboo stretcher.

On it lay an unconscious young man, face ashen with pain.

"What happened to him?" Jin asked.

Emar glanced over but didn't slow his pace. "He's just been through his initiation. All imperial mages must offer their manhood to Heaven to be allowed into the deepest mysteries of magic."

Jin recoiled. She had heard wild rumors about imperial mages but thought they were all just bawdy inn talk. As they kept walking, she tried to quell her unease. The further she walked into this palace, the further she left everything she knew behind.

When they reached the doors, Emar lowered himself onto a long teak bench with legs carved as dragons, and waited. He gave Jin no indication of what they were doing or whether she should sit on the bench with him, and so she stood, gazing at the ceilings and the surrounding carvings.

The moments passed in silence. Jin tried reaching out to Rayshan, but only heard a distant hum, like the sound of a faraway stream.

"Distance makes hearing your dragon difficult," Emar said. At her look he leaned forward. "I've trained enough dragonriders to recognize that look. You're trying to reach him. Your bond is too young; it's not powerful enough to cross any distance greater than a dragon's wingspan."

A flood of questions entered Jin's mind, but she bit

them back. There was no point asking about her future when she might not have one.

"What are we waiting for?" Jin asked.

Emar looked at her. "For the empress to summon us."

Jin tried to tame her nerves. The Empress Wu. Sole ruler over every living thing in the empire. A thief in the shadows heard all the whispers, admiring and scathing. Jin knew countless tales about the concubine who had risen to become wife to the former Emperor Kaizhong. Officially, Emperor Kaizhong had, on his deathbed, named his empress sole ruler—not just as regent until the crown prince came of age, but for life. Plenty of gossip flowed about the powerful woman, though anyone who valued their head made sure to speak carefully. For the secret police, known as the Royal Veil, were everywhere, and the empress did not tolerate detractors.

At some point, when Jin's feet started to ache, she heard footsteps from down the hall. Prince Tai walked toward them. He had donned a yellow robe over his leathers and redone his hair to tame it from the ride in the dragon carriage. His boots were no longer dust caked, and he had clearly washed his face, though the faded bruise remained. Only the most inner circle of the royal family could wear yellow. She fervently hoped he was not the son of the empress, or worse, the crown prince.

He reached them and raised an eyebrow at Emar. "You haven't gone in?"

"We are waiting for the summons," Emar said.

The prince smirked, then opened the door.

The servants, seeing Tai, held the door and ushered them in. They glanced in veiled surprise at Jin, who looked exactly like what she was: a street rat caught in some forgotten corner of the empire.

They entered a luxurious office with windows that overlooked the palace. Gold was everywhere, and there was enough teak, Jin decided, to feed an entire kingdom for a year. All the chairs bore silk cushions, and finely carved lanterns hung at regular intervals. A luxurious silk carpet covered the floor, and at the far end a woman in light linen robes and a glittering nest of jewels in her hair sat on a raised dais, a low table covered in documents before her. Standing to one side, holding half a dozen scrolls, was a man dressed in ash gray silk, with a black headscarf marking him as an official. His plump figure contrasted with his thin nose, thinner mouth, and carefully groomed mustache, which hung just past his chin. A man in a headscarf stood opposite, his face lined but stoic. Jin noted he looked much kindlier than the plump official. Sitting at a line of low tables against one wall were half a dozen clerks, busy writing on scrolls of paper.

"Greetings, Your Highness. Greetings, War Minister Gao, Legal Minister Wei," Prince Tai said, striding forward and bowing. Emar motioned for Jin to kneel and began to do the same, the effort clearly paining him.

At first, only the whisper of paper disturbed the silence.

"Rise."

Jin stood after Emar struggled back to his feet, and stole another look at the empress. She was, Jin decided, one of the most unique women Jin had seen in her life. The woman was beautiful, yes—the stories of her beauty were all true, perhaps even diluted. But she emanated a powerful magnetism, even when she was sitting still. Everything about her seemed groomed to perfection—from the powder on her face, to the small vermillion dots on her lips, to the black lines highlighting bright and intelligent eyes that Jin sensed missed nothing. Everything about her spoke of the highest authority, even without the conspicuous gold dragon seals hanging about her neck.

The empress took the new arrivals in at a glance, pausing at the bruise on Tai's face. "What happened to your face, my son?"

Son? Jin's heart sank as she glanced at Prince Tai, who stood looking the empress in the eyes, something no one else would dare. This was the crown prince. Her fortunes were deteriorating rapidly.

To Jin's surprise, Tai's tone was dismissive. "It's but a bruise. Don't worry yourself about that. But we had an incident along the way. The dragon hatched and bonded to someone else."

The empress's eyes widened, and Jin thought there was hope mixed with surprise. "You bonded to the dragon?"

"No, Mother, it was not I."

The war minister's lip curled. "Then who? Surely not to you, Master Emar?"

Emar stiffened, and Jin sensed a private insult in the words.

"No, Minister Gao, not to me. We have brought her to you, Your Highness," Emar said, indicating Jin.

There was a moment of perplexed silence.

"But Master Emar," the one Tai had called Minister Wei said. "Dragons do not bond to girls." He cast the empress an uncertain look. "Do they?"

Emar took a breath. "It seems this one did."

"Then we unbond her," the war minister said. "Send the dragon to the king of Khitan. We gave our word."

Emar looked from the ministers to the empress. "It's not that simple. The dragon, as fate would have it, is a Jade."

A chilly silence descended, and Jin noticed the shock on both ministers' faces. The empress's was hard to read, but her very stillness made Jin suspect that the news had affected her more than she wanted to admit.

"Clerks, you are dismissed," the empress said. "Girl, wait outside until you are called."

One of the clerks, whom Jin guessed was a head clerk due to the large seal hanging from his neck, looked to object, but at the empress's hand gesture, he bowed. He and the clerks stood and filed from the room, closing the door behind them. Jin followed and joined the clerks, who kept a haughty distance. No one spoke, but Jin knew her fate was being decided within those closed doors.

CHAPTER 5

*P*rince Tai knew his mother's moods better than anyone and caught the telltale loss of color beneath her makeup.

"How did this happen?" The empress stood, the beads in her headdress clicking as she came down the steps from her raised dais.

"A group of thieves tried to rob us, Your Highness," Emar explained, then corrected himself, "did rob us. This girl stole the dragon egg, and then it hatched and bonded to her."

"That's ridiculous," the war minister scoffed. He glanced at Wei, who had remained silent. "As Minister Wei said, dragons don't bond to girls."

"I'm sorry, respected Minister Gao," Tai said, "but this one did. It tried to defend her. No hatchling would do that unless bonded." The previous days had seemed like a long series of unexpected twists: first, fighting a woman and losing. Then, finding the dragon had somehow hatched a month before their estimates. And last, discovering the same woman had bonded with the dragon. Though he had been taught that dragons refused to bond with women, he had seen enough bondings to recognize it when it happened.

"My prince, you must be mistaken," Gao insisted, face dark. "Dragons are noble creatures. They wouldn't choose a peasant off the street, much less a thief and a woman."

Prince Tai snickered inwardly at Gao's gaffe. The empress turned a cool gaze on her minister. "Women are ignoble, Minister Gao?"

Tai enjoyed the reddening in Gao's face but hid it with the practiced ease of a natural diplomat. Tai knew the man's contempt for his mother, despite Gao's efforts to conceal it. He had been genuinely sorry when Gao's father died five years prior, as it meant the title of war minister passed, as was customary, to his eldest male heir. Gao the son was proving to be much more antagonistic to the empress and Tai than Gao the father had been, but Tai knew removing him was out of the question—the man had tight, blood relations with every noble house.

"That is not at all what I mean, Your Highness," Gao replied smoothly. "But Dragon Class expressly forbids women riders. Not to mention that traditionally, dragonriders are chosen only from noble families of good standing."

"Then what do we do with the Jade, respected minister?" Emar looked from him to the empress, who still seemed to be digesting the news.

"We cannot break a promise to an ally, especially the king of Khitan," the war minister said. "Your Highness must agree."

"Perhaps this is a blessing, Mother," Prince Tai cut in. "We almost sent a Jade to the king of Khitan. Think of how dangerous that would have been." Despite his fear of the Jade, he also knew the classic advice to keep your friends close and your enemies closer. Keeping the Jade, and its rider, out of enemy hands made good political sense.

"And you think it's less dangerous now?" Gao turned on him, eyebrow raised. "A Jade in the grasp of some lowborn girl?" He swept them all with a stern gaze. "What if she turns out to be another Mengkhis Lai?"

The air in the room cooled further. Tai inadvertently glanced at Emar, who kept an impassive face. The two of them had debated this repeatedly on the journey back to the capital, and Tai had to admit that his first reaction to the Jade hatchling had been a primal stab of fear. To him, a jade dragon was synonymous with his uncle—Mengkhis Lai, the dragonrider who had killed his father and nearly killed him and his mother. Not to mention the chaos Mengkhis Lai had rained down on the empire. Tai's mother had taught him from an early age that together, they had to do everything in their power to ensure Mengkhis Lai never came back. The empire's safety lay in their hands. They were an inseparable team, he and his mother, destined to protect the dragon throne at all costs, no matter the sacrifice. But Emar had argued that a Jade presented possibilities they could not ignore.

"You lost your dragon to Mengkhis Lai," Gao said to Emar. "Or have you forgotten?"

Tai wondered if Emar would abandon all protocol and leap upon the minister. Emar, like any rider whose dragon died before him, had been gutted. Gao's words only flayed a wound that had never fully healed.

"With all respect, Minister," Emar said in a voice that sounded as if it was coiled so tightly it would snap, "I don't need to be told the price we have all paid for Mengkhis Lai."

"Then you agree we must get rid of her," Gao said. "The risk is too great. If the king of Khitan finds out we've cheated him of a Jade, he may refuse to guard the Well of Ice."

Unease slid over Tai. The empire's most powerful mages had imprisoned Mengkhis Lai's dragon, Baikalan, in the Well of Ice. But if he was somehow released . . .

"But then what?" the prince said. "If we get rid of her, we have to bond the dragon to someone else. Whom would we entrust a Jade to?"

"Why not you, Prince Tai?" Minister Wei spoke up.

"Who better to trust with a Jade than the crown prince and the head of Dragon Class?"

Tai held back his sigh of exasperation. His mother had ordered him into the hatchery, with no other candidates present, when the last harvest came in. To his mother's great disappointment and his own relief, none of the dragons had bonded to him. His fear of heights made his duty to ride frequently in an airborne carriage bad enough. Riding those things every day would have been torture.

Hopefully, his mother sensed Wei was just feeding her her own secret fantasy. How convenient to have her son command the empire's most powerful dragon, in a public show of might. But the thought of something being forcibly bonded to him was distasteful. Repulsive, really.

The empress went silent, as if considering. Indulging a daydream, Tai supposed. But as he knew she would, she put the fantasy aside in favor of practicality.

"A prince, bonded to a dragon who didn't choose him? I can hear the derision now." She tapped the gold-painted nails of one hand against her palm. "I agree with my son. We let the girl stay. But we keep a close eye on her. There is to be no talk of Mengkhis Lai around her. We must make sure she never has a chance, or even the desire, to follow his path."

Minister Gao shook his head. "Your Highness, that still doesn't solve the diplomatic nightmare this raises.

The king of Khitan will be livid that he hasn't received his dragon, never mind that it's a Jade."

"But he doesn't know it is a Jade, does he?" the empress asked.

"And he needn't know." The prince paused, turning to Emar. "Isn't that right?"

Emar nodded. "I can have the men keep it quiet. And if we send another convoy immediately, the king of Khitan shouldn't sense anything amiss. We could blame foul weather for the delay."

The war minister's face contorted. "Your Highness, please consider the dangers. Not just of angering our ally, but the repercussions if we let this girl remain bonded to a dragon. It isn't done."

His mother was silent for a while, then swept her dress around to face the minister. "Girls don't become empresses in their own right either. Yet here we are. And sometimes we must do things we'd rather not. Master Emar, I trust I can leave you with arrangements for dorms."

Emar frowned. Tai had not thought of the minutiae of taking in a female dragonrider either. "Dorms, Your Highness? We don't have dorms for—"

The empress's expression remained unchanged. "She trains, eats, and dorms in the same place as the men. Special treatment will only make her enemies."

Tai felt a momentary pity for the girl, but his mother was right. Gao and others who opposed a girl in Dragon Class would argue that any special treatment only proved how unfit a female was as a dragonrider. He hoped Jin was as tough as he thought, because she would need it if she was going to live day in and day out with the men.

Minister Gao shook his head. "I respectfully make my objections known, Your Highness. This will never work."

"I have noted your objections," the empress said. "The girl will prove herself, or she will prove you right. But we cannot afford to give a Jade to the king of Khitan. Now I don't want to discuss this matter further, Minister. This stays between us."

The minister bowed in submission, but Tai caught the displeasure on his face.

Emar also bowed. "Your servant is here to serve, Your Highness."

The empress nodded. "Then I believe we are done. You are all dismissed. Tai and Emar, ready a convoy to go to the king of Khitan. I expect you to accompany it, my son. Send the girl in. I wish to speak to her. Alone."

Tai glanced at his mother, surprised. She always let him stay for official meetings, and as this was a Dragon Class matter, he should naturally be present. But her expression told him she wanted no arguments, and disappointed, he bowed, then followed the other men out of the audience hall.

* * *

"Stand, girl."

Jin did as she was told. She had watched Emar and the others file out, the minister of war giving her a stinging glance as he left. Then Emar had motioned for her to enter and instead of following her in, shut the door behind her.

She had entered and knelt as expected, and there had been a moment of quiet before she was told to stand.

The empress's eyes rested on her, and Jin understood how even the bravest might flinch under that gaze. The woman had dark, arresting eyes that seemed to see all Jin's thoughts.

"What's your name, girl?"

"Wang Kway Jin, Your Highness. Most simply call me Jin."

The empress came over and peered at Jin's face. Her delicate brows rose. "How old are you?"

"Twenty. Twenty-one including my womb year."

She didn't know her exact birthday, but she knew the year, for everyone knew the Year of Chaos, before the empress had restored order.

"Born in the Year of the New Empire. Perhaps a fortuitous sign." The empress paused. "I'm not sure how you had the gall to steal a dragon from me, Jin. And I'm hoping it wasn't pure stupidity. But if it was, you'll have to grow some wits. I am giving you a chance to rise from your life of squalor and insignificance, not to mention utter dishonor that would land you in the lowest levels of hell. You have a rare chance to pursue a life of integrity amongst my Dragon Class."

Realizing the empress expected her to say something, Jin replied, "I am unworthy, Your Highness."

"Indeed, you are," the empress agreed. "But you are also a first. No dragon has ever chosen a woman, and women are barred from the hatchery. I'd be lying if I said I wasn't intrigued."

She circled slowly around Jin, eyes narrowing. Jin tried not to think of a snake wrapping its prey. "You will join Dragon Class and serve along with your Jade. Make no mistake, this is not forgiveness for your stealing from the empire and me. This is atonement. Dragon Class is the pinnacle of the empire's military, but that means it is demanding. We only accept the best, the most disciplined. It's a place of men. You will serve in it with no complaints, and at the first sign of weakness or the first snivel, I will not hesitate to remove you and send you to the salt mines. Do you understand?"

"Yes, Your Highness," Jin said.

"I'll also give you some free advice." The empress drew closer and stood before her. "I rose to where I am because I am the fiercest and the smartest. I make no mistakes, or at least none that I cannot correct by killing or appeasing someone. But I have more enemies than I can count who believe a woman should never sit on the dragon throne. I cannot afford to give them extra leverage against me by having an example of a woman failing. If you fail, you will be a burden to me, and I will remove you, quickly and with no regrets. Do you understand?"

"Yes, Your Highness," Jin said.

"Good. To make sure you understand, I'll tell you now: to be a woman in a man's game, you will have to not just pass the Dragon Class trials, but be the best. You must be unassailable." The empress paused. "The trials will be hard, and the salt mines might just be more merciful. Are you certain you want to choose this path?"

"Will I be parted from Rayshan if I go to the mines, Your Highness?"

"Who?"

"My dragon," Jin explained. "The Jade. Will I be parted from him if I go to the mines?"

"Of course. A Jade would be wasted on the mines."

Jin bowed. "I will join Dragon Class."

"Then welcome to the capital. You're dismissed, Little Jin."

*E*mar was waiting for her in the corridor, but Jin saw no sign of Prince Tai.

She expected him to ask her what had been said, but if he was curious he gave no sign, walking with the clear expectation she would follow.

When they had emerged back into the outer court-yards, Jin sensed Rayshan prowling anxiously at the edge of her mind. Though she couldn't hear his words, she sensed a fluttering sensation—his relief that she was alive.

"Now, some rules: tell no one how you really came to bond with Rayshan or where. If anyone asks, you tell them you broke into the hatchery to steal an egg. Understood?"

She nodded.

"Good. Now what knowledge do you have of dragons?"

"Very little. The Tang empire is the only nation with them."

Emar grunted. "Every child knows that. Very well, I'll assume you know nothing. The empire has over four thousand dragons, not including unhatched eggs. Dragon Class is divided into four 'banners': warriors, messengers, transport, and agriculture. Don't listen to all the nonsense about warriors being better. Each is important. And all dragons have a rider, to whom they are bonded."

"But they don't automatically join Dragon Class?" Jin asked.

"All riders must pass the two trials, the snowfire trial and the geography trial, then serve under a banner."

"What if I fail?"

"Then you'll likely be sent to the slave mines. They'll forcibly bond Rayshan with a worthy rider if you fail."

"Why don't they just force Rayshan to bond with someone else then?"

Emar's cheek twitched, as if the thought was distasteful. "Forced bonding can have consequences. It diminishes the dragon and sometimes damages the mind. It's not our first choice, and certainly not with a Jade."

"What if I succeed?" she asks. "What's in it for me?" Was there a way to flee with Rayshan? She had inadvertently cut herself free of Haitao. Could she not do it with the empire, as mad as that seemed?

From Emar's reaction, he clearly had never fielded this question. "Most join for the honor, girl. Dragonriders are heroes. Some, like Oyang Kang, become legends. And," he added, "if you pass the trials, you start on a salary of twenty gold bao. A month."

Jin's jaw dropped, and Emar chuckled. She had never had money of her own, much less a gold bao, or twenty. Everything she stole went to Haitao, and if he was in a generous mood, he might bestow her a few coins to spend on herself. With that kind of money, she could find Lu, if he was still alive. The empress's words came back to her: this was a chance to live an honorable, respected life—a life as far away from the gutter as she had ever known. The best a thief like her could hope for working for Haitao was a life with enough to eat and perhaps the chance to see another day without a knife in the ribs. Was this what Lu had always wanted? He had insisted there was another life to thieving, a life that involved good things.

"Here we have the mess hall."

Emar's words broke into her thoughts as they crossed several courtyards and arrived, judging by the sun, on the northern side of the palace. Like every Han household, each courtyard and house was arranged on a north and south axis, where the head of household and honored family members occupied the northern rooms, with everyone else in descending order toward the south, where the front door would be.

This large courtyard held dining halls on one end, and even now servants hurried to and from the kitchens, bearing platters of flatbread stuffed with mutton and spices, jars of wine and goats' milk, bowls of tripe soup and dumplings that smelled of coriander and cumin. Jin's mouth watered, and though this was likely a coarse meal for the soldiers, to Jin it was a feast.

"You will have three meals a day here, and if you need anything extra, you'll have ration cards for jerky, dried beans, and spiced tofu," Emar said. Her stomach growled audibly. He paused but continued, "You'll have an allotment of clothes, bedding, shoes, and tickets to the bathhouse." He stopped, seemingly just having thought of the logistics of a girl using what Jin assumed to be an all-male bathhouse. "I'll arrange for you to have a private time each day for bathing."

He took her through another moon gate, and she reluctantly left the smell of food behind. They crossed several courtyards until they came to a large arena carpeted in sand, surrounded by double-storied halls. Racks of weapons lined one side, and ropes and bridles lined another.

"What are those for?" Jin asked, pointing at the roof where iron bars curled out the top.

"Roosting sites for the dragons," Emar explained. Just then a flight of dragons passed overhead, their roars resounding as they called out to companions below. There was an answering chorus of roars from behind the dorms to the east, distant but very audible. Jin looked in that direction.

"That's where we stable the dragons," Emar said. "In the caves we call Dragon City, behind the dorms. Each dragon has their own alcove, and though there are servants there who will muck the caves and provide food, you're ultimately responsible for your dragon's health, including keeping him free of any lice or scale rot." He raised a hand at her retort. "We'll go over all that later. For now, just try not to get lost in the palace. You'll primarily spend your days here, in the barracks which we call the Hall of Bright Fire, and in Dragon City. Here, take this."

He pulled a metal coin strung on a thong from his pocket and handed it to her.

"What is it?"

"It's a Dragon Class medallion. I'll have one with your name made, but for now, use this. You'll need it to enter Dragon City."

She slipped it over her head, feeling the cold metal settle against her collarbone.

They arrived at a set of doors. He pushed them open and led her into a spacious courtyard where vats of clothes were being dyed and aired on racks. Workers glanced at them before returning to stir their dyes or beat out fabric with paddles.

A thin but immaculately dressed man with a long

face came to greet them. "Master Emar, welcome. What can we do for you today?"

Emar motioned to Jin. "Tailor Chen, I need some clothes and an initiate's package for our newest dragonrider."

The man looked at Jin, as if doubting his eyes. "This is a girl."

"Yes, it's a girl," Emar said patiently. "Her name's Jin."

Jin noticed some workers had stopped, overhearing this conversation. The tailor snapped at them, "Back to work! This isn't a theater performance."

The workers hastily returned to their tasks, and the tailor nodded. "Come with me."

He led them inside an office, where a tall girl marked cloth next to a jumble of measuring string, pins, and chalk. The girl cast curious glances at Jin.

"Forgive my assistant," the man said. "Neither of us has tailored clothes for a female Dragon Class officer before." He frowned, thoughtful. "We'll have to improvise as we go. Come, stand here on the box, arms out."

Emar nodded to Jin. "I'll be back for you."

"Where are you going?" It wasn't any of her business, but he was the only person she knew here, and she felt vulnerable without him.

"I have to gather a few other Dragon Class items," he said. "Master Chen will take care of you."

She watched him leave, then stepped onto the box, tense as the assistant came forward and ran measuring tape across her breasts; around her neck, wrists, waist, and hips; and down her inside leg. The girl called out measurements while the tailor wrote them down with a brush and ink.

When the girl had finished, the tailor pinched his nose, as if pained. "We can't have you looking ridiculous in the uniform. The empress will have my head. I'll have to design something for you specifically." He rummaged on a back shelf until he found a package wrapped in cotton and string, and held it out to her. "Try this on. It should be roughly your size. I will have something workable designed in a week and make the clothes in a fortnight."

She stepped down from the crate, and the tailor motioned toward a latticed door.

"Go. There's a room back there."

Jin went into what turned out to be little more than a storage closet. She opened the package and saw dragonrider leathers: tight pants, a loose linen shirt, and a *pao*, or short-sleeved jacket, which slipped over the shirt. She pulled these on. The tailor was right. They weren't a poor fit, though the legs and sleeves were too long.

She stepped out, and the tailor appraised her. "That will do for now. Take them off and I'll adjust the hems."

Jin changed back into her clothes and gave the leathers to the tailor. He instructed her to sit on a chair while he went to another back room, muttering about why the scissors were never where they were supposed to be. The assistant followed to help him look, and Jin found herself alone in the waiting room.

A man about Jin's age entered, a jacket draped over his arm. His topknot was bound with expensive green silk, but his clothes marked him as a dragonrider. He would have been handsome if not for his eyes. They locked on Jin, judging and categorizing her by the time he blinked.

"I need you to sew these tears," he said, pulling the jacket slung on his arm and tossing it to her. She caught it, wrinkling her nose at the overpowering soap smell in the fabric, and was about to tell him she wasn't the tailor, but he didn't give her the chance. "I need it by tomorrow, so make sure you get to it now."

"I'm not a tailor."

His face darkened with impatience. "Of course you're not. Tell your master what I need. Understand?"

"I'm not the assistant either."

He seemed to notice her men's pants, boots, and tunic. "Then what are you, a messenger?"

"Ah, Master Madu!" The tailor emerged, his assistant behind him. "I will be with you in one moment." He held out the leathers to Jin. "Here you are. They should be your size now."

Madu looked from the clothes to Jin. "Those are dragonrider leathers." He examined her. "What family are you from?"

"She's your new classmate, Madu." Emar's voice

made them all look at the doorway. "So as her elder I hope you'll be an example to Jin."

Madu bowed. "Master Emar, forgive my surprise. I was just curious about Jin's family, as I am familiar with all the noble families." There was no mistaking the haughty pride in the statement.

"Jin is . . . an exception," Emar said. He took the jacket in Jin's hands from her and held it out to Madu. "If you paid more attention during the gear care lessons, you wouldn't need to bother Tailor Chen with your rips."

"Yes, Master Emar."

Jin snickered inwardly at how Madu's haughty bearing changed instantly before a higher authority. The rider humbly took his jacket back from Emar.

Emar motioned toward the assistant, who had brought out a pile of bedding topped with a pair of boots. "These are your fresh supplies. Take care of them, for if you lose or damage them, you'll have to pay to replace them. Now come with me. I'll show you your sleeping quarters."

She scooped up the supplies and followed Emar out of the courtyard, noting the assistant's wide-eyed stare and Madu's surly one. If all the other riders were like Madu, then she was not looking forward to her time here.

After the tailor's, Emar led Jin to a double-storied building with carved wooden doors and pillars. He opened the doors and led the way upstairs. More doors lined the corridor here, with labeled wooden plaques on each one.

"You and the other initiates who haven't yet passed the first trial are in these rooms," Emar said, opening one door. There was a flurry of movement inside as four young men about Jin's age leapt to attention. Three were Han and dressed in various pieces of dragon leathers, but the fourth, Jin noticed, was decidedly not Han, and she stared for a fraction more than polite. He had olive-colored skin, with a head of curly black hair in a loose warrior's knot. The man caught her look but didn't react.

"Riders. Meet your wing's new recruit," Emar said.

The riders stared.

"And, yes, she's a girl," Emar said, clearly deciding to address their silent question. "This is Ezho, Panshalar, Jao, and Aadan."

Jin took stock of them. Ezho had long braided hair that he wore slung like a scarf around his neck, and though of average height, he exuded quiet authority. Panshalar was the giant of the group, towering a head above everyone else. His height and breadth, along with his broad face and distinct cheekbones, marked him as Mongolian. In glaring contrast to Panshalar was Jao, whose diminutive height looked absolutely puny next to the Mongolian. He wore his hair slicked into a ponytail, and like many shorter men Jin had met, he looked like he spent all his spare time lifting rocks and training in an attempt to look bigger. The last of them, Aadan, was the huren. His thick goatee, light-colored eyes, and curly hair made him stand out like ink on paper. He gave a polite nod.

"You'll be eating, training, and living together," Emar continued, "so I suggest you show each other courtesy. Treat her as your own."

Jao smirked, standing taller but thereby only drawing attention to his short form. "One of our own? Her female yin force will weaken us," he muttered under his breath, but Jin heard all the same.

And so did Emar, for he fixed Jao with a piercing look made all the more formidable by his white eye. "If your yang is so weak that one girl's yin will cripple all of you, you have no business being in Dragon

Class." He paused, apparently waiting for Jao to argue. When Jao stayed silent, he continued, "Now, as I was saying, treat her and her Jade dragon as your wing mates."

At the mention of a Jade, the boys' expressions changed, and she wasn't sure whether they were shocked or scared. Perhaps both. "Help her learn her duties here as a dragonrider. Ezho, as wing leader, I expect you to enforce that. Is that clear?"

"Yes, Master Emar!" Ezho said.

Emar nodded, satisfied. "I'll see you at the evening meal when the bell rings."

Once he had gone, the others lapsed back into slouching shadows. Aadan glanced at her again before lying back on his bed, where he picked up a book and began reading, but the other students drew closer, eyeing Jin with a mix of curiosity and challenge.

"You can have the pallet at the end," Ezho said. "Follow the rules and you'll be fine."

She didn't bother replying.

"You mute or something?" Jao said, crossing his thick arms.

"Probably just speechless at our looks." Panshalar grimaced at her cold reaction. "Just a jest."

"Everything's a jest to you," Ezho said irritably, punching Panshalar on the arm before retreating to his bed and what looked like an unfinished letter he had been writing.

Panshalar shrugged his meaty shoulders. "And you

lot are all painfully serious. Jin, is that *jin* meaning 'gold'?"

"Probably because her father paid a paltry gold piece for a night with her mother," Jao scoffed.

Ezho shook his head, while Panshalar had the decency to wince. It wasn't the first time Jin had heard that jibe, but deep down it still stung—not because she looked down on song girls, but simply because not knowing her heritage was a blot she couldn't erase. She had no ancestors to pay respects to at the Grave-Sweeping Festival, no parents to honor.

"Well, you're not Han, so what are you?" the giant Mongolian asked, curious.

"Leave her alone, Panshalar." Aadan didn't even raise his head from his book. She hadn't known what she had expected, but Aadan didn't speak with even a hint of an accent. If she hadn't seen his face, she'd have thought he was born and raised in the palace with the best of tutors, for his Chinese was flawless. "Panshalar is a good man deep down, but tact isn't his strength. Would that be fair?"

The giant shrugged his beefy shoulders. "Matter of opinion."

Ezho looked up from his letter. "Is it true, what Emar said? Dragons don't bond with girls."

"You haven't met my dragon," Jin said, and walked past him. She noticed ten beds in the room, with a rod and curtain for privacy next to each one. "There are others in this room?"

Jao smirked. "You can count. That's a good start."

She summoned her patience. Jao was like a dog, she decided—the smaller ones were always the most combative. The best tactic was to ignore them. "Where are the others?"

"Well, I guess I should have known you'd be assigned to the milkmaids' section."

She turned and saw Madu, the rider from the tailor's, standing with three other students in the doorway, who all bore such a striking resemblance to each other, especially with their square jaws, that Jin thought they must be brothers. Ezho and the others stiffened.

"This is the new dragonrider, Jin," Jao said, clearly eager to appear as the one with information.

Madu tossed him a dismissive look. "We've met." He strode toward Jin and made a disapproving noise. "Dragon Class is falling into disrepute." He indicated Panshalar. "First bastard children, then foreigners— though he at least is of noble blood. And now women."

The brothers followed him in and snickered at this.

Aadan closed his book. "Perhaps you should complain to the minister of war, if it upsets you so."

This seemed to rile Madu. "Maybe I will."

Panshalar's ears were still red from being called a bastard, but he crossed his arms in defiance. "Her dragon's a Jade, Madu."

This gave Madu pause, and the three brothers narrowed their eyes at her. "A Jade chose *her*?"

"Why the surprise? Because he should have chosen you?" Aadan asked. "Just because you're the war minister's nephew?"

Jin digested this. Minister Gao's family likely shared his views about women entering Dragon Class. She sensed Madu's hostility toward her wasn't about to change soon.

The rider's expression curdled, but the sound of a gong being struck drew everyone's attention.

"Dinnertime," Madu said. He turned to Jin. "Let's show you the kitchens. You may want to ask for a transfer there, as you would probably feel more at home."

Anger flared in her, but she ignored the bait, waiting until the others had filed out. Aadan gave her a nod, as if to encourage her to follow. In the corridor, she noticed other students making their way toward the dining hall. She followed at a distance, not wanting to miss out on any meals that were being served. Food was vital, and right now she wouldn't skip a meal if she didn't have to.

Jin walked down the staircase as dorm doors flew open. Students ranging from eighteen to twenty-five years of age were walking out, donning robes and bantering. She felt even more singled out and alone in this sea of males. She mentally reached out and touched Rayshan's comforting answer. This time, she caught a snippet of a sentence.

. . . alone . . . give it time . . .

Perhaps their bond was strengthening, if she could hear words now at this distance. She followed the crowd to the dining hall, enduring the curious looks of all who noticed there was a female in their midst who wasn't a kitchen maid or servant. Back home with the Red Crows, she had also been the only girl, but she had been accepted. She never thought she'd miss Haitao and her old life, harsh as it was. But now, she found herself wanting to contact him—if only to say goodbye and ask if they knew Lu's whereabouts.

In the mess hall, long tables and benches filled the room, lined up end to end. At the front of the room was a brazier with blazing coals and a spit, where a hump of meat sizzled, the aroma of mutton and spices heavy in the air. A gong sounded as the riders found their seats, many gesturing her way as news spread. She sat down with the others in her wing, taking a seat across from Aadan. Jao turned away, clearly wanting to disassociate himself.

Emar came through a door and made his way to the dais before the brazier. He clapped his hands loudly until the whispers died down.

"Dragonriders and initiates, I salute you."

"We salute you, Master Emar!" the hall called back in unison.

"No doubt you've already noticed our new initiate." He waited for the inevitable reactions as people turned to peer at Jin. "We have never had a woman as a dragonrider, and we thought dragons do not bond to women, but today Jin has proven us wrong. I advise you all to remember what unites you rather than divides you and to treat her as a brother." He himself seemed to realize the ridiculousness of his words as sniggers broke out. "As a comrade," he corrected himself. "In Dragon Class, we must all be willing to help each other and stand shoulder to shoulder, because we are the pillars of this empire's might, the steel in the empress's sword, whether on the battlefield or in peace. And tonight," he surveyed the crowd before gesturing toward the hall's main doors, "I have a special surprise. We are honored to welcome back our brothers who have returned from subduing the rebels of Parhae!"

An excited murmur swept the room, and the doors swung open. A dozen dragonriders in shining leathers and brilliant wool capes strode into the mess hall. The room erupted into welcoming whoops and cheers as riders stood and clapped or pounded the tables while the new arrivals soaked it in and walked to the head dais. They greeted other riders as they passed, and the leader of the group, a small man with an undeniable charisma about him, paused at the sight of Jin. Madu's expression, Jin noticed, was particularly awe-struck.

A chant began around the room of "Oyang Kang!" and soon the room reverberated with the sound. Jin recognized the name as the rider Emar had mentioned, and she studied the man, curious. Oyang Kang raised his fist in reply before bowing to Emar and mounting the dais.

The rest of Oyang Kang's riders each bowed to Emar before taking their seats at the table, and the hubbub only died down when the last one was seated and the gong called for food to be served.

In the excitement, the others in Jin's wing seemed to have forgotten about the awkwardness of having a woman amongst them. As Aadan returned from the communal sideboard with bowls and chopsticks for each member of the wing, including her, the students talked, their excitement palpable.

"What I wouldn't give to ride with Oyang Kang," Panshalar said wistfully.

Jao scoffed. "You and everyone else."

"I'll bet the head table will be hearing all about his single-handedly killing fifty Parhae fighters," Ezho said, casting envious looks at the dais.

"Is that what makes him famous?" Jin asked. "Because he kills people?" She didn't relish the thought of a future killing others.

"You don't know about Oyang Kang?" Jao asked, incredulous.

"Even if she doesn't," Aadan interjected, "she has a good question." He turned to her. "He's famous for being a skilled rider and fighter, it's true. But I admire him because he brought down the Parhae city of Yalufu without any casualties. That's worth emulating."

Panshalar gave Aadan a rough slap on the arm.

"How did they let a pacifist like you into Dragon Class, anyway?"

The others laughed and continued their awed retellings of Oyang Kang's exploits, and Jin studied the hero at the high table. What was it like, to live in the light rather than the shadows? To be admired rather than shunned? To be a hero rather than a criminal? The possibility threaded her with excitement, but she kept her hopes in check. Though they were all riders and divided only by the length of the room, they might as well have been separated by a sea.

Servants streamed from the kitchens bearing giant platters, and Jin forgot all other thoughts of anything but food. Someone clanked down a goblet before her and filled it with goat's milk. Then a woman with an apron and thick arms was ladling a hearty soup into her bowl, along with flatbread and a heaping spoonful of rice, a side of pickled vegetables, and a piece of mutton the size of her fist.

The serving maid gave her a tentative smile. "Peace upon your evening, initiate."

Jin murmured a return greeting before diving into her food. She had never eaten her fill like this, much less had her pick of the various meats and river fish, along with the delicacies like wood ear mushrooms and watercress the maids brought. She hesitated momentarily when a server asked if she'd like seconds.

Before she could answer, a shadow fell across her and the serving maid hastily stepped back. Jin looked up to see Oyang Kang and his wing mates standing before her. Her table seemed to have gone silent.

"Wang Kway Jin, is it?" Oyang Kang asked, unsmiling. Jin noticed a jagged scar puckering one eyebrow, as well as a hairline that was receding despite what she estimated to be his thirty-odd years of age.

"Yes." Jin braced herself as all eyes seemed trained on this exchange.

"Well, I never thought I'd see the day a woman entered Dragon Class," Oyang Kang said.

"Neither did we, Rider Oyang," Madu snickered.

The older rider looked gravely over at Madu. "On the battlefield, your wing mates are your family. A smart dragonrider supports his wing mates." He turned back to Jin. "It is good to have you in Dragon Class. I am honored to have met the first female dragonrider, and I wish you luck, rider Wang Kway Jin."

Oyang Kang bowed, then strode out of the hall, his wing mates following. Madu looked sullen, while the others at the table all seemed at a loss for words. Jin was similarly surprised at the man's encouragement.

The maids came to serve soup, and she resumed her seat. Madu stood and leaned across the table, holding out a tray of onion bread. She eyed him, wary.

"Oyang Kang's right," Madu shrugged. "You're our wing mate, and we should stand by one another. Please, take one."

She hesitated. Just as she was about to decline,

Madu tilted the plate, dropping the contents in her soup. The liquid exploded against her cheek and neck.

"How clumsy of me, Rider Jin."

Jin glared at Madu and stood. The nearby tables broke into a clamor, itching for a fight. Part of her wanted to give it to them, especially when Madu's face broke into a grin.

Rayshan's bond pressed in on her, pulling her.

Jin wiped the soup from her cheek and walked out of the dining hall. Whoops and hollers erupted behind her as everyone acknowledged Madu's victory, and her stomach burned with the desire to take him down. But she knew that would be unwise. Her ears flushed hot with shame and fury as she left the hall.

*A*adan finished his bread at the table, trying to ignore the surrounding ruckus.

He watched the girl flee from the room. Well, perhaps *flee* wasn't the right word. She stalked, really, reminding him of the cats his father loved to keep about him as living ties to his homeland.

Someone jostled him as he sat down, and Aadan sighed. It was difficult being the one who loved quiet. He finished his bread and wiped his hands, then stood and took his bowls to the kitchen and slid them into the waiting tubs of soapy water there. When he stepped out into the fresh air of the courtyard beyond the mess hall, there was no sign of Jin or Oyang Kang. Instead, he was surprised to find another familiar figure, as if waiting for him.

"Your Highness," he said. "I thought you were in the North?"

Tai didn't answer and instead motioned with his head toward two saddled horses held by grooms. "Enough formality. Let's hit some targets."

Aadan followed him to the horses. He occasionally taught Tai Persian techniques in archery, but that was usually on rest days, and not at dusk. He noticed a bruise on Tai's face but decided to ask questions later.

They mounted the horses and cantered out of the Blood Oval, through the Da Ming palace, and to an outer training area where Dragon Class students came for archery drills. At this time of day, the range was deserted, the straw targets standing in a somber line against one far side.

Tai dismounted, and Aadan followed. The grooms that had accompanied them handed over a selection of bows. Tai examined two before selecting a long, fine one made of mulberry wood. Aadan took a shorter one of bamboo, which he favored for its flexibility. The grooms then gave them both quivers and a selection of thumb rings and stood back. Out of earshot, Aadan noticed.

"Your technique has improved," Aadan said as Tai drew back and loosed an arrow, hitting the straw figure through one leg. Tai had always been excellent at archery from a standing position. But he had recognized his weakness in many other techniques that involved a fast aim or only using fingertips. Thus he had sought Aadan's help, and a relationship of teacher and pupil had, if Aadan could be presumptuous, turned into one of friendship.

Tai grinned. "Thanks to you. Though I'll have to miss this week's lesson, I'm afraid."

Aadan checked his thumb ring, aligned his shot, and loosed. The arrow pierced the neck. Too bad he was aiming for the eye. "Official business?"

The crown prince nodded. "Always. To the king of Khitan."

Aadan glanced over, surprised. "I thought you'd already been."

"There was a complication," Tai replied.

"The girl dragonrider?" The timing seemed a little coincidental.

Tai's arrow went wide, hitting Aadan's target. "I'll be gone for a while."

Tai's avoidance of Aadan's question made him suspect he had been right. "Well, don't let your archery get any worse," Aadan replied drily. He received a jab in the ribs in revenge.

"I have a favor to ask."

Aadan drew out another arrow. "Oh?"

"I want you to keep an eye on the new dragonrider."

Aadan hesitated in taking his shot, distracted. "The girl? Because she's bonded to a Jade?"

"Yes," Tai said. He sighted and loosed. The arrow thudded into the straw target's chest. "The empire needs to know what kind of person she is. I need to know what kind of person she is."

Aadan didn't need Tai to elaborate. He read more books than anyone, and therefore knew more about the empire's history than even most Han students themselves. He knew the notorious Mengkhis Lai and the last jade dragon the empire had seen. But beyond that, Mengkhis was the ghost that stalked Tai in his nightmares. The demon who had almost ended Tai's life.

"You want me to befriend her?" Aadan wasn't sure why this all sat ill with him. True, his Zoroastrian faith prized honesty, but he would be first to admit he was not the most stringent follower of the one true god's teachings. No, it was more that the girl seemed to have enough problems without being spied on. And as for Aadan, he had enough trouble making genuine friendships, much less false ones. It occurred to him now that Tai was perhaps the only friend he had. Everyone else tolerated the dark foreigner and gave him the respect his royal lineage required, whereas Tai seemed to truly enjoy his company.

Tai shook his head. "You don't need to go that far. But just—see what you learn while I'm gone. Tell me anything you think I should know." He looked over. "Can I rely on you?"

Aadan couldn't refuse the prince. The prince was second in command in the empire and had shown Aadan nothing but kindness.

"Yes. I'll keep watch for you." He loosed his last

arrow, and even in the thickening dusk he saw the shaft buried straight through the target's painted eye.

Jin followed an innate sense of where Rayshan would be. She realized she had no idea where she was going, as Emar hadn't shown her the caves, or Dragon City as he had called it. But something invisible drew her, and she sensed it was Rayshan guiding her. She left by a large eastern gate to the dorms and saw before her the caves rising behind the Hall of Bright Fire barracks.

When Jin reached the guards at the doors, they looked as if they would stop her. She remembered Emar's words, that she was ultimately responsible for her dragon. She showed her necklace with the dragon insignia. "My dragon needs extra provisions."

They stared, clearly startled by a woman rider, but then nodded and let her through.

When she reached the foot of the caves where the dragons were kept, she found Rayshan almost by instinct. It was like having a second sense, and she was unprepared for her relief when she climbed the steep staircases and paths carved into the rock and entered his cave. She couldn't put it into words, but being near him made her feel safe, despite his size. It was a steadying, a grounding of her soul.

"You're chained!" she said, appalled. Somehow she had thought that here, the dragons would be free to come and go as they pleased.

A precaution, Rayshan said, his voice amused rather than angry. *The grooms fear us, as we aren't as gentle with them.*

As if on cue, a lanky boy with a scowl peeked around the alcove. "Who are you?"

"I'm Jin. Rayshan's rider."

The boy looked suspicious. "The girl rider? Don't feed him anything without telling me first. I have already fed him his ration, and I don't need to be mucking out more dragon dung than I do already."

He walked on.

I dislike him.

"I can see why."

He smells bitter, like his personality.

"Wonder why he's so grouchy."

You'd be better to speak through your mind, Jin. Another dragon told me this boy, Ping, lost a finger to a dragon once. Hasn't forgiven any of us since.

I'll bring you more food if you need it. Did you eat?

Yes. Despite what he says, the rations are good.

She sat down cross-legged. He jumped into her lap and pushed his scaly head against her shoulder roughly.

What kept you?

She scowled. *Meeting my fellow riders. Who are all horrible.* Or mostly horrible. It would be unfair to paint Aadan with the same brush.

Things will improve. At least we both have full bellies.

This was true. And Haitao was not here to berate her for eating too much. *The wolf that gorges itself is the slowest of the pack,* he often reminded her. She wondered where he was and hoped he and the clan were safe. Haitao had been brutal, but at least she had known where she stood with him. The rules were always clear.

Who is Haitao?

She started. She wasn't used to someone else being in her thoughts.

I can't hear everything. Only when you are unguarded.

Haitao was my father. Or at least the one father I had. He found me during the Year of Chaos. He thought a girl would be useful, so he raised me and made me a thief. Taught me to trust no one, especially those closest to you.

Is that what a typical human parent does? Rayshan asked.

I can't say, she said. She had seen parents who treasured their children. But she had also seen parents who treated their children worse than their own livestock, which perhaps simply made Haitao average when it came to parenting.

Did she miss him? In a strange way, she did. She couldn't remember a life without him. And though he had been brutal, he had also protected her more times than she could count.

I have never had a family, but our bond feels . . . stronger than that.

It is, Rayshan agreed. *Like I said, dragons almost never know their parents. It's not something we miss.*

Jin remembered an identical conversation with Lu. Lu had been sold to Haitao as a boy and so remembered a loving family, a home. According to Haitao, he had found Jin the day she was born. So he was her father, mother, and world. But Lu had told her of everything she was missing, things she didn't miss only because she'd never experienced them.

The only thing I know about my parents is that one of them must be a Jade for me to be one too. Rayshan glanced at her. *Your coloring is different. Surely that must tell you something of your parentage?*

She thought about this. *There must be foreign blood in me, but that's all I know.* That was what made all the taunts about her birth, like Jao's, cut so deep, for she would likely never learn the truth.

It doesn't matter who made you, Rayshan said. *What matters is what you make of yourself.*

Maybe. Jin was unconvinced.

Why do you rub that spot behind your ear whenever you talk of your parents?

Jin pulled her hand away.

You can tell me, Jin.

She swept her hair aside to let him see the hairline behind her ear. He placed his front claws on her chest and craned his neck to see.

Is that a scar?

A brand. It says Kway, as in precious.

Who put it there?

Haitao said I had this on me when he found me. That it was newly burned on me, still weeping. It's why he named me Kway Jin: precious gold. He hoped I would bring him riches.

You think your actual parents marked you?

She shrugged. *I don't have many explanations. It's not a usual slave mark, which makes me think I wasn't from the slavers. But why would they mark me, or give me away?*

Many children were taken during the Year of Chaos. Sometimes she liked to think that her parents had marked her as "precious" before they died, out of love. But something about it made little sense, and in her darker moments she wondered if it really was a slave brand.

Rayshan seemed puzzled. *You are sad that you do not know your parents?*

Yes. *She frowned. If you have no one to care for you after hatching, how do you dragons survive?*

Rayshan made a little quiver of his skin, in something she sensed was like a shrug.

We grow quickly in the first couple of months, and it's why we have this webbed ridge, to scare off attackers while we are small and more vulnerable. Other creatures have parents to defend them when they are weak, but we must learn to fend for ourselves or die.

That's a very harsh beginning, Jin said. She understood so little of dragons, or how they came to be.

Another shiver rippled over Rayshan's shoulder in a shrug. *It is how life is. We absorb much information through the insides of our eggs, which tells us about these things and how to learn. That gives us an advantage, as I have the imprint of thousands of years of dragon history in my mind.*

Jin's thoughts spun. *So you are born with all this knowledge?*

Some things, yes. It comes to me in pieces.

Do you know much of Dragon Class tradition?

I can guide you to an extent. But nothing I say will take away the odd notion these humans have that only boys can be dragonriders. There is nothing in my collective memory that says that.

You were meant for a king, Rayshan.

He cocked his head. *So?*

Well, you were on your way to a king. And I stole you. I am sorry. She realized she meant it. She had never regretted stealing anything in her life; it was all a job. But her stealing Rayshan had changed the course of his life forever.

You are worth more than a thousand kings, Jin.

That now familiar hum reverberated through her, the strength of the bond beating like another pulse. A week ago she had wanted to get away from the egg, but this week she couldn't imagine living without Rayshan's pulse just under her own.

Thank you, Rayshan. That . . . means so much to me. She had never been good at expressing her feelings, but here, speaking in her head, was different.

Rayshan's tail curled around her wrist. She leaned her head against the wall, feeling the smooth scales and thrumming warmth against her hand, as if he had absorbed the sun during the day and now gave off its heat. Soft noises emanated from his throat and mind.

Are you singing?

He hummed louder in affirmation.

I didn't know dragons sang.

We sing all the time, but it's a different kind of song. We call it the Firesong. It's like a tapestry of dragon history and memories. But you need to listen not just with the ears.

What do you mean?

Listen with your being. Try it.

She relaxed, closing her eyes, and focused. At first she couldn't decide what made this different. The sounds were in her head, but this didn't sound like Rayshan's voice or any instrument that she had heard before. And it wasn't just something that played in her mind; it was a beat that reverberated in rhythmic patterns through her body. When she leaned into it, the music made her see colors she couldn't name.

You don't see all the colors we dragons do, Rayshan explained. *But through the Firesong you can.*

She relaxed again, sinking deeper into the rhythms, until the colors melted together and formed shapes, and the shapes puddled into complex figures, and then she realized she was watching scenes, as if from a play and yet not a play. She saw dragons winging across a wind-scraped sky and heard the song of hundreds of them as they headed for a jagged mountain that pierced the clouds. Nine Claw Mountain, she was sure, where the dragon queen laid her eggs and chose those to gift to the Tang empire. White smoke drifted from the peak, and she saw an egg nestled in a hollow on the side of the mountain. Not just any egg, but Rayshan's egg, and then it was being retrieved by a rider and his dragon and rolled into a box lined with hay and silk before being carried over the fields to the royal city of Changan. The scene dissolved, then reformed into a nest of warmth, where she heard singing. It was Rayshan, singing in his egg, growing and transforming. Tenderness flooded her for this unborn Rayshan, this Rayshan that she hadn't yet met.

The image seeped away until all was dark. She drifted in it, at peace, but then the darkness shifted. It moved and gathered into a ball before her, then burst apart and rained down. It rained upon the city, a city she wasn't sure was Changan.

She saw a chaotic time, of people killing each other with daggers and swords, trampling others with their horses, or setting dogs on the young or the maimed. Over the smoking city a dragon rose, a Jade, with a towering rider on his back that seemed to be made of shadows. He didn't seem solid, and yet when he sliced down with his sword, heads and limbs rolled. He plowed through the people and dragons before him, and as he came near Jin, she heard the Firesong hiss a name: *Mengkhis Lai.*

The warmth in her shrank into a sudden, numbing cold. She had heard of Mengkhis Lai, the notorious man behind the Year of Chaos. He was flying toward her, sword raised. His dragon opened its great green jaws and descended while she stood and watched, unable to run. The roar from its throat made her ears bleed.

She woke with a jerk. Dusk was leaking into black along the cave edges, and she scrambled to her feet. Rayshan looked spooked.

What was that?

Rayshan's flicking tail showed his agitation, and he made a noncommittal noise. Clearly he was just as unsettled by the visions in the Firesong as she was.

She heard the distant peal of a bell and realized it must be much later than she realized. Emar had, during his instructions, mentioned a strict curfew that all students were to observe. She placed a reassuring hand on Rayshan. *It was in the past. Mengkhis Lai's time is no more.*

Rayshan snorted uneasily but nodded.

Jin rushed from the cave, calling out a hasty mental goodbye as she went. She smiled encouragingly before she turned her back, trying to tame the unsettled feeling that lingered. She had heard of Mengkhis Lai. But she had never known that he rode a Jade.

CHAPTER 10

*A*fter she had rinsed her mouth with tea and rubbed her face with cold water from the kitchen, she made her way to her room. Almost everyone was already in their own beds or preparing their blankets. Jin pulled her curtain closed, then spread her clean sheets over her cot, but a gut instinct made her climb under the covers fully clothed.

"Hey Jin," Madu called out, "if you get lonely or scared, you can always sleep with Panshalar. You'll be safe with him, since he's got no—"

"Shut your hole, Madu!" Panshalar shouted, clearly riled.

There were laughs and whistles at this, but Jin said nothing.

A few more taunts followed, but getting no response, Madu and his friends settled into disgruntled silence. Jin put her hands behind her head and thought of what Haitao had often said: "The empty vessel makes the most sound."

Jin closed her eyes, feigning sleep. The lights fluttered out as the warder on duty extinguished them, and a bell marking the curfew hour rang out. Soon the door was shut and the sounds of night settled in: tossing in beds, the warder's footsteps receding as he went to the next rooms, the swoop of bats just outside the eaves.

She listened to the sounds of breathing evening out, and after a while she opened her eyes. To her surprise, the room wasn't dark. She turned her head and peeked around the curtain to look, and saw Aadan, propped on one arm in bed with a small lamp lit.

He didn't seem to notice her, but concentrated on the book in his hands. She let the curtain slip back and lay down, frowning. She had never seen anyone so interested in books.

Something tickled her innate sense, and she listened. She heard the sound again, the groan of a bed, but this time not that of someone rolling in sleep. Rather, it was that telltale slow creak of someone who was trying to get out of bed without waking others.

She waited, and the sound came again, followed by the soft slide of feet on the floor. And another creak, from a different bed.

She balled her fists and was ready even before she heard Aadan's voice.

"Jin!"

She rolled off the bed in a flash, hearing the fists hit the place where she had been. She sent a swinging kick against her attacker, propelling him back against the next bed, which woke everyone. The light from Aadan's lamp was enough for Jin to see the three shadows gathering on her.

Madu was definitely one, for she recognized the broad shoulders and smelled the soap he used—the same smell from the jacket. The others—she wasn't sure, but neither of them was from her wing, she was fairly certain. The one who had fallen rushed her, leaping over the bed between them. She ducked his fists and landed a blow to his groin. As he doubled over, her knee met his face, crumpling his nose.

"Son of a reptile!" the downed one's voice gurgled with blood.

Jin bent into a horse stance, ready.

The two rushed her together, and an excited murmur started amongst the other beds as the students all got into watching the fight. Some stood on their beds, while others seemed concerned about the warden.

Madu reached Jin first and tried to grab her from the side so his friend could land a blow. She drove her elbow into his midsection and brought her heel down hard on his foot. He cursed but stayed the course, trying to crush her with brute strength. She flipped him with a deft cut of her other foot, taking his weight out from under him and sending him crashing to his back. She straddled him as his friend came to his rescue, pressing his arm hard around her windpipe.

Jin let him lift her, but not before delivering a brutal kick to Madu's face. The man clutched his jaw in pain. Her attacker wrapped one hand around her throat while his other pinned her arm to her side. She jabbed up and back sharply with her free hand. The first try hit a brow, but the second connected with the eye, making her attacker drop her.

She stood, wheezing from her bruised throat, and glared at the other riders. Someone had lit another lantern, and a row of faces stared back at her, some shocked, others sullen, a few reluctantly impressed.

"If any of you want to come for me, do it now. But you won't ride for weeks." She stared at them all, challenging.

Her gaze settled on Aadan. "You. Why did you warn me?"

"What do you mean?"

"Why did you help me?" she said. No one did anything for someone else without wanting something in return. Haitao and bitter experience had taught her that.

"I don't understand," Aadan said slowly. "I helped you and you're upset?"

"Thank you, but I don't need help. And I don't owe you anything. Are we clear?"

"Very well," he replied angrily, "Next time I won't say anything. Die if you wish."

Her attackers began crawling back to their beds, and she was about to do the same when the door flew open.

The warder entered, raising a lantern that revealed the bloodied faces and bruised bodies of the men.

The warder gaped, and then seeing the blood on Jin's face, he snapped, "You, girl, come with me."

She rubbed her sore knuckles and complied, apprehensive. Closing the door behind them, the warder led her through several corridors to the northern part of the compound.

The warder hissed, "Stay here," before entering a door. She heard rapping and then voices. One of them sounded slurred. Before long the warder came out and jerked his head.

Emar, wearing a thick robe, sat at a round table. His gloves were gone, revealing a left hand with the same unnatural white hue and texture as his face. A wine jug with a single cup, along with a tapered pipe and the cloying sweet odor of poppy hinted at Emar's interrupted activities.

"Master Emar, are you sure you should be—"

The head trainer didn't give the warder a chance to finish. "I said I'm fine. Now leave her and go. I'm in charge of my recruits, and I'll handle this."

His words were slower than usual, yet still carried

the same unflinching authority. The warder bowed and with one last disapproving look at Jin, left.

Emar poured a cup of wine and looked at her over it. The chalk-colored side of his face appeared ghoulish in the lantern light. "You intend to do this every night?"

Jin said nothing. Would he punish her or Madu? She only hoped the empress wouldn't change her mind and send Jin to the salt mines. Emar downed his wine. He poured another cup and catching her look, said, "This keeps me alive. That and the poppy."

"I wouldn't know, Master Emar."

He regarded her with his one good eye, as if trying to assess whether she mocked him. "No, you wouldn't. And you'd best pray to Buddha that it stays that way."

"Is it . . . painful?"

He glared at her, as if again sensing that she was being flippant. He softened upon seeing her expression and offered his left hand. "Very. Go on. Touch it."

She didn't really want to but also didn't want to offend him. She placed her fingers on the hard, unnaturally smooth surface of his hand—not soft enough to be skin, not hard enough to be marble, yet icy cold. She pulled back, unnerved.

"Best you understand now, this is what awaits if Rayshan dies," Emar said. "It starts as a tiny piece of you turning to ice and then spreads. Usually the rider is gone in a year. Most choose to kill themselves before the time comes, rather than endure the pain."

Jin reached out for the reassuring hum of Rayshan. "I am sorry. You lost your dragon recently?"

Emar pulled away, grimacing. "Yalongma died in the Year of Chaos." At her confused look, he said, "Yes, twenty years ago. I'm cheating death and all eight levels of hell with the help of wine, poppy, and the skills of the imperial mages."

"Why?" Realizing how rude her question sounded, she added, "I mean, if it's painful and most choose death, why did you choose to live?"

He pondered this, then grunted. "That's my business, rider." Emar poured himself another drink. "But right now, I need to decide what to do with you. I cannot have you maiming my students, even if they are to blame. I can, and will, punish them for their behavior. But I can't change their hearts and minds. That's up to you."

What if their hearts and minds are unchangeable? Jin thought, bitter. "Please, do you have to report this to the empress?"

"We will deal with this in the morning." He ordered a servant in. "Find a carpet, a blanket, and a pillow."

The servant rushed to obey. When he came back, Emar motioned at the floor, and the servant hurried to place the items out in the semblance of a bed.

"Now try to stay there without breaking anyone else's nose." He pushed himself off his chair and limped from the room, closing the doors behind him. She lay down on the makeshift bed, curled around herself, and reached out for Rayshan. Though the distance meant she couldn't hear his words, just feeling his muted hum was enough to comfort her to sleep.

Thankfully, this time she had no visions of Mengkhis Lai or his Jade.

CHAPTER 11

The next morning, she woke before Emar but didn't move off the mat, still worried about what punishment he might give her. Emar appeared, clearly worse for wear after the previous night, pulling on an outer robe. He let her visit the night soil bucket, then ordered her to follow him, without offering her breakfast.

He led her through the dorm courtyard and out the gates, through the private back streets that connected the Hall of Bright Fire with the imperial city.

"Master Emar, I will take your punishment, but do we need to bother the empress?"

"Yes, we do," Emar growled. "Now please, my head hurts almost as much as my dying limbs, so leave me in peace."

They walked the remaining half hour in silence. Jin tried to keep control of her nerves, for the empress learning of the fight last night would not win her any favors.

They navigated a maze of walkways before arriving at a guarded courtyard and announcing their presence to the sentry. The guard bowed and slipped behind a set of doors with ornate phoenix and dragon carvings. He re-appeared a moment later and motioned them to enter. When they did, Jin saw they were in the empress's private quarters, and the ruler was clearly not pleased. She was seated before a lavish breakfast with Minister Wei and a beautifully made-up girl in a peach-tinted gown who seemed to have a permanent smile on her face.

"What is so important that you had to come see me at my breakfast?" the empress asked. The empress looked immaculate, even at this hour.

"Your Highness, we must make alternate lodgings for the new dragonrider, Jin."

The empress turned to Jin. "I made it clear, did I not? If you can't survive in the men's dorms, then you aren't worthy of Dragon Class."

Emar cleared his throat. "I'm not worried about Jin, Your Highness. I'm worried about the men."

The empress looked from him to Jin. "Oh?"

"If we don't move her, there may be only half the students left by the trials."

The empress looked back to Jin, and she steeled herself for the woman's wrath. Instead, a hint of a smile crept into the empress's eyes.

"What kind of damage?"

Emar sighed at the empress's amusement. "Broken noses, Your Highness. So far. But injured hands or feet will prevent riding."

The empress nodded. "Very well. We shall arrange for separate rooms, purely for the safety of the male riders." Her smile faded, and she fixed a contemplative gaze on Jin. "I think it may be good for such a wild woman to have female friends. Let us find a suitable lady of the court for her to room with."

Jin's heart clenched. The thought of living with women filled her with anxiety, for she had little idea what was expected of her. Better the demon one had wrestled than the one you hadn't, as the saying went. But she thought better of protesting.

"Yes, Your Highness," Emar answered. "I may have a lady in mind. Lady Jiang would welcome another person in her household."

The empress scoffed. "Lady Jiang can't distinguish her nose from her foot when it comes to etiquette."

"Lady Shu? She is well respected at court."

"And she couldn't teach a fish to swim."

"Your Highness, I'd be happy to have her live with me."

Jin looked up, surprised. The girl at the table had spoken, drawing a frown from the minister.

"My aunt recently went back to the country, so I have rooms to spare, and I was just thinking how lonely I'll be without my aunt."

The empress raised an eyebrow and then turned to the man. "What say you, Minister?" the empress said. "Would you be willing to have our newest dragonrider stay with your niece here?"

Minister Wei cast a look at Jin and seemed about to disagree, when the girl spoke again.

"It's no inconvenience for me, and I am sure you'd agree, Uncle, we'd both do anything to be of service to the empress."

The minister looked unsure, but at his niece's beseeching eyes seemed to swallow his protests. "Yes. Of course. If Meipin agrees, then I'd be happy to allow the girl dragonrider to stay in Meipin's quarters."

"Then it's decided." The empress turned to Emar. "Have her things moved today."

The empress dismissed them. As they walked away from the empress's quarters, Jin's misgivings must have been obvious.

"Consider yourself lucky," Emar said. "Lady Meipin's rooms will be luxurious, so in my eyes you're being rewarded, not punished. Be glad."

"Yes, Master Emar." She let a pause settle, then ventured, "I don't mind sleeping in Dragon City. I'd be happy to—"

"That is strictly forbidden. We do not have riders and dragons dorming together."

His tone made it clear that it was risky to push this further, and so she let the matter drop. She was running out of rope.

"You are half huren. You should understand you need to step carefully," he added under his breath.

She glanced at him, and at her look, he sighed.

"I very much want to see you succeed, believe it or not."

"Because I'm a huren?"

He grunted. "I don't care about that. You have the makings of a fine rider, if you can ignore those who want to bait you to fight, and . . . " he hesitated, as if he wasn't sure whether to continue. When he did, it was with a tinge of defiance. "And you remind me of someone."

"Who?"

He regarded her, then shook his head, almost sad. "It doesn't matter. Someone long gone. Now try to make less trouble, and focus on the tests. Or you'll be that much closer to the mines. Let's get you to training. We're late as it is."

MORNING EXERCISES, she learned, involved several laps around the training grounds, called the Blood Oval, before they were assigned different exercises: there was an obstacle course with hurdles and rope webs, buckets of water for muscle strengthening, and a beam for practicing balance. Today, Emar made them all do an extra two rounds, until everyone, Jin included, was practically on their knees at the last stretch.

"You can expect more of the same every time you mistreat a fellow rider," Emar said affably. "When it comes to working you lot, my ideas are as plentiful as the scales on a dragon, so feel free to sample them all if you wish." He limped down the line of students as he spoke. "Now as you may already know, you'll have to pass two physical trials to enter Dragon Class: the snowfire trial and the geography trial. The first you have to pass is bringing back a snowfire bloom."

Jin glanced at the others, suspecting the trial was more difficult than it sounded.

"You will fly with your dragons up Ice Beard Mountain to retrieve a snowfire bloom. The flowers are rare on the lower reaches but grow best in the higher reaches. This is to test your flight abilities, how you deal with height and cold, and, of course, how observant you are." He let his words sink in. "As long as you bring back a flower, you pass." He paused. "But some of you might like to set yourself the challenge of coming first, as there is special honor in that."

Jin caught Madu standing taller and his friends tossing superior glances at the other riders. In their minds, he had already won.

They were allowed a quick toweling off before heading to the classrooms. In the dorms, she followed the other riders out and down the corridor, to a large hall with rows of low tables and cushions.

Everyone found a spot, and Jin stood away from the others, toward the back. She had never set foot in a classroom and wasn't sure what to do. She saw Aadan sit cross-legged at a table near the front. He seemed the most practiced of the lot, so she modeled her behavior after his, sitting cross-legged at one of the back tables.

A wooden clapper sounded, and Jin's attention flew to the front of the room. A tall figure wearing a short-sleeved *pao* over his crisp blue shirt stood there, surveying them with stern eyes.

"Peace upon your morning, class."

"Peace upon your morning, Teacher Shu!" the class shouted in unison.

"Today we continue our lesson in—" The teacher frowned at Jin. "You there. You are the girl dragonrider, are you not?"

"Yes."

"Bow when you speak to your teacher!" Shu said sharply.

Jin lowered her head to the table, uncertain. She had learned how to behave at feasts, official parties, bathing houses, and theater shows so that she could blend in and lift valuables. But a classroom was an entirely new environment.

"Now understand this, girl." Shu strode over to her table. "There is to be no corrupting of my students, do you understand?"

Corrupting? At the snickers nearby she realized what he meant, and she flushed.

"I would not corrupt your students if you offered me a thousand bao," she retorted.

There was a roar of laughter at this until Teacher Shu rapped his fan on the table and restored silence. "Good. You'll treat my classroom with respect, girl."

He swept back to the head of the class, and Jin cautiously rose back to a seated position.

Shu picked up a thick scroll from his desk. "Let us review the week. Who can tell me the history of Dragon Class's founding? You, Student Li."

A short student at the front answered, "Dragon Class was born when the First Emperor united China. He found Nine Claw Mountain and made a treaty with the Dragon Queen, who allowed him to use her children to unify the warring kingdoms."

"Very good, Student Li. That is all. And Student Aadan, tell me the rules that the Dragon Queen decreed in exchange for the use of her children?"

"The empire can only use her children by following three laws: riders may only bond with male dragons, no one may kill a dragon or his rider, and no one shall blood bond with a dragon."

"Very good," Shu said in a tone that Jin recognized despite never having set foot in a classroom. It was the tone of someone speaking to their prized apprentice. Aadan was clearly the favorite here, despite his foreign blood. Good to know, she thought.

"And why is it we do not blood bond?" Shu asked. "Student Wang, can you guess?"

All eyes turned to her, expectant.

What even is blood bonding? Jin thought to herself.

Rayshan's voice came to her in snippets: *. . . blood . . . strengths . . . a dragon shares . . .*

Realizing the silence had become long, Jin said, "Because it's against the three laws?"

Shu's frown melted into an approving smile. "That is right. It's against the law."

"Teacher Shu, why did Mengkhis Lai blood bond if he knew it was dangerous and wrong?" someone piped up.

A somber hush settled on the room. Jin turned and saw a thin rider who seemed almost more awkward than she was. He turned a bright crimson at everyone's gaze and pulled into himself like a snail.

"Because Mengkhis Lai was of sick mind and even sicker heart," Shu replied. "Now I am not teaching a class on Mengkhis Lai, so I will answer no more of those questions, Bo Tan."

Student Bo Tan nodded, chastened, and Jin caught a scoffing sound to her left. She looked over and saw Panshalar, his bulk making his table look like a toy.

"His family's one of the richest ones," Panshalar whispered. "He's only here because of his birth."

Jin heard the bitterness in his tone. Clearly the Mongolian's illegitimacy was a sore point, especially amongst dragonriders who all came of noble blood. They were sparrows amongst swans, as the saying went. So be it. Sparrows were faster and survived better.

After what seemed like an interminable lecture on

the history of war technology and battles with neighboring kingdoms like Silla, an assistant sounded the gong to end the lesson.

"That is all for today, class," Shu intoned. "And I hope you took notes, because you'll need them for the written exam at year's end."

Everyone bowed and said in unison, "Good day, Master Shu."

Jin bit her lip. A written exam. Throughout the class she contemplated her options, but all involved sacrificing her pride. She stood and filed out into the hallway, craning her neck until she spotted Aadan's tall frame.

She wove through the crowd until she drew alongside him. He slowed until everyone else had left the halls and it was just the two of them.

"I need to ask for something."

One eyebrow rose. "You don't need my help, remember?"

She took a breath. "I don't trust others easily, that's all."

"Clearly," he replied. "Is this about you not being able to read?" At her look of surprise, he added, "You didn't write a word the whole class."

"So will you teach me? I need to pass the written exam."

"Very well. But you won't be able to learn in one lesson. This will take weeks, you understand, and we haven't much time."

She nodded.

Aadan motioned for her to follow.

"Where are we going?"

"To the Dragon Class library. We might as well start now."

Of course Dragon Class would have its own library. She was still getting used to the luxuries available in the palace.

As they walked, a thought occurred to her. "Do you speak many other languages?"

"Chinese. Farsi, my father's native tongue. Aramaic. Greek. Hebrew. Tigray. A smattering of Mongolian."

She barely knew where half the languages were from.

"Do you speak any?" he asked, and she could see him contemplating her foreign appearance.

"A bit of Turkish," she replied. But this was stretching the truth, for she had really only learned a few key phrases while working merchant caravans that passed through Gaozho.

They strode through outdoor corridors until they reached a wide courtyard with open blue doors, guarded by carved dragons on either side. They entered and found round study tables with benches, and shelves filled with scrolls and books of every size and color. The shelves reached the ceiling and ran several stories high.

Jin looked around, awed by the sheer amount of

paper in the place. She hadn't known that so many books existed in the world.

"Let's sit here, and I will show you the basics."

She sat obediently while Aadan rifled through a few of the shelves and came back with an armful of scrolls.

"Can you write any words? Your name?"

She shook her head, an unexpected shame jolting her. She was grateful he kept any judgment to himself.

"I'll start with your surname. See if you can follow," he said. He took out parchment from where it sat in a teak holder.

"Paper is free to use?" She had difficulty imagining such a luxury available to all.

He seemed amused. "Yes. Scholars at the library can use as much as they like. Now pay attention. You do know how to hold a brush, don't you?" At her hesitation he changed tack. "Alright, books aside for now. Let's start with some basic numbers."

Though she chafed at asking for his help, she reminded herself why she was here. She couldn't afford to fail Dragon Class.

Within the first hour she had mastered how to hold the brush, and with one of the readily available ink stones, she could write the numbers one to ten fairly confidently. It wasn't pretty, but it was readable, as Aadan pointed out.

"You are not from the noble families, I take it, given you don't read."

She practiced a brushstroke, the talk of family

making her think of Lu and Haitao, Little Mole and Fox. She firmly kept her tears in check. "I grew up with a strict Confucian. He didn't believe in educating girls. Are all Sogdians so studious?"

"I'm Persian, not Sogdian," he corrected her. "My father is studious, at least. He made sure I read all the classics, all our traditional religious texts. Then he taught me other languages so I could read books from other lands."

"What's so interesting in all those books?"

He gave her a look of surprise. Seeing she was in earnest, he appeared momentarily at a loss for words. "Books are the gateway to . . . to everything. You can learn anything you want from them, go anywhere. Through books I have learned how to speak languages, communicate better with my dragon Wanli, learn the history of my country, which I've never seen."

"You were born here?" For some reason, she hadn't thought about the possibility that he had never seen his country.

He nodded. "I know China much more than I know my own home." The sadness in his voice was unmistakable.

"That must seem strange."

"My father worries I'm Han in all but my skin," he said. "He wants me to learn Persian history better than China's history, but I think it's a draw at the moment."

"You must know almost everything, reading so much."

He shrugged modestly. "Not everything. I don't know how a woman becomes bonded with a Jade, for instance." He leaned forward. "How did you encounter your dragon, when women aren't allowed into the hatchery?"

"I stole my dragon," Jin explained, remembering Emar's instructions, "breaking into the hatchery."

"Stole? Why would—" he broke off, astonished. "Did you realize you could have been killed?"

"At the time it seemed worth it." Which was true. She and Lu had thought the cargo would be their salvation, not knowing the Dragon Class was transporting an actual dragon.

To Jin's relief, a gong sounded outside, signaling the end of the hour and interrupting Aadan's next question.

"Same time tomorrow?" Jin said. She wanted to avoid spinning more lies than she had to.

Aadan nodded. "Same time tomorrow. I'll see you on the Blood Oval later."

He left, and she sat back, looking at the surrounding shelves. Was Aadan right? Were these portals to other worlds, to wells of knowledge? She thought of all the libraries she had robbed, always seeking jewelry people kept hidden in secret drawers and scroll boxes. But if Aadan was right, then all those paled in comparison to what was inside the books. She was going to learn to read.

She grinned.

CHAPTER 12

Emar and Jin walked an interminable maze of corridors and courtyards, past moon gates and through gardens.

Jin was exhausted, in mind and body, from her first full day at Dragon Class. After Aadan's lesson, she and the students had gone to Dragon City for a long demonstration of proper dragon care, then spent the afternoon doing training exercises to strengthen their mental bonds.

Now, the shadows had stretched to thin wraiths when at last Emar conferred with a guard at a large complex with double-storied rooms on all sides. The guard nodded and let them enter a well-kept garden with fishponds cloaked in lotuses. They crossed a marble bridge to the main rooms, but before they could knock, a voice called from behind them.

"Master Emar! I've been waiting!"

They turned. Standing on the path was the plump girl from breakfast, her hair coiffed and her peach-colored gowns flowing about her. Her smile hid her teeth, the perfect rendition of a court beauty.

Emar bowed deeply, and Jin followed his example.

"Lady Meipin, peace upon your afternoon. Dragon Class thanks you for sharing your accommodation with dragonrider Jin."

Meipin made a demure gesture. "Oh, it's a pleasure. My uncle lives in service to the empress. Come, I can't wait to show you your new home, and you and I will be like sisters!"

Jin doubted that, given how many hours she'd be in training, but she smiled politely. "Thank you."

Emar looked relieved and turned to Jin. "Remember, staying here means you need extra time to reach the training grounds. I won't tolerate tardiness, so make sure you still attend all your classes on time."

"Yes, Master Emar."

He nodded. "I will see you then."

When he had left, Meipin took Jin by the arm and began leading her around the luxurious quarters. "This is your wing," she said, throwing open the latticed doors to a suite of rooms.

Jin thought she'd misheard. A *wing*?

"Your bathing quarters are through there," Meipin continued. "Here's a study room, bedroom, and receiving room. But I'm hoping you'll dine with me in our shared foyer at night."

Meipin tugged her along, showing her the spacious hall that connected the two wings of the mansion. A round rosewood table dominated the center, with beautifully carved wooden chairs. Three long *kangs* covered in silk cushions lined the sides while scrolls with flowing calligraphy and ink paintings covered the walls.

Jin turned to Meipin. "Thank you for hosting me. I hope you gain favor with the empress."

The girl's smile turned mischievous. "Oh, that's why my uncle agreed. But I admit I suggested it for selfish reasons. The entire palace is so amazed to have a woman as part of Dragon Class! And to think you're staying with me! This is incredible. I want you to share all the details."

"I don't know all the details," Jin said.

Meipin laughed. Now that they were alone, Meipin showed her teeth and laughed as raucously as any man. "Is it true that you hatched the Jade? And that you maimed several of the imperial men?"

"I didn't maim any imperial soldiers, no." Jin looked around and caught the sun hanging low over the roof. "I must take leave. I have to tend to my dragon and—"

"If you must," Meipin pouted, disappointed. "But tell me, do you prefer jasmine or lotus? I'll have flowers put in your room. Do you like peach? I adore peach shades. I always buy extra, so you're welcome to have all the spares. You don't even need to return them."

"Thank you," Jin said, bowing and backing out. "But I must go, I'm late."

And before the girl could try to stop her, she slipped away, eager to leave Meipin and the prospect of awkward conversation for the frictionless communication with Rayshan.

* * *

OVER THE NEXT TWO WEEKS, Jin tried to adjust to her new life. Her days started just after sunup and ended only an hour or two before dusk. Emar pushed her as hard as the others in a strict regime of running, weight exercises, and practical skills such as knot making, dragon care, and drills. And though she found the training hard enough to make her nauseous, she refused to give anyone the satisfaction of knowing.

Her days settled into a routine. She had to arrive at the Blood Oval by sunrise for morning drills and exercise, where her endurance slowly improved. Next they had an hour to clean themselves and have breakfast, before classroom lessons in history, math, and botany followed, but Jin used this hour to learn to read with Aadan. In the afternoons they all returned to the Blood Oval for training with their dragons before they were expected to carry out a roster of chores that included cooking, saddle maintenance, and dragon care. Jin enjoyed dragon care best. They walked to Dragon City at the same time each day and gathered oils, brushes, clippers, and hemp cloths to clean their dragons' scales, teeth, and nails. All the other dragons were double Rayshan's size, as they had hatched earlier.

Each student also had to choose a specialty class for the afternoon. The alchemy class was full, which left Jin with the choices of medicine, astronomy, foreign languages, or engineering. She decided on medicine. The way her life was going, she would never travel beyond her borders or have need of the stars. But being able to stitch a wound or heal herself would always be useful. That the only recruit from her year in the medicine lesson was Panshalar was also welcome, for besides Aadan, Panshalar seemed the warmest toward her, and she found him bearable once she became accustomed to his humor. The rigorous physical training and classes left her sore and trembling every night, but she made sure to never join in any complaints. The empress would, she was sure, make good on expelling her for the first sign of whining.

At the end of the second week, Meipin excitedly showed her a package that had arrived from the tailor: new dragon leathers especially cut to fit a woman's form, along with her own Dragon Class badge.

"It's too bad it doesn't come in peach," Meipin lamented, smoothing a hand over the leathers.

But Jin didn't care. They were high-quality, tailored leathers with fine stitching and stretchability, more expensive than anything she had ever owned. Putting them on gave her an unexpected sense of protection and belonging.

That same day, their usual history class was exchanged for a biology lesson. Jin followed the rest of her class into the part of Dragon City that housed the dragon hatchery.

She wasn't exactly sure what she had expected—a hen house or shelves lined with eggs. But the hatchery was more like a cave, with a furnace in one corner and pipes running along the walls. The heat struck her first, a pressing wet heat that made the air cling to her skin.

"The dragon eggs mature faster when warm," came a voice behind them. "So we pump hot water through the stone nests to keep the hatchery a stable temperature."

They all turned to see a rotund man with leather guards on his forearms. Sweat beaded his forehead and upper lip, but he didn't bother wiping it, as he was clearly used to the constant heat.

"Welcome, students. For those of you who don't know me, I am Master Lo, Chief Caretaker of the Imperial Hatchery. Fourth-generation caretaker, I might add. And today you will help me check the eggs for warmth, size, and movement. Let's begin."

Master Lo paired them into teams, and Jin was relieved to be paired with Aadan. Master Lo handed out scrolls and ink and brushes to them all.

"We keep records of the eggs' growth to estimate when they hatch. You will see tags next to each egg, with their number. Write the number, and then measure the egg and note this down. You should also handle the egg and make sure it's warm. Any egg cooler than your hand is sick or has died and should be removed. All eggs have a mark to show which way is up. If you find an egg on its side or upside down, very gently reposition it the right way. Questions?"

Jin looked around at the twenty or so eggs, all of different hues. Some were larger than others, and no two shells looked the same: some were spotted, others pale, one black as ink. "What if one hatches? Will it try to bond with us?"

A few sniggers broke out, but Master Lo beamed, clearly eager to talk about his passion. "No, no, a very good question. Baby dragons are highly sensitive and intelligent. They can sense when a rider is already bonded to another."

Master Lo assigned each team two eggs, and Jin followed Aadan to theirs.

"You want to do the writing or the measuring?" he asked.

"I'll measure," she said, taking the roll of marked silk from him. She didn't fancy drawing ridicule from Master Lo or anyone else who would read her writing. She placed a hand on the first egg they came to, a ruddy one marbled with dusty yellow. Warmth radiated beneath her hand, reminding her of the day Rayshan had hatched.

"Is this where you bonded to Wanli?" she asked.

Aadan shook his head, clearly fond of the memory. "He was already hatched when I met him, so he was in the nursery. Warm?"

Jin nodded, and Aadan wrote this down.

"What about him?" Jin asked, indicating Master Lo, who was busy showing Panshalar and Madu how to turn an egg over. "What if a dragon bonds to him?"

"The master of the hatchery and his assistants all wear a lead vest," Aadan said. "The dragon senses a weak connection and rejects them."

Something clicked in her memory. Rayshan's egg had been in a lead box, to prevent him from bonding in case he hatched. That explained the box's weight, and she expected the mage had worked a spell to make the box lighter for transport.

"How big is this one?" Aadan's question brought her back to the present.

She wrapped the silk around the middle of the dragon egg and quickly counted the lines. "Twelve." She looked at the nearby eggs. "Do any not hatch?"

Aadan glanced over. "It's rare. But even the smallest will hatch within the year."

An excited shout erupted from the far side of the hatchery. A baby dragon was squirming free of its shell, jaws snapping, and Jao and his partner, Bo Tan, were scrambling away from it. Bo Tan was clutching his fingers, where blood seeped.

"Coming through!" Master Lo said, striding forward between the fascinated students. He pulled a pair of thick leather gloves from his pocket and gave a short whistle. Two assistants emerged from a side room and at Master Lo's signal pulled out similar gloves. They stood in a circle around the egg, which was a large pale yellow, as the cat-sized dragon smashed the last of its shell with its tail. It surveyed those around it with filmy eyes, sniffing the air, then rushed for Master Lo's ankle, jaws open. The man clamped his hands around the beast and lifted, not even wincing as it sank its teeth into his glove and tried to shake. Bo Tan was still clutching his injured hand as one of the assistants pulled out a cloth bandage and began wrapping his wound.

"A magnificent silver!" Master Lo crowed, his sweaty face beaming. "Who would like to help weigh and measure him?"

Ezho raised a hand, along with a wiry rider with a shaved head whose name Jin didn't recognize.

"You," Master Lo said to Bo Tan, "see the infirmary after class and have some rice wine put on it." He turned to the room. "The rest of you, continue on!" He disappeared into a side door with his assistants and the hatchling, who was still trying to gnaw his glove.

"Are you alright?" Jin asked as Bo Tan sat down heavily next to her and Aadan.

He moved his fingers. "I'll live."

"You've been fine every time you've been bitten before," Aadan said, moving on to the next egg.

"How often does this happen?" Jin asked.

"Quite a bit," Bo Tan replied sulkily, examining his hand. "Don't you know how the bonding works?"

"Jin stole her dragon."

Bo Shan looked at her, incredulous. "You could have been killed."

"How does everyone else come into the hatchery without getting killed?" Jin asked.

"Every five years after the dragon harvest, five hundred rider hopefuls are allowed into the palace." Aadan tossed her the measuring silk, and she dutifully began measuring the next egg. "We are allowed inside in batches, with Master Lo overseeing us, so no one gets seriously hurt if an egg hatches and the dragon doesn't bond to anyone."

"What happens to the dragon who doesn't bond?"

"It's very rare," Bo Tan said. "But if so, it's forcibly bonded, right, Aadan?"

Jin frowned. "I thought forced bonding lessens the dragon."

"It does," Aadan said. "But it's preferable to having a wild, unbonded dragon. They can't be loosed in the wild, and the Dragon Queen won't take them back once they've hatched outside her nest. So it's either kill them or bond them."

When they had finished measuring the eggs and handed their scrolls to the assistants, Jin asked, "What about the riders who don't get chosen?"

Bo Tan shrugged. "They can come back and try their luck in five years if they are under twenty-five."

He held up his injured hand. "Sometimes without all their fingers."

That afternoon, Emar summoned the first-year students to the Blood Oval with their dragons and spaced them all at intervals in a circle.

"Each dragon has an inner power according to his type," he said, moving along inside the circle and surveying them. "What are they? Bo Tan?"

Bo Tan nervously recited, "Bronzes have the power of strength. Silvers the power of water. Golds the power of metal. Blacks the power of air?"

Emar nodded. "Good." He looked at Jin, as if sensing her unspoken question. "Jades are unknowns. Each displays his own inner power in his own time."

Jin placed a hand on Rayshan, who had folded himself in her lap. She didn't know what any of those powers meant.

You will see, Rayshan said. *And we will find mine.*

Emar turned back to the students. "I want you all to focus on your bond, draw your energy inward."

He waited until they had all lowered their heads and their dragons had stopped pacing or fiddling to lie down next to them. Jin closed her eyes and sensed the pulse of her and Rayshan's bond, then grasped it and gently pulled. The energy came willingly, gathering like a ball of yarn as she wound it closer and closer to her, until it thrummed.

"Now sink deeper," Emar said. "Ask your dragons to

push down hard on the energy of your bond. And then harder still."

Jin frowned, trying to do as Emar said, but the locus of energy scattered, and Rayshan snorted.

Sorry. Let's try again.

They practiced all that afternoon, and little cries of triumph or wonder rose around the circle as the dragons successfully harnessed, even briefly, their inner power. Jao's bronze grew larger for a heartbeat before shrinking back to his normal size. Aadan's Wanli gleamed with a layer of water droplets he made appear on his scales, and shook off in a happy spray. Panshalar's gold dragon clinked the metal clasps on his rider's boots without touching them, and Madu's black dragon ruffled Madu's hair without moving.

Only Rayshan and Jin had nothing to show after an hour's attempts. Each time Jin tried to harness the gathered energy, it shattered into wisps around her.

"Good work," Emar called out at the gong, signaling the end of class. "Do not worry if you cannot harness your dragon's power yet, as this takes great effort. I encourage you to practice in your spare time as well, with small attempts."

Don't let it frustrate you, Rayshan said. *I am not like the others, which means my power is harder to find.*

But it was difficult to ignore the speculative looks the other students tossed her and Rayshan as they stood and accompanied their dragons back to Dragon City—and even harder to keep her anger in check when Madu made sure she overheard him remark to the brothers who always trailed him, "My uncle says that women can stunt a dragon's development. That's why they're not allowed in the hatchery or to bond."

Don't mind his drivel, Rayshan growled.

And though she appreciated her dragon's confidence, a grain of doubt chafed her. If no female rider had ever bonded to a dragon, then who was to say Madu was wrong?

CHAPTER 13

As the larches and firs brightened from green to a pollen yellow, the palace prepared for the empress's annual pilgrimage to the Temple of Heaven in the city's southern quarter. Master Chen and his assistants had no time for repairing leathers, as everyone was put to work readying silks and brocade for the two hundred carriages in the empress's entourage. The royal stables worked into the night polishing harnesses, readying saddles, and shining stirrups. Some of the older Dragon Class students were selected to form an aerial escort for the empress, and the sounds of the imperial musicians practicing could be heard whenever Jin passed through the courtyards on her way from the Blood Oval to Meipin's quarters.

Jin could hardly believe her ears when Emar told them they would have the day off. Since the empress only left the palace for sacrificial rites at the temple, the whole city would be celebrating the rare chance to see their ruler's procession through the streets.

Jin's wing mates were, like her, eager to leave the confines of the palace and have a day in the capital to join the festivities. But Jin looked forward to the holiday for very different reasons. In the week before the holiday, she gave two *fei* from her first monthly stipend to Meipin's maid, Ahlu, and instructed her to buy cotton trousers, a simple pao, and a plain brown shirt. She roughed them a little with a rock from Rayshan's cave, so they wouldn't appear too new.

Will you be long? Rayshan grumbled, a little sulky.

I'll be back by noon. There will be plenty of time to try to fly. They had been helping him try to get airborne, even if for just a wingbeat, but with limited success. Seeing he was still unconvinced, she added, "I'll bring oranges."

He hummed, appeased.

On the morning of the pilgrimage, Jin rose at dawn and pulled out her clothing. She dressed, checked the coin purse she had prepared the night before, and took a cold meat bun she had saved from her evening meal. Meipin and her household had already left the day before for her cousin's in the city's east, and so the rooms were deserted. When Jin arrived at the service gate leading from the imperial city into Changan proper, she saw a line of dragonriders already impatiently queuing in anticipation.

"Interesting choice of clothes."

She turned to see Aadan's tall frame behind her. In stark contrast to her outfit, he was dressed in clean, bright winter robes with soft felt boots that looked new.

"I don't have much besides dragonrider leathers," she said.

"Are you visiting the song houses?" Jin had overheard a few of the initiates mentioning the women with whom they intended to spend the holiday. The thought that Aadan might have a female companion somehow disappointed her.

He gave a surprised laugh. "Hardly. My father and I meet at the Persian temple this time every year."

She felt a flicker of relief. She had never experienced romantic feelings toward anyone, and her only experience of relationships had been what she'd seen at song houses.

Just then, a lusty cheer arose as the gatekeeper came with his keys and unbolted the gates that led to the city. The line moved quickly, and soon she was striding out onto the wide boulevards that radiated out from the palace. Aadan raised a hand in farewell before he pulled up his hood and walked toward the city's west.

She turned directly south, pushing thoughts of Aadan from her mind. She had never run the streets of Changan, but all major Chinese cities emulated the capital, so this would be a magnified version of Gaozho. Markets would be located in the heart of the city, and she hoped that even on a holiday such as today, the most ardent of vendors would still be there to earn a fei.

Already the streets were filling with vendors and stalls hawking all sorts of breakfast items and sweets. Fried dough floated in woks, pancakes made from egg and scallion sizzled on hot plates, and the smell of sweet candied apples on sticks beckoned. She burrowed like a rat into the throng, happy to lose herself in the city's rhythms.

As she walked, Jin reveled in the sights and sounds, awed despite herself. The sheer mass of people made her own city seem like a village. People of all ages and ethnicities thronged the streets. Though huren in Gaozho were common, they seemed to be everywhere here in the capital. Blond-haired women with blue eyes served tea and fermented milk at the inns, and Indian monks stood outside Buddhist temples with bowls for alms. Musicians from Persia and Khitan played rollicking tunes on instruments Jin couldn't name, and people in traditional Nanzhao dress sold finely embroidered raw silk, delicately wrapped packets of tea, and glittering beaded hats.

She was so engrossed she nearly missed the scribe. The man, dressed in a threadbare scholar's robe and holding a basket of brushes, ink, and paper, was working a cheap teahouse whose tables and chairs were all outside. The few customers he approached all waved him away.

"How much for a letter?"

The man turned and took in her clothing and worn shoes. "Two coppers a page."

She drew out her coin pouch and paid him, then paid for a cup of mare's milk for both of them. She had never hired a scribe herself, but she had spent enough time at teahouses and street corners to know you were expected to spend coin in exchange for a table and chair. And though her writing was improving steadily with Aadan, it was not so refined that she could compose an entire letter unaided.

As the serving boy brought them two steaming bowls, the scribe busied himself with his tools of trade.

"Please begin," the scribe said, brush poised over a sheet of paper.

Jin had thought through her message the night before. "Most respected third uncle. Sixth aunt sends her regards and wishes you to know her cough is much improved. We are grateful for the fei you sent, but please don't trouble yourself sending more. How is second cousin's shop doing now?"

The scribe dutifully wrote this in long, flowing script. She invented other banal family events to fill the page, just to make a show of getting her money's worth, and watched as the scholar blew on the ink. Haitao would recognize the coded message and hopefully send a reply.

Just then she felt a whisper of fingers at her waist. Instinctively her hand clamped down, grabbing a wrist. She whipped the thief forward, ready to force his palm open, but instead found herself looking into the defiant eyes of a girl no more than seven years old. She wore tattered clothes two sizes too large while grimy feet protruded from shoes that looked like they'd fall apart if washed. One hand still clutched Jin's purse.

Jin froze, stunned. Even in their leanest days, Haitao had never kept her in rags or let her go barefoot.

In an instant the girl sank her teeth into Jin's hand, and Jin let go with a surprised cry. The girl shot away, melting back into the sea of pedestrians. Jin knew she could catch the girl if she wanted—after all, Jin had been pulling this trade far longer than the child—but decided against it. The girl needed that money more than Jin did, and she hoped it bought her some better treatment from her handler.

"Thieves are everywhere these days," the scribe sympathized, clearly relieved he had been paid upfront.

Jin checked her hand for blood, then patted her inner pocket where she had kept a few *fei* separate. It should be enough to pay for what she needed. She took the letter from the scribe and rose to leave. "Do you know which way to the nearest central market?"

"The eastern market will be closed today," the scribe said, packing his things. "You might find the western market open. Cross the central boulevard and head toward the Temple of Mercy."

Jin followed his directions. The walk gave her time to think about the girl at the tea house, which only made her think of Lu. Her determination grew to find out if he was alive.

The western market turned out to be the size of an entire neighborhood, and the holiday had clearly swelled business. Taverns and teahouses with colorful flags lined the streets while stalls hogged every inch of space. Rich aromas of cooking lamb, burnt sugar, and dates surrounded Jin, but she forced herself to focus on finding her target. After wandering through a few blocks, she finally found what she was looking for: a trader's teahouse.

These hubs for roving merchants were recognizable by the number of horses tethered nearby, as well as the universal sign they had emblazoned on their flag: a carriage with an abacus painted on the side. She walked in, grateful that most of the men smoking their pipes seemed too engrossed in business dealings to pay her much mind. She found the boss near the back, his fingers flying over an abacus while his assistant measured sacks of spices for a garrulous man that both the proprietors ignored.

"Peace upon your morning," Jin said. "Do you have merchants traveling to Kwannay?"

The boss didn't look up. "Foodstuff or wares? We don't guarantee food preservation for that distance."

"Letter."

The boss still didn't look at her. "Five fei. We only deliver to cities, and by law, all mail will be read, you understand?"

"Five fei?" Jin asked incredulously. She had never sent a letter, but she instinctively knew this was a premium price. She also didn't have that much left after being robbed.

The boss jerked his head to the side. "Don't like it, find someone else."

Jin left the shop, tears of frustration welling. She wouldn't have another payday for a month, and then she'd need to find a window of time to return to the city. She'd missed her chance to ask for news about Lu, all due to her being soft-hearted with that child thief. She was so engrossed in berating herself that she nearly collided with a figure carrying a bundle of wrapped wood.

"Take care where you're—" Aadan frowned. "Jin? What are you doing here?"

"I—I was exploring the market," Jin said, blinking back tears.

She could tell Aadan wasn't convinced. He looked over her head at the flag outside the trading hub. "You transporting goods?"

"It doesn't matter. What are you doing here?" Jin countered. She looked at the bundle in his hands, the smell heady. "Is that . . . sandalwood?"

He nodded. "For the fire at the Persian temple. It's just north of this market." He glanced at the trading hub again, seemingly debating, and then lowered his voice. "Look, if you need to send something, why not use a dragon?"

She stared, uncomprehending. "What do you mean?"

"How do you think the government communicates with the provinces?" Aadan asked. "There's a whole network of dragons used only for messages."

Jin frowned. "That's not for private use, though, is it?"

"If you know the right dragonrider it is."

She glanced back at the trading hub, unsure.

"If you want to wait half a year for a reply, use this lot. But a dragon travels in half the time, and I'd trust another dragonrider over these thieves any day."

She winced, and he colored.

"I'm sorry, I didn't mean . . ."

"No, you're right. They are thieves, charging me five fei a letter." She deliberated. "Who's the rider?"

"Someone who owes me a favor. Let me deliver this package, and then I will take you." He began walking, and she followed as he wove through the crowds. She noticed people who bowed when they passed, and others made a sign with their hands. Occasionally she heard them murmur something that sounded like, "Shahansha."

"What are they doing?" Jin asked.

"This is the Persian quarter," Aadan said, clearing his throat. "They all know my father and, hence, me."

"Why? Who's your father?"

"His name is Peroz."

"He must be well respected."

"You could say that."

"What are they saying? Shahansha?" She tried out the word.

"Oh, that." Aadan seemed uncomfortable. "Shahan-shah means 'king of kings.'"

She slowed. "And why would they call you that?"

"Because they all see me as the one who will take Persia back from the Arabs."

She glanced at him. "Why you?"

Aadan dipped his head in acknowledgment to a gnarled woman in a doorway bowing to him. "My father is the king of Persia. He fled here with his brothers when the Arabs invaded our kingdom. The Tang emperor at the time, Tai's father, welcomed them. My father joined the army here and received a general's title, and I am expected to do the same. We hope that with Wanli, we can free my home kingdom."

"But dragons are not allowed outside the kingdom. How will you . . . ?"

"I'm working on it," he answered.

"Sounds like a big task."

He sighed. "Trust me, I know."

She studied him. An exiled prince. Clearly the expectations weighed on him, and she wondered if this was why he studied so hard, strove to be the star pupil.

They walked in silence after that until they reached a whitewashed stone building with foreign script over the doorways.

"I won't be long," Aadan said apologetically. "I'm afraid those not of the faith are not allowed in."

"I understand." Jin watched from the outer court-yard as Aadan stepped into the temple, still carrying his bundle of sandalwood. An older man who had Aadan's same cheekbones and stoic countenance greeted him before the two disappeared into an inner chamber, along with a flow of other worshippers. Jin knew little of the Persian faith, except that like Buddhists, they valued performing good deeds and prayer.

When Aadan e re-emerged, he was dusting ash from his hands, followed by his father. The two hugged warmly before his father strode over to Jin, Aadan following.

"Greetings!" The man she assumed was Aadan's father was all smiles. "I am Peroz, Aadan's father. He tells me he must come late to the family meal because he needs to help a comrade-in-arms."

Jin bowed. "I am sorry, I didn't realize—"

"Don't apologize!" Peroz shook a ring-studded finger. "Helping a comrade is one of the greatest deeds one can do. Good thoughts, good words, and good deeds make a good man." He patted Aadan's cheek. "I shall see you later, my son. Your mother is eager to hold you, so be quick. May the Wise Lord protect you both."

Aadan bowed and helped his father into the horse carriage that had arrived at the temple gates. Jin wondered at how different her life might have been had she had a father like Aadan's.

Aadan led her out of the market and toward the main imperial thoroughfare.

"Where are we going?" Jin asked.

"To seek the friend who owes me a favor."

By now the crowds had thickened into a dense river of people lining the central axis, eager to catch a glimpse of the imperial procession when it came. Jin felt strange, being amongst people who had this one chance to see the empress, when she herself had stood before the woman multiple times.

Aadan threaded through various streets and alleys until they came to a canal crowded with barges plying the waters. A few flat-bottomed boats were moored to the platform, and Aadan led Jin onto one, dropping a copper in the boatman's leathery palm. The boatman pushed them away with his bamboo pole, and soon they were jostling amidst other watercraft. Many, like theirs, served as transport for people on their way to see the procession, while others were piled high with goods and snacks to be sold to the crowds.

"You've never been on one of these before?" Aadan asked, seeing her apprehensive face.

She shook her head.

"Can you not swim?"

"I can." Seeing his inquisitive look, she added, "I nearly drowned once. I haven't liked the water since."

"You should have said. We could have taken a sedan."

She didn't bother to explain that she had nearly drowned because Haitao had deliberately put her in a submerged bamboo cage to test her escape skills. She still had the occasional nightmare of being in cold, rushing water, of the sense of powerlessness as she was swept into the current with no sense of up or down. If Lu hadn't secretly snuck out of their clan's base and helped her, her bones would likely still be at the bottom of the river.

"Here we are," Aadan said. They bumped gently against a platform, and Jin gratefully followed Aadan onto solid ground. He led her through winding alleys before arriving at a broad street that was clearly a theater district. Vendors selling wooden puppets and glass candy shaped like animals called to passersby while ushers shouted out the names of the operas that were playing.

Aadan ducked into one theater with brightly painted doors, and Jin followed past flowing brocade curtains. Aadan scanned the small crowd seated around the stage, then pointed. "There."

Jin saw a tanned youth of roughly twenty-two years sitting near the stage, a dreamy look in his eyes. Aadan smiled. "Mao fancies the lead actor. He comes here every chance he gets."

Aadan led her over, and they took the two seats

next to Mao. Seeing them, Mao colored, but Aadan smiled. "You must know all the words by now."

"What is she doing here?" Mao eyed Jin, curious.

"You know Jin, don't you?" Aadan said. "She needs to send a message." He glanced at Jin. "Nothing sensitive, just private. Can you help?"

Mao glanced at the stage, then back at Jin. "Where?"

"Gaozho. Kwannay province."

Mao nodded. "You have the letter?"

Jin hesitated.

"You can trust Mao," Aadan said.

Jin reached into her inner pocket and pulled out the small, folded paper. She held it out. "Give it to the proprietor of the pawn shop opposite the main pagoda. Please."

Mao tucked the letter into his *pao*. "You want a reply?"

Jin nodded.

The orchestra came in and settled themselves, and a girl began threading through the audience collecting pay. Mao indicated the exit. "I'll be in touch within a moon. You'd best go if you're not staying for the opera."

Aadan put his hands together in a show of thanks, and Jin bowed. The two of them made their way out of the theater before the usher reached them, stepping out into the feeble autumn sun.

"Thank you," Jin said.

"Don't mention it," Aadan replied, then seemed to

think something over. "Would you like to come to my father's for the day? My parents would welcome you."

Jin almost accepted, but then remembered her promise to Rayshan. "I swore I'd help Rayshan with his flying today. I'd best head back."

Aadan nodded, and she wondered whether that was real disappointment in his face or practiced courtesy. "Some other time then."

He insisted on her taking a carriage back to the palace, as it was a long walk, and only after he had paid the driver and stood watching her leave did she understand the emotion in her: regret that she hadn't accepted Aadan's invitation. She felt at ease with him, something she hadn't felt with anyone besides Lu.

She thought of telling the driver to turn back. But to her disappointment when she glanced behind them, Aadan had already disappeared.

CHAPTER 14

*P*rince Tai had only just stepped inside his chambers when the onslaught of messengers began.

The journey to Khitan had been long, with foul weather and even fouler food. Tai had been forced to drink endless jugs of wine with the king, until even now, days after having not touched a drop of alcohol, he wondered if the pounding in his head would ever fade. The carriage ride back courtesy of a great rough bronze had not been kind either, and the flight had made him sick multiple times. He didn't want to see any liquor for the rest of the month, if possible. All he wanted was a hot bath, some privacy, and a talk with Aadan. He'd been increasingly curious about what he'd learn about Jin and her dragon.

But a prince rarely had the freedom to do as he wanted, as his mother kept reminding him. He looked at the pile of scrolls on his desk and the messengers waiting outside and decided that with several hours left in the day, he might as well soldier through. He bade his servant let the messengers in, and one of the first was his mother's private clerk.

"Welcome back, Your Highness." The man bowed. "Your mother sends her greetings and requests you join her as soon as you are able."

"Where is she?"

"The polo grounds, Your Highness."

No wonder she hadn't greeted him upon his return. The only thing she loved more than the throne and her son was polo with her ladies-in-waiting. He nodded. "I'll be there soon."

He washed his face, then changed into more respectable clothing, a rich silk robe and palace boots. He called for a servant to dress his hair and tie an official headscarf around his head. As he looked at himself in the mirror, he wondered again at how much he must resemble his father. He had never met Emperor Kaizhong, and Tai had only portraits to go by. Physically, he saw little resemblance to his mother. In spirit and goals, however, they were mirror copies of each other, united by their dedication to the throne.

He rose and made his way to the polo grounds. Even from a distance he caught the whinnies of the horses, the thunder of hooves, and the excited feminine whoops as the players chased the ball with their mallets.

A servant showed him to a silk tent erected on the sidelines, safe from the flying turf and any stray balls. He sat on a pile of cushions at the low table and held down his bile when an attendant offered wine.

Soon a player scored a goal, and a scorekeeper rushed out to the field to call a halt. One rider dismounted, her royal gold trousers and loose tunic marking her as empress. His mother tossed her mare's reins to one groom and her polo mallet to another, then strode toward the tent, her face flushed and her eyes sparkling. Tai marveled at how alive his mother was out here, in the field, away from the throne and its gaggle of officials.

"Welcome home, my son," she said, sitting down and patting his hand. "Wine?" At his expression, she laughed. "The king of Khitan still loves wine, I take it?"

"Drinking himself to an early grave."

"We should be so lucky." She took a cup of water from a nearby servant and downed it, but even this gesture was ladylike, refined. His mother could, as Tai heard one courtier put it when he hadn't realized Tai was listening, pass wind in such a way that it sounded like music.

"He suspected nothing about the dragon?"

Tai shook his head. "Seemed happy enough with the replacement. How was the pilgrimage to the temple?"

"Fine," she said drily. "Another year where Heaven didn't strike me down where I stood." Tai smiled. Her detractors liked to hint that Heaven took umbrage with a woman on the throne, and every year that she made the sacrificial offering at the temple was another strike against their enemies.

"Now let's talk of matters at home," the empress said. "We've lost much time in planning the spring festival ball. You'll have to meet with the astrologers and rites minister as soon as possible."

Tai felt a headache coming on that wasn't related to drinking. The spring festival banquet was the traditional opportunity for the nobles and imperial family to present their daughters, hopeful of securing the crown prince's favor and possibly winning the title of empress. Last year, he and his mother had managed to put off selecting a bride. His mother's view was that keeping the empress title vacant was a choice piece of bait to hold the nobles in check.

"Who do we need to flatter?" Tai asked.

"Duke Ning has been a right pain about the grain tax," the empress said, grimacing. "Dance with all four of his daughters on the night."

"I thought he only had three?" He remembered them well. Ill-tempered girls who constantly begged him to take them riding in his dragon carriage. The last thing he ever wanted to do on any day.

"His fourth has come of age," his mother said. "If Duke Ning thinks any of his girls has a chance at the royal bedchambers, he'll be docile as a sheep for the year."

"Very well, I'll flirt and show my best charm, like a

singing girl," Tai replied, glib. His mother shot him a reprimanding look, and he realized he sounded more bitter than he'd intended.

"Have you forgotten why you must do this?"

"No, Mother. Of course not," he reassured her. A prince served the empire, and though he chafed against many of the restrictions that came with that title, he shared his mother's view that their duty was to the empire and the throne.

"I sacrificed everything to be here," she continued, and he knew he was in for the familiar lecture. Her hands went, as they always did when she tried to impress him with his duty, to the official dragon seals she wore around her neck. "To give my only son an empire and give the people much-needed peace. If I hadn't sacrificed everything I held dear, we'd be rotting, unburied somewhere, our ghosts wandering the land, and the people would be suffering under Mengkhis Lai. Not to mention the many enemies who would tear us down from within. I cannot let that happen. You cannot let that happen."

"Then why don't I marry soon? The sooner I beget an heir, the sooner we secure our future." He had no eagerness for marriage, as he wasn't naïve enough to think there would be any love involved. His mother constantly reminded him that any woman throwing herself at him was merely throwing herself at the throne. Either besides this or because of this, he wasn't sure, he had never even been in love.

Except for Peilah. Had that been love? He couldn't say, and he'd never know. The budding relationship with Peilah had been tragically cut short before he understood his feelings. For the sake of holding onto the throne, however, an heir was necessary, and one needed marriage for an heir.

"Once you are married, we will have given the prize spot of empress away. We must play that move as best we can while we can."

He knew the more jaded whispers circling court over his still being unmarried at twenty: the empress Wu didn't want an empress in waiting, as she feared another woman having sway over him. The more vicious rumors whispered that she had ordered Peilah's death. But he dismissed those rumors, knowing they were there to drive a wedge between him and the empress. His mother was right—she was buying him time before he had to deal with the onslaught of nobles, courtiers, dukes, and petty princes all vying to get their claws in him through marriage. He had to remember his mother's most important lesson: the Dragon Throne above all. And if that meant harnessing his polished charm and stringing along noble ladies at the spring banquet while feeling like some high-class courtesan, then that was the price he had to pay.

"I understand, Mother. I just—never mind."

She nodded, satisfied. "You should go visit the Lady Meipin and pay your respects. Today if possible. It will give her and her uncle Minister Wei great face to have you visit on the day of your return."

He caught a thoughtful look at his mother's mention of Meipin. "What's wrong?"

"Nothing." His mother plucked a piece of fruit from a nearby bowl and nibbled it. "Well, I might as well tell you. I had to lodge the girl dragonrider with Lady Meipin."

That was a surprise. "What happened to saying she should survive the dorms?"

The empress frowned, but Tai knew she was trying not to laugh. "She, apparently, wasn't the one in danger. The boys ambushed her, and several nearly got themselves maimed."

Tai cursed softly and glanced at his mother. "You're not worried, given she might follow Mengkhis Lai?"

The empress shook her head. "I'm not worried. Yet. Besides, it is good for those men to be given a lesson. It will keep Gao quiet about women not being strong enough for Dragon Class."

Did this happen because he'd asked Aadan to keep an eye on Jin? He hoped Aadan was unscathed. The girl had more bite to her than he had imagined, even knowing she had bested him at the inn. This latest fight in the dorms should have worried him, as her being dangerous was exactly what he feared. But he felt something else unexpected—a fascination. She had only been defending herself, after all. "I'll go visit Meipin now."

The empress watched him stand, smiling. "That's my dutiful son. You will make a fine emperor when I die."

He bowed and offered the expected words to ward off the fates. "May you live ten thousand years."

As he strode away toward the imperial quarters and the Wei residence, he realized that for once, he wasn't calling on Lady Meipin out of duty. In fact, he was actually looking forward to it.

CHAPTER 15

Jin was stripping off her dirt grimed outer robes in the hall she shared with Meipin when the girl threw open her own room doors.

"Ah! You're back!" the girl beamed. "I have a surprise. I've ordered a special dinner for us, as I'm sure that muck in the barracks is insufferable." She wrinkled her nose.

Jin didn't bother saying that the "muck" was hearty and luxurious, far preferable to the court delicacies Jin had glimpsed on Meipin's table: fried ant eggs and simmered turtle.

"Your ladyship is too kind, but I am afraid I promised to have dinner with someone else." This was partially true. She almost always took an evening meal to Rayshan's cave. She suspected Meipin viewed her as an exotic pet, a source of court gossip that would allow her to dominate conversations with other ladies. Jin had no desire to suffer through a meal being polite in order to increase Meipin's social value and had devised various excuses the last three times Meipin invited her to join a meal or a game of chess with her friends.

Jin turned to walk to her rooms, but froze at the figure walking in.

"Prince Tai!" Meipin immediately slid into her demure lady demeanor. "It's such an honor to have you here. I did not know you had returned."

"Lady Meipin," the prince said, then looked at Jin, who also bowed. "I arrived back today and wanted to pay my respects."

"Your Highness honors me. I am sure you have already met Wang Kway Jin," Meipin said. "Jin is sharing my quarters now."

"I heard." The prince raised an eyebrow. "I'm not sure who's being punished, you or her."

"Oh, stop it!" Meipin said playfully, feigning as if to rap him with her peach-colored fan. "You are just in time for dinner. Would you care to join, Your Highness?"

Prince Tai gave a dazzling smile. "Nothing would delight me more."

The blatant flirtation made Jin even more eager to leave the two. She nodded to both.

"Excuse me, Lady Meipin, Your Highness. I am late."

"You are not joining us?" Tai's tone of disappointment was very convincing.

"She has another dinner appointment," Meipin said, touching the prince's arm with her fan. "Clearly more pressing than Your Highness. Come, I want to hear all about your time away."

As Jin bowed to retreat, the prince added, "I heard about you beating your own classmates, by the way." The prince seemed unperturbed by Jin's discomfort at this. "Quite the damage. I urge you to be polite to your new roommate, Meipin. On the other hand, you may sleep more soundly knowing you have such a good bodyguard in your rooms."

"Why do you think I offered to have her stay with me?" Meipin looked over at Jin. "My new roommate is quite the dark horse." She turned back to the prince. "Would you care to make a wager?"

Tai gave a smile so charming it could make birds drop from the sky, as the saying went. This man differed greatly from the one Jin had fought at the inn. "As with all wagers, it depends."

"I will put money on Jin passing this next test and beating all the other riders. Care to bet against me, Prince Tai?" Her smile was both coy and challenging.

Tai bowed, gracious. "I wouldn't dream of refusing the chance to take part in a game with you, Lady Meipin. Very well, I will bet six bao that our female dragonrider does not pass the next test."

"Six bao?" Meipin huffed. "Such a petty sum for a prince."

"Ten then."

"Money is no object for the rich. We might as well be gambling grains of rice," Meipin protested. "Let's bet the loser must give the winner any gift they choose."

"That sounds like high stakes."

"Are you afraid of what I might ask for, Your Highness?" Meipin's sweetness would have made honey taste sour.

Prince Tai glanced at Jin but then gave Meipin a broad smile. "Of course not. Whatever the Lady Meipin asks for, I'd be delighted to give if it is in my power."

Meipin clapped her hands. "We have a bet then! Go train, Jin, and show the prince we shall win!"

Jin bowed, but it was more to hide her fury than to show respect. Being a pawn in two spoiled royals' game felt humiliating.

She hurried out and made her way back to the caves. By the time she reached Dragon City, she wasn't sure what she disliked more: her new lodgings, her new housemate, or the prince that headed Dragon Class.

＊ ＊ ＊

ONE MORNING as autumn deepened and the air smelled of snow, Jin rose before the sun and reached Dragon City before the bell tolled.

You couldn't let me sleep just a little longer? she complained.

Rayshan huffed with impatience. *Not today.*

She took tools and cloths and examined his claws and teeth, admiring his growth. He was now the size of a deer, which was still several hands smaller than the other dragons. But his jade and white scales rippled a beautiful water green in the dawn light, and the gold spikes that lined his back gave him a regal air. His eyes glittered with mischief, and Jin knew he was eager to start the day.

For now that the dragons were a certain size, Emar had promised to take them and their riders to the feeding grounds.

A dragon doesn't want to be fed. A dragon wants to feed.

When she had Rayshan groomed, she led him to the Blood Oval, where he watched her go through her morning exercises with the rest of the class. Each rider brought their dragon to the Oval. Jin heard Rayshan's humming in her head, growing more excited and urgent by the moment. At last, all the riders swung onto their dragons' backs, following Emar, who led the way on his horse. Even from up here, she sat lower than anyone else.

Once I feed myself, I'll grow faster, Rayshan promised.

I hope so. We can't afford to fail the snowfire competition.

We won't.

She cheered silently at his confidence but said nothing. They walked through a series of courtyards, led by Emar on his horse, until they came to the Dragon Lore

Gate, two great iron doors that separated the hunting grounds from the rest of the palace.

Emar signaled to the guards, and they shouted down to another pair on the opposite side. Jin heard the grinding of levers before the gates slowly opened to reveal a holding area where another double door waited. Only when the doors they had entered had sealed closed did the opposite doors open.

Jin stood in wait with the other dragonriders, sensing the dragons' excitement in their flared nostrils and craned necks. Their tails whipped back and forth, and some even had their mouths open, clearly anticipating their meal.

She saw Aadan stroking his dragon Wanli's silver scales with one hand. A good third taller than Rayshan, the silver towered over them, his great claws as thick as Jin's thumb. A ridge of white bones ran along his spine, and his scales rippled over powerful muscle.

I like his dragon. He has the cave next to mine.

You speak to him?

Rayshan huffed at her surprise. *I speak to all of them. Wanli is the most levelheaded. He says Aadan is a good man.*

Perhaps he's biased, Jin said. Though deep down she believed Wanli was right. Aadan had helped her send that message to Gaozho. *Don't all of them like their riders, if they chose them?*

True, but Wanli has better taste than the others.

The doors opened, and Jin looked beyond. Parkland sprawled into the visible distance, with trees and rolling green hills, and a man-made stream dividing it. She knew from the size of the walls that she was seeing only one small part of the hunting grounds.

"It's divided into quarters," Aadan said, her awe apparent.

"What's in each?"

"This part is for the younger dragons," he said, pointing, "who have the run of the smaller beasts. Then in the other quarters, there are deer and oxen and camels, along with fish in the ponds. Though few dragons besides Wanli care much for fish."

Jin looked back out at the park. This must cost a fortune to maintain. A herd of wild goats ran up a slope, seeking brush to hide in. The dragons practically pawed their own riders in their eagerness to hunt.

The guards shouted to each other on the wall, and at some unknown signal, Emar called out, "Loose them!"

Each rider gave the mental nudge, including Jin, and Rayshan was off from her with a start. He pumped his wings, though he still couldn't fly, and soon he had flushed out a ram and pounced on it. The dragons hunted, clearly happy, and gorged themselves on wild goats, pigs, and even a deer. None of them were large enough yet to bring down the bigger yaks Jin saw roaming the distance. Each defended his own catch, and Ezho's dragon even received a sharp nip when he tried to steal a morsel of the buck Madu's black dragon had brought down.

Have you had your fill? she asked Rayshan.

Not nearly. I feel like I'd like to eat ten horses.

Grow big enough to catch them first.

He growled at her in mock reproach but kept eating.

"Any news from Mao?" Jin asked Aadan.

Aadan shook his head. "Nothing more than what I told you: he delivered the message, but the proprietor said he hadn't received a reply."

Jin gnawed on this information. Haitao had always stressed that if any of them were arrested, they were not to contact the clan for at least three months. But it had been over three months now, yet he hadn't sent a reply via his designated point person. Was he still angry at her for the heist? She supposed he had every right to be. But this meant she still didn't know whether Lu was alive.

"Maybe he'll have a reply when he next returns," Aadan said encouragingly. He looked over to the drag-ons, who were still happily feeding. "Rayshan is growing into a magnificent dragon. I wouldn't be surprised if he outgrows the others someday."

She watched Rayshan happily crunch a bone between his teeth. "Is that why the others dislike me so much? Or is it just because I am different?"

He glanced at her, then looked at the boys from their class. "I suspect it's a combination of the two. People need someone to hate. It used to be me."

"And now they like you?"

"They tolerate me."

"Why?"

"Because I fit in and I can beat them at their own game. Everything about me is Han except for my skin color, remember."

She used to be good at fitting in. She would deflect attention, follow Haitao's rules to the last brushstroke, and never rouse sleeping tigers. Now, she had broken more rules and taken more risks than she had in her life. And no matter how hard she tried, it seemed her just being here was causing unwelcome ripples.

"Well, at least they tolerate you." Jin scanned the other boys. Panshalar was shading his eyes while watching his gold dragon wade into a lake. Jao was busy pulling himself up on a branch, training his arms. There was no sign of Ezho, Madu, or any others. "They'd push me into a fire given half a chance."

"They're not all like Madu." He paused. "My father always told me that hatred for others usually comes from hatred of oneself."

Jin regarded him. "Meaning?"

Aadan indicated the boys. "Jao is the smallest in the wing. He feels he has to constantly prove himself and be bigger and meaner than everyone else to earn his place. Panshalar? Madu never lets him forget he's here only because his father needed to get rid of his illegitimate child. Ezho's dream is to be wing commander, if only to win his father's respect. Madu simply wants power and envies you and your Jade."

Jin thought about this. "And knowing all these things excuses their horrible behavior?"

"No." He smiled with a hint of wickedness. "But if you know their weaknesses, you know where to hit back."

She laughed despite herself. "Have you hit back?"

He shrugged, grinning. "I try not to, as it's against my faith. I find it helps to keep sight of my end goal, my dream. Then the rest becomes insignificant."

"Your dream of taking back your kingdom?"

He nodded. "And you? What do you hope to do? What dreams do you have of joining Dragon Class?"

The question took her by surprise. No one but Lu had ever asked her what her dreams were, and during her life as Haitao's thief, it had seemed a waste of time to contemplate such things. What was the point of dreams when you couldn't make them come true? Lu had dreamed of leaving Haitao, opening a tavern. That was partly why he had wanted to rob the Dragon Class convoy in the first place—a daring gamble to change his fate. And they had changed their fates—just not at all in the ways they had planned. Thinking of this still made her ache. "I simply want to survive," she said quietly. "With Rayshan."

Aadan contemplated her thoughtfully. "It's good to have dreams. We are directionless without them."

She stood, seeing that Rayshan had apparently finished eating and was calling for her. "Princes, even those without kingdoms, can afford to dream. Girls like me cannot."

Jin walked away, pushing away thoughts of Lu and all his dreams that might never come true.

* * *

"She resents the rich. Nobles in particular."

They dismounted and examined the targets. Aadan's had hit true. He seldom missed a target on horseback. Tai's, meanwhile, wavered and then fell to the ground, having barely pierced the straw enemy.

Tai retrieved the offending arrow and put it in his quiver. "Resents them enough to kill them?"

Aadan plucked out his own arrow, thinking. "No, she doesn't seem the power-hungry or ruthless sort. Nothing like what I've heard of Mengkhis Lai." He looked over at Tai. "Are you truly that worried?"

Tai mounted his horse, gathering the reins. "I just want to be cautious."

Aadan nodded. He understood. Which was why he and the prince had met like this each week since his return, though Aadan thought there was little information to cause alarm. But he also wanted to reassure one of the few people he considered a friend. "I don't think you need fear. Jin's . . . well, she's not vicious."

"And no reply to her letter?"

Aadan shook his head. He still felt torn about

divulging the fact that she had sent a message, but Jin hadn't asked him to keep it secret.

"Mao says the proprietor told him no one came to claim it." He looked at Tai. "A lie, you think?"

"Possibly. Though if she told you she expected a reply, then it wasn't meant to be a one-way message." They walked their horses back to the starting line. They had been practicing loosing their arrows from moving horseback at fifty paces. Tai was clearly focused on Aadan's words, as he hadn't shown his usual quiet frustration at missing the target many times. "I can tell you were about to say something. Out with it."

Aadan shrugged. "I was just going to say she seems a bit too vulnerable to be a Mengkhis Lai. I think she's simply trying to make sure a friend or friends are safe." Tai had explained the real story to Aadan after he had asked about her hatchery robbery. "She has a tough exterior from her life as a thief, but I think it's a wall she's built in order to survive. She's not a bad person." He realized he meant it. For all her wariness and reticence about sharing a past she clearly wanted to keep secret, Aadan sensed a good, if scarred, soul—a soul he could relate to.

Tai glanced at him, assessing. "You've always been an excellent judge of character. I believe you." He clapped a hand on Aadan's back. "Thank you for keeping me informed."

Aadan shrugged off the praise. "I wouldn't want

another Mengkhis Lai any more than you would, Your Highness."

"And no inkling of what her dragon's latent power might be?"

The Persian shook his head. "I think she's just as eager to find out as the rest of us." Everyone would be watching for similarities to Baikalan, Mengkhis Lai's famed and feared dragon. "May I consider my assignment finished?"

Tai adjusted his horse's stirrup, which had twisted. "Until we know his powers, I think it's best to watch her closely. Let me know as soon as you have an idea, or if you think she knows and is hiding it."

"Of course, Your Highness." Aadan hid his disappointment. This spying was leaving a bad taste in his mouth.

Aadan watched Tai gallop toward the target, this time loosing an arrow that hit true. He smiled and clapped as Tai raised a triumphant arm, but he realized why he disliked the prince's task: he felt a connection with Jin, perhaps because of her huren background, or perhaps because she, like him, was an outsider having to prove herself. But ultimately, he increasingly disliked having the prince's agenda hanging over him every time he spoke to Jin.

CHAPTER 16

Over the next few weeks, Jin was relieved to see that Rayshan grew rapidly after his first hunt. His limbs filled out, and his head lengthened. His jaws were now the length of her arm, and his neck and tail thickened. His wings stretched out, growing until he lifted off the ground for several wing beats before crashing to the ground again.

Like the other riders, she had also spent hours trying to find his inner power. Or rather, it seemed every other rider was already honing their dragon's skill, whereas she and Rayshan couldn't even find it, despite hours of Jin trying to push on their bond as Emar had instructed. Like all dragons, Rayshan could breathe a small amount of flame when provoked, but where the others seemed to grow increasingly skilled at manipulating air, water, metal, or their own sizes, the Jade didn't show any sign of a special ability. And where the other dragons could now fly short distances, Rayshan remained earthbound, as his wings hadn't grown large enough.

Her worry only increased when she reached the Blood Oval one morning after the first snowfall marked the start of winter. Minister Gao stood to one side, wrapped in luxurious furs as he observed the initiates. He was not only a physical reminder of how everyone wanted her to fail but also an indication that today's training was going to be different.

Assistants marked a circle in red-dyed chalk. When they had finished, Emar motioned for the riders to bring their dragons into the training arena.

"Students!" Emar bellowed. "Today we'll spar and allow our dragons to use their abilities."

There was an excited ripple amongst the initiates, and Jin noticed Madu and his friends looking particularly eager.

"This does not mean, however, that we want you to injure each other," Emar said. He seemed to be speaking directly to Madu. "May I have two volunteers?"

Madu stepped forward.

"Thank you, Madu. Who would like to challenge Madu and his dragon, Tian Pao?"

The hulking black dragon arched his neck and splayed his ridges, silently echoing Madu's open challenge.

There was a pause before Aadan stepped forward. Wanli flicked his silver tail.

"Good," Emar said. "Come and take your places opposite each other."

Jin watched the riders do as they were told, with the dragons following. When they were standing on opposite ends, Emar said, "Your goal is to use your dragon's power to push the other dragon's rider out of the ring. Begin when you're ready."

At first, both riders and their dragons stood motionless. Then the two dragons leapt into action in such a blur that Jin barely understood what was happening. Her hair whipped her face as what felt like an instant storm ripped through the Oval. She saw Aadan knocked on his back, skidding toward the outer edge of the Oval before Wanli's tail caught him and tossed the rider onto his own neck. Aadan gripped his dragon's ridges as wind whipped around them.

She thought she heard him shout something but couldn't be sure. She looked at Tian Tao, Madu's dragon, and saw him crouched, concentrating. The air storm seemed to only be affecting Aadan.

Is his dragon doing all this? Jin asked, incredulous.

Yes, Rayshan answered. *Black dragons can control the surrounding air, drive it against an enemy like a weapon. That's why he's called Tian Pao: cannon of the sky.*

Madu and Tian Pao must have been honing their skill for a long time to have such power, she thought, heart sinking at how behind she and Rayshan were.

Wanli scuttled out from the trajectory of Tian Pao's air storm, taking a moment to blink the dust out of his eyes before he turned on Tiao Pao. Madu was climbing Tiao Pao's back when a spray of water pummeled him. The rider flipped over his dragon's back, landing with an audible thump on the other side.

Jin looked over at Wanli, who stood with jaws open, water dripping from his mouth.

Silvers can absorb and store water, even from the air itself, then spray it back out.

Wanli took a breath and sprayed again, but this time Tian Pao blocked the water and charged, giving Madu time to recover. Wanli took to the air, leaping over Tian Pao and landing near his rider, who was scrambling to his feet, soaking wet.

Aadan leapt to the ground, pulling Madu down, and the two wrestled, each trying to push the other across the Oval's outer line.

Just as Aadan was about to shove Madu over, a blast of air from Tian Pao sent both of them flying across the line and into the dust. They picked themselves up, Madu glaring at Aadan as they spat the sand from their mouths.

"Well fought," Emar clapped. "And your dragons' powers are clearly improving rapidly. Though Madu, work with Tian Pao to make sure he directs his powers only against your opponent and not you as well. He turned to the group. "Who's next?"

Jao and Panshalar stepped forward, Jao with his bronze dragon, and Panshalar with his gold.

Emar nodded. "Let's see how Nakkalan has progressed in transforming. And Panshalar, I hope your gold Bayan has been honing his concentration. Take your positions. And remember, you are not to use maiming force on each other. Understood?"

The riders and dragons took their spots. As soon as Emar gave the signal, Nakkalan began to swell and grow until he was nearly twice his size and filled the Oval. While he was growing, his rider, Jao, began stripping off his metal-studded chest armor.

Jin knew golds could manipulate metal, but seeing it in action was very different. Jao looked like he was in a physical fight with an invisible enemy. He was being dragged on his back across the Oval, his boots leading the way, and he madly scrambled to pull them off. Meanwhile, Panshalar was running away from Nakkalan, who had grown into a giant and was trying to scoop the rider up in his jaws. To his credit, Panshalar was fast despite his great size and raced between Nakkalan's legs before the great beast could bring his cumbersome tail down on him. Jao had managed to pull his boots off but was now trying to fend off various swords and shields that came flying off the weapon racks, as if thrown by invisible hands.

Jao rolled, just missing a dagger that embedded itself in the earth.

"No weapons from outside the circle!" Emar bellowed.

Jao must have signaled his dragon, for Nakkalan bent toward him and opened his mouth, which due to his new size was more than big enough to fit a rider. Jao leapt in, and Nakkalan closed his mouth.

Smart, Rayshan said. *Now Panshalar and Bayan will have to push the big bronze if they want to win.*

The giant bronze turned to face his opponents, and Jin thought that if he didn't have his rider in his mouth, he might have almost grinned.

But his triumph was short-lived. A shimmering wall of sand rose in the air and swirled around the giant bronze. The beast shut his eyes and swung his head, trying to keep the tiny grains out of his nostrils and eyes.

Metals, Jin realized, incredulous. Bayan was controlling all the metal pieces found in the grains of sand and using them as a weapon now that he wasn't allowed to access the blades outside the circle. Nakkalan snorted and pawed at his nose, turning to avoid the flying sand. This only made Bayan focus harder, crouching and snarling as he made the grains of metal fly faster. Panshalar patted his neck, urging him on. Gradually, Nakkalan turned and stumbled, trying to escape the stinging sand, until he crossed the circle.

Emar clapped. "Well done, Panshalar and Bayan. And, Jao"—he turned to the other rider, who was on his knees in the dirt, wiping his dragon's saliva from him —"that was good thinking."

Jin noticed Nakkalan had shrunk back down to his usual size and seemed exhausted.

They can grow big and twice as strong, but it costs them in energy afterward. He won't be training anymore today.

After everyone had had a turn and Jin was bracing for her and Rayshan's time in the ring, Emar said, "Good work. Now, Aadan, are you willing to take on Ezho and Turuchi?"

"What about Rayshan and me?" Jin interrupted. "We haven't had a turn."

Emar shook his head. "You don't know your skill yet. When you do, you can spar with the others."

She heard Madu's snicker and clenched her fists.

"Madu," Emar barked, "be glad none of you are sparring with Rayshan yet. When he finds his ability, he may very well beat all of you with his eyes closed."

"Master Emar," Jao said. "Is it possible for a dragon to never find his power?"

There was a murmur amongst the students, and Jin noticed Gao watching with great interest. Anger surged in her, for she knew the insinuation: a female rider stunted a dragon's abilities.

Emar gave Jao a hard stare. "That's never happened. Jades can take longer to manifest their talent. I advise you to not make an enemy of the Jade." Emar gave Madu a pointed look. "Or his rider."

Madu nodded in a show of agreement.

Rayshan stretched one wing and huffed near Jin's ear. *As he says, my skill will come.*

At the end of the lessons, Jin asked Rayshan to wait in the Oval, then stayed behind after all the dragons had been led back to their caves and Gao had left the grounds. She waited for a chance to talk to Emar privately, and when the other students had filed out to the midday meal, the big man looked at her and nodded.

"You have questions."

"Yes. Clearly everyone thinks a Jade is powerful." She glanced over at Rayshan, who was intently watching snowflakes fall on his snout. "And he is." She paused. "But what is it exactly that Jades can do that others can't?"

Emar took a breath, as if debating. "A Jade is born only every quarter century, so they are rare. We know less about them."

"But?" Jin sensed her instructor was holding back.

"But they tend to have compound abilities, where they first discover one, and then perhaps a few more manifest. The books speak of one who could travel instantly between places; he didn't actually need to fly. And another could—" He stopped, hesitant.

"Could what?"

"Could turn invisible," Emar said. Had she imagined it, or was he avoiding her gaze?

"How did other Jade riders find out their dragon's special abilities?"

He sighed. "You can't hurry such things. They found out when they found out."

She tried to contain her impatience. "There must be some trigger. Did they find out in battle? During stress? After a growth spurt, perhaps?"

"I know you're frustrated and want to prove yourself, but you'll just have to let nature take its course," Emar said. "He's a fine dragon. Just have faith in him. And in yourself."

Jin looked back at Rayshan. All that would be easier, she thought, if she didn't know that people like Minister Gao were fanning suspicions—including her own—that Rayshan would never manifest his power. All because of her.

CHAPTER 17

"Today we'll work on your tack and saddling skills," Emar said the next day at training.

Several pages came forward, carrying leather saddles, cinches, and saddle cloths. "It's essential you become so familiar with this that you'll know how to saddle your dragon in your sleep," Emar said, "for if you don't, you'll be like stones falling from the sky. I can't tell you how many we have lost to falls from dragons."

Assistants pushed in carts piled high with dragon saddles. Though she was no expert, these were bigger than any horse saddles Jin had seen. Horses had been a luxury, used only when they had done highway heists. They were useless for inner city thieving, where you needed to dart and weave, then disappear.

Emar hauled one off a cart with his good arm and dropped it to the ground. "It's different from a horse saddle, as you'll see. You have your pommel and grips but no stirrups."

Now that Jin had a better look at the saddles, she realized they were shaped to fit between the dragon's spikes, with a curved pommel at the front and a matching one at back that went halfway around the rider's middle to keep them in place. Two pockets of leather, wide as a foot, were stitched to either side.

"Those are footholds," Emar explained, indicating the grooves on the sides. "You'll be leaning forward, as close to your dragon's neck as possible, to avoid wind drag. This is how the buckles work," Emar continued, motioning an assistant forward to demonstrate. "You need to strap all three properly, or you'll slide."

They lined up at the cart to be given saddlecloths and saddles. They were heavy in Jin's arms, and when she brought them to Rayshan, she saw her problem immediately. Besides the saddle being heavy, it was also much too large, especially on the relatively small Rayshan. Jin caught sideways snickers from her classmates.

She pulled it off, and Emar approached her. "Practice the buckles for now, so you're ready when he is." Emar looked Rayshan over, assessing. "He won't be able to take the saddle, or you, for a while yet. Feed him often. That will spur his growth. Otherwise he won't be ready for the snowfire trial."

Rayshan lashed his tail, growling.

"I'll order extra food ration tickets for him," Emar

said. "Take those tickets to the hunting grounds, and they will allow you extra hunts."

Rayshan growled louder, and Emar grinned at him.

The dragon hummed in anticipation as Emar walked off.

I like him.

Because he offered you food?

No, I sense he's a good man.

I wonder how he lost his dragon. What was it like to live with the pain he had, every day of every year?

She began removing the saddle cloths from Rayshan's back, and with the help of the assistants hung the saddles in the tack room with the other students. She spotted wooden plaques above each hook and recognized her name on one toward the end. A flicker of pride surprised her. She had never seen her name written, outside Aadan's demonstration and her own writing. Reading the characters carved in wood moved her and made her more determined to keep her place in Dragon Class.

SOON AFTER THEIR SADDLE LESSONS, Rayshan proudly showed her his ability to fly from one roost to another on the roof of the training grounds, and her heart warmed. Between the lessons and the physical training, Jin couldn't wait for the day that Rayshan was big enough for the saddle, so she could join him in the air.

And one mild winter day, when a bitter storm had abated and left the palace in thick carpets of snow, it finally happened. The saddle cinch was on its furthest hole, but that was all she needed. She triple-checked the straps and found that the saddle stayed.

Climb on, Rayshan said, lying down.

Are you sure?

In answer, he gave her an insistent shove with his head.

Jin hesitantly stepped up onto the first hole in the saddle strap, then pulled herself up using his spikes and threw one leg over him. She folded her legs into the saddle straps and fixed her toes deep in the footholds. Rayshan had grown to the size of a large buffalo, and he shifted as he adjusted to her weight.

Does that hurt?

Not at all. Just takes getting used to.

Me too.

Now hang on.

He didn't have to tell her twice. She gripped the ridge before her in both hands and held her breath as Rayshan took a running start, then leapt. His wings snapped open and caught the air. His scaled muscles worked, his wings pumping as they lifted up, up past the rooftops and over the tiles. The wind swept her face and tugged at her hair, the chill autumn air bearing tendrils of smoke and incense from the temple.

Jin leaned in close over him as he banked, and heard

the song in him turn into a triumphant roar, joy radiating off him.

This is to be a dragon!

She gripped with her legs, suddenly aware of how high she was, that eight stories of empty air, and death, awaited her should she slip. They swept over the imperial gardens and watched the goats scatter beneath them, bleating as they ran for cover. Rayshan roared again, then trumpeted loudly as he swept down, skimming over the bushes.

Jin clung on as he banked and soared, and in that moment she knew she wanted to win the snowfire competition at Ice Beard Mountain, wanted to be a dragonrider for the rest of her days. Everything else could go to the eight levels of hell. For dragonriders soared where others walked. Dragonriders experienced this every day. *This* was living.

Rayshan agreed with a deep hum of satisfaction, his scales almost glowing in response to her joy.

When the bell for supper rang, Rayshan defiantly burst into new speed, spiraling higher into the sky as if to escape everything below. Reluctantly, Jin urged him to land.

Rayshan huffed petulantly but obeyed. He swirled in lazy circles before slowly coming back to the Blood Oval and landing on the hard-packed earth. Jin impulsively wrapped her arms around his head.

Thank you. The words seemed inadequate, for he had given her the world.

He butted her in reply, his scales hot with the exercise. Jin's cheeks were still stinging with cold, but she relished the feeling.

We will win the snowfire test, she said to him.

Yes we will, Rayshan answered.

* * *

WITH WINTER DEEPENING, Jin threw herself into training with renewed vigor, for she had learned that flying required a fitness very different from thieving. She ran extra laps every morning before all the other apprentices woke. She carried buckets of water to work her muscles and sat with bent legs against the sparring pole to strengthen her thighs. Sometimes she noticed that the kitchen maids and other female servants would gather to watch her train, before some superior came out to send them back to chores. She also flew every chance she had, staying out late to take Rayshan over the city and surrounding hills.

Her saddle became her prized possession, and she kept it pristine and oiled in the tack room. With her and Rayshan's ability to speak in sentences, they had expected communication in the air to be easy, but early in their first flights, they quickly discovered how wrong they were once they had to do more complicated moves.

"A clear bond over which to communicate requires a clear mind," Emar had explained when they had come back frustrated from one of their training flights. "Your dragon can become so excited in flight that he forgets everything else, and you as the rider must always keep the bond unclouded."

When Jin concentrated on her next flight, she understood what Emar meant. Fear or anxiety on her part made the bond turn cloudy and dark, where she couldn't hear Rayshan's words. And Rayshan's excitement to be airborne often overwhelmed the bond, making it hard for Jin to reach him. But the more they flew, the more they understood each other and learned to even read non-mental signals—he would know which way she wanted to turn, where to go, how high, whether the chill winds were too much for her or whether she needed to shift her balance to stabilize. She came to understand the small nuances in his body —the tension in his shoulders as he prepared to fly higher, the folding of his wings that came with a sharp drop in altitude, the way he bobbed his head when he was about to bank to one side. And soon she became an extension of him, able to shift and adjust her own weight so she wasn't yanked one way and then another in the saddle.

And she loved every moment. The joy of it almost swept the trials from her mind, until one frost-bitten day she walked out to the Blood Oval and noticed everyone much more tense than usual, and several of the cadets stiff and anxious.

"What's wrong with everyone?" she asked after stopping her run to stand, bent double, next to Aadan.

"It's only a fortnight until the first test," he said. "You've not forgotten?"

The reminder dampened her spirits, for she knew there was more at stake than not advancing. Failing would mean a future at the salt mines and never flying again.

He raised an eyebrow. "Wanli and I have been practicing flying at higher altitudes, to get used to the thin air. You should do the same. It will help."

She nodded. "Good idea. I will."

"Why not come along with us?" Aadan suggested.

His invitation warmed her, and she realized she welcomed his company. "That would be good. Thank you."

Emar drilled them in the rules of the snowfire trial every chance he had between their flight training. "You will have the morning to reach the summit and return with a flower from the peak. Remember, these flowers grow sparsely. You must not only reach the top but also have sharp eyes to find them."

He dismissed them to their noon meal, and Jin and Aadan ate their rations of rice and steamed fish with black beans before heading to Dragon City. They flew as high as they dared until her head turned giddy. Each day, they flew a little higher, the cold thin air like knives in their lungs.

When they returned, they would see to scales and claws, and occasionally Jin slipped both dragons the oranges she had scrounged from the kitchens. Aadan always accepted gratefully, while Rayshan's eyes lit at the sight, and he would wolf down the fruit, licking his jaws.

Jin found herself sad for the evenings to end, for she had been increasingly enjoying Aadan's company.

Wanli tells me he's fond of you, you know, Rayshan said lightly one night after Aadan had left early to return to the dorms.

Aren't you dragons quite the gossips, she replied, flushing. Then trying to sound casual but failing, she asked, *What else does Wanli say?*

Give me the last orange and I'll tell you, Rayshan said, butting her shoulder. She tossed it to him, and he snapped it in two ecstatic bites.

So? she prodded.

Nothing, that was all, Rayshan replied, his words thick with laughter.

She slapped his side. *Trickster. Why do dragons like oranges so much anyway?*

The same reason humans do, Rayshan answered, as if the question was obvious. *They taste of summer.*

You haven't even seen summer, she said, amused. Rayshan had hatched at the end of the warm months. *How do you know what it feels or even tastes like?*

He licked a drop of juice that had fallen on his foreclaw. *Firesong.*

She remembered the first time he had shared his

memories with her and shivered; all thoughts of Aadan and Wanli washed away.

Mengkhis Lai frightens you as well.

Jin nodded, thinking. *What else do you know about him?*

What you saw is what I know, Rayshan said. *But I sense what you sense, that he was terrifyingly powerful. And I've heard the stories. I know he is buried in the South and his dragon Baikalan is imprisoned in the North. They are kept apart so they can never find each other and wreak the havoc that they did.*

Haitao told me that during the Year of Chaos, brother turned on brother, child on parent, and mother against child, Jin said. *That it was a terrible time and he would never want to see it again. In his kinder moments, he said I was the only good thing to come of that year.*

On that, Haitao and I agree.

THE DAY of the snowfire test came, and nearly all the riders woke early. Jin had had a restless night, and when she slipped from her bed and threw on her furs, she knew Meipin had not yet risen. The girl rose late after her nights of dice games and playing popular songs on her stringed *pipa* with friends, and rarely saw Jin when she left. Jin grabbed a few of the leftover buns that were sitting on a plate in the living area and then ran through the courtyard to the Blood Oval.

There was already much activity there, and Emar was giving orders to the servants to ready everything, including the saddlecloths.

Jin strode over to the tack room to fetch her saddle, but froze when she entered. Hanging there on the peg, where she had carefully hung the saddle the night before, was nothing but shreds. Someone had destroyed the one saddle that fit Rayshan's small build. She held the tattered cinch, the slashed pommel. This wouldn't hold on a donkey, much less a dragon.

Her heart plummeted, even as rage swarmed up to greet it.

"Problems with your saddle, Jade rider?"

Madu's voice grated her raw nerves. She turned to see him lounging in the doorway. He was wearing an expensive fox fur robe and hat, with a broadsword at his waist, and his false look of concern made her want to rip his throat the way he had her saddle.

"Guess you won't be flying," Madu said with feigned sympathy.

Emar appeared at the doorway and frowned at the sight. "Madu! Do you know anything of this?"

Madu stood straight. "No, Master Emar! I do not know who would do such a heinous thing!"

Emar shot him a thunderous look. "I bet you don't. Get your tack on and mind your own business before I disqualify you."

"Yes, Master Emar!" Madu left, but not without a suppressed smirk.

Emar stepped in and looked at the saddle for a long moment. "I'm afraid I can't prove it was him, so there's little I can do."

"There must be other saddles," Jin said. The tack room stored spares, she knew.

"In Rayshan's size?" Emar shook his head. "We'd have to send for one, and there isn't time. You'll have to sit this out, which would disqualify you."

"There is no rule against riding bareback, is there?"

His face darkened. "Riding without a saddle is dangerous. Beyond dangerous."

"The other option is the mines, no?"

"I can speak to the empress."

Jin shook her head. To ask for pity or leniency would not go well.

Emar hesitated. "Are you sure?"

"Yes."

"You're brave or foolish, I'm not sure which."

I'm a girl with few choices, she thought bitterly. Some things hadn't changed since her days with Haitao.

Jin began hunting for a rope along the tack room's back wall. She knew they kept ropes here for various sparring exercises, to be used in tug-of-war and other tests of strength. Choosing a sturdy one with a short lead, she looped it around herself. She remembered a heist with Lu, where he had lowered her through a hole in the ceiling down into a rich merchant's house below. He had shown her how to knot a rope so that it held but could also unravel with one pull if she had to escape quickly. She pushed the memory aside.

She walked out to the Blood Oval and saw the huddle of initiates stamping to stay warm, their breaths wraith-like in the frigid air. Aadan was amongst them and seemed about to come toward her when the dragons began landing on the roosting perches. The familiar hum began in her veins even before she spotted Rayshan's bulk on one of them.

Madu's surprise when he saw her was little comfort.

"You must be very sure of yourself, Jade rider, to not need a saddle?"

She ignored him and instead reached out to Rayshan. *We will have to improvise.*

A hum of support rushed over her. *I will not let you fall.*

"Students, today you have your first test as Dragon Class hopefuls," Emar said. "I trust you all to not disappoint. We will escort you to Ice Beard Mountain in formations of five squads. Each squad will consist of three wings. Follow your squadron leader, and do not deviate from the route. When we get there, there will be an audience of important guests, but try not to let this distract you."

The dragons swooped down from their perches to land next to their riders. Emar designated the wings into squads, and Jin was relieved to not be in Madu's.

Shortly after, the squadron leaders flew into the

square with their dragons. A black dragon and his rider stood in front of Madu's wing, and the students lined up obediently behind him. A bronze stood before Jin and her group.

"I will lead your squadron today," the bronze's rider barked. "You will address me as Squadron Leader."

"Yes, Squadron Leader!" the group shouted in unison.

"Follow me, and we will be at Ice Beard Mountain within the hour. A raised fist means fly. A sideways arm to the right means slow. A bent elbow means to land. Do you understand?"

"Yes, Squadron Leader!" everyone shouted again.

The squadron leader frowned at Jin. "Student, where is your saddle?"

"I don't have one," Jin said, pushing down her fear while tossing the rope around Rayshan's middle and double knotting it.

The squadron leader clearly thought she was mad, and Aadan looked about to protest, but at a look from Emar, the squadron leader nodded and shouted, "Very well. Riders, mount!"

A horn sounded, strident and rousing, and the squadrons took to the skies. Jin's squadron flew last. Rayshan lifted off, and despite having no saddle, Jin reveled in the feel of being airborne and watching the earth pull away from her.

She watched the servants on the ground scurry away before turning and waving brightly colored scarves, cheering on the dragons and their riders. The squadron leader and his bronze climbed to a comfortable height where the cold bit but did not shock.

The squadrons fanned out into a wedge formation, and Jin's squadron leader set a comfortable pace for all. Jin stayed in last place, flying behind Jao before her and Aadan, still looking concerned, on her right. She spotted Madu ahead in the leading wedge.

She felt oddly naked without a saddle and gripped harder to compensate so she wouldn't slip. But Rayshan soon calmed her.

Not having a saddle means I am lighter and faster.

She didn't answer, simply wound part of the rope around his ridge and gripped tighter as they flew over the city and then over increasingly deserted countryside. Fields carpeted in snow passed beneath them, with only naked trees and the occasional mud hut to break the monotony. Eventually a high mountain emerged, its peak gleaming bone white with heavy snow.

Ice Beard Mountain.

They flew in formation for a while longer, and then Jin saw the squadron leader raise his arm, fist up. They slowed and banked to the right, following their squadron leader, who then held his arm out, fist down. Jin sighted frozen pastures beneath them and torches outlining a landing oval.

The dragons spiraled down, first Madu's squadron, then the second, then Jin's. They landed in a clearing lined with stones and torches, with Emar waiting in the middle. Lining the sides were various nobles from court. Jin spotted Prince Tai and the War Minister.

When all the dragons had landed and the squadron leaders had retreated to the outer edges of the circle, Emar stepped forward.

"Students, this is your initial test in entering Dragon Class. You will, on the horn blow, fly to the mountain peak. Do not be deceived; it is further than you think. Near the summit you will find a flower—a snowfire blossom—and bring it back. This is how we know you have reached the peak, for they only grow on the upper reaches. Bring this flower back to this oval before noon, and you will advance to level two of Dragon Class. Fail, and you will not advance to the next test." He paused, looking at all of them in turn. "Good luck, and may good fortune favor you."

He stepped back and nodded to a boy with a bugle standing to one side. The boy put the horn to his lips and waited.

Emar looked to the war minister and Prince Tai. Jin thought Gao glanced at his nephew Madu, but it was so quick she couldn't be sure. The minister raised his palm. Emar turned back to the boy and nodded. The bugle blew a long, piercing blast.

The test had begun.

Rayshan leaped. The thunder of dozens of wings beating the air drowned all other sounds as the dragons flew, roaring.

Hold on, Rayshan said, pumping his wings. Most of the other dragons sprinted, but Jin mentally reined Rayshan in.

Easy, Rayshan. Remember what Emar said? It's a long way to the top. You cannot afford to tire yourself.

She soon realized the wisdom of Aadan's training and glanced over to see him bent close to Wanli's neck. The dragons spread out, ascending the mountain's stony face. The air thinned quickly as they flew higher. On their way to Ice Beard, they must have already been ascending, and the mountain itself was higher than it looked. Her lungs burned within moments of their ascent, and her head grew giddy. The dragons seemed much less bothered by the cold, but the thin air was clearly affecting them equally.

Are you alright? Rayshan asked.

I will be, she reassured him, double-checking the rope around her waist.

Rayshan slowed his ascent, and his heartbeat evened out under her own. They passed other dragons and their riders, some of whom had already stopped on precipices to rest. Many, having ascended too quickly, were on their knees, busy being sick. Jin silently thanked Aadan for helping her avoid this. She had lost sight of him in the ascent and hoped he hadn't also been overcome and had to stop somewhere.

The temperature dropped with every wing beat, and twice Jin's fingers froze into nonresponsive lumps, even through her thick gloves. She didn't dare take them away from the rope, as she worried she would fall and never be able to grip it again. Time seemed to stretch and bend, and Jin struggled to remember how long they had flown. Her body ached as if they had been flying for hours, but that couldn't be right. Clouds swarmed in, and higher up, the weather turned downright malicious. Soon biting snow whipped down from the clouds, swirling around them in icy blasts.

Do you need to stop?

Jin didn't want to, as she spied several figures ahead of her in the flurry. A bronze and his rider, the furthest ahead, were curled under a woefully small ledge, clearly waiting to see if the storm abated. She recognized Bo Tan.

Jin wanted to rest, but she knew the trap that waited. She needed to keep moving, stay active. She mentally shook her head in response to Rayshan, and though he gave a worried huff, she sensed his agreement that it was for the best. He gave an extra burst of speed.

Lean in close to me. Take my warmth.

She did so, squeezing her legs and trying to blow warm air on her stiff hands. She wore gloves, but they seemed useless against the savage cold, and already her fingers felt numb. The rope holding her was already brittle with ice. They passed the bronze on the ledge and kept climbing the rock face, flying ever toward the top. The air seared her lungs, not just because it was cold but because it seemed like she was breathing nothing. No matter how big of a breath she took, her lungs seemed to collapse on themselves, and her head was aching. But at least they were nearing the top and there was no one ahead of them. Now, she just had to find the flower. And keep from freezing.

Rayshan pushed harder, and then they punched through the cover. Jin felt the sun on her, and incredulous, she gazed about her. They had broken through the mountain's icy beard that gave it its name, and now they were in the frigid upper regions of the peak, but at least they didn't have to deal with the wet snow cutting into them.

Here, Jin's fingers tingled with a sudden warmth, and she looked down at the mountain. It was craggy, but here and there shrubs on spindly branches wound out of the crevices. And on those spindly branches were the odd blood-red snowfire bloom. The flower that would seal her advancement in Dragon Class.

There! She called to Rayshan, but she needn't have bothered. Rayshan was already negotiating the winds and skimming close, but there was nowhere to land.

I'll sweep by, but you'll need to grab the flower, Rayshan said. *Are you ready?*

Jin flexed her fingers, pulling one hand away from the slippery, frozen rope. She gripped as hard as she could with her numb legs and used her other gloved hand to hold on to his ridge.

Yes. As slow as you can.

Rayshan banked and swept in toward one particular shrub that stuck out more than the others. As they passed, Jin grabbed the branch, but it broke before she managed a firm grip, and the flower tumbled out of sight.

Curse it!

Never mind. We'll go again. Ready?

She focused. *Yes.*

And this time she would be sure. She flexed her fingers again, focusing on the flower. Rayshan swept in once more, from the same angle, beating his wings backward to give her some time to aim and grab. She had her hand around the branch, her heart thudding, when something slammed into them.

Everything around her spun wildly. The rope cut into her middle like a knife as it broke her free fall, Rayshan wheeling and trying to regain his wings.

From the corner of her eye, she saw the blur of a large black flying by, its scales flecked white from snow, a rider in fox fur on his back.

Madu.

CHAPTER 19

She swung, held only by the rope, and felt a brutal pain in her side she knew would hurt for days. If she lived. For her head was spinning, and her stomach was in danger of coming up her throat.

Can you climb? Rayshan shouted.

Her limbs felt frozen, and she barely distinguished up from down, though she glimpsed Madu and his dragon sweeping in toward the shrub. She was about to call out to Rayshan when the rope holding her snapped, as if made of wood instead of fiber.

She plummeted, icy wind needling her back as she flailed for a hold, any hold.

Breathe! I'm coming!

She tried to tame her terror, the certainty that this time death would have her.

Brace yourself.

No sooner did she sense his words than she saw her

dragon beneath her, wings outstretched, his ridges folded down to give her the best landing spot possible.

The impact knocked the wind from her, but she knew it had also saved her life. She scrabbled until her hands closed around one of Rayshan's ridges, which he raised now to create a crude saddle. She gripped him hard with her legs and craned her head skyward.

Madu wheeled above, and when he spied her looking, he waved the red flower in his hand. She could almost hear his laugh of triumph, even though he was too far away.

Madu and his dragon disappeared through the cloud cover below.

Ready? Rayshan asked.

Yes. And we'll need to catch up. She remembered the empress's words about having to come in first in everything. She wanted to not just survive Madu's underhanded tricks, but beat him. She wanted to come in first, wanted to make Madu eat his laughter. The remaining rope around Rayshan's ridge was too short and stiff to tie around herself, leaving nothing to hold her to Rayshan. She would just have to rely on her legs and her dragon.

Rayshan banked in close to the mountain, and Jin took out the knife she had strapped to her belt. As she came in, she hacked at the branch closest to her, and soon the whole thing gave. It had four blossoms on it, all blood red, and she grabbed it as it fell onto Rayshan's wing.

Rayshan trumpeted, echoing her own feelings. He turned, tail whipping, and then began the descent.

Hang on now. This is going to be fast.

He wasn't lying. As the air hurtled by them, Jin nearly strangled his ridge with her grip. In her other hand was the branch, cradled to her chest within the folds of her robe. They approached Bo Tan's bronze on his outcropping and noticed his saddle was empty. The bronze was clearly distraught, trying to push his head into a crevice in the rock floor.

What's he doing?

The dragon raised his head and called out to Rayshan, *Bo Tan tried to mount but then slipped into that crevice. He can't get out; the opening is too narrow.*

Jin struggled with what to do: if she stopped to help, she would lose to Madu.

Wait, Jin said.

They wheeled in, and Jin shouted to Bo Tan. There was no answer.

Ask his dragon whether he can hold out a wing for me to climb on, Jin said.

Rayshan nodded, and soon the bronze stretched out his wing, growing it to twice its size to make it better able to hold Jin's weight. Rayshan hovered close, and Jin leaped out onto the wing. She tried not to think of the deathly drop below her and instead crawled along the bronze's great wing until she reached the rock. She jumped off, happy to have firm ground, and peered into the crevice.

The hole was about half her height, and she saw Bo Tan's unmoving, slumped figure at the bottom. The opening was wide enough for her shoulders to get through but too narrow for his dragon's head. She reached in and shook the rider, hard. No reaction.

Jin cursed. There was no way to get Bo Tan out except to haul him. She climbed over the lip of the crevice, trying not to trample the man. She maneuvered her hands under his arms and pulled. He was thin, which helped, but his dead weight still made her arms and back protest. She worked a knee under him, pushing him upright until she wormed her shoulders under his. His head lolled, revealing a bloody gash on his temple. She pushed him up and over the lip of the crevice.

Tell his dragon to be ready. I'm going to push him over, but he needs to make sure Bo Tan doesn't tumble over the side.

She sensed Rayshan communicating, and then on Rayshan's signal, she pushed with all her might. Bo Tan's body teetered on the lip, and then she grasped his legs and pushed him the rest of the way until he collapsed on the other side, his dragon blocking the ledge to prevent a fall. Jin clambered out, sweat prickling her under her furs, and watched as the dragon butted Bo Tan's face until the rider's eyes cracked open.

"Wake up!" Jin said.

"I failed . . . yet again . . . " Bo Tan muttered.

Impatience stabbed her. Nothing was worth him

losing his life. She reached into her belt and broke her branch in two. "Here."

He looked at it in confusion but made no move to take it. Clearly, his mind was still clouded by the thin air and the blow to his head.

Hurry, Jin, he says he can't keep his wing strong for much longer.

Jin secured the branch in Bo Tan's belt, then scrambled across the bronze's now trembling wing. Rayshan positioned himself as close as possible, and taking a deep breath, Jin leapt off the bronze just as his wing shrank back to its normal size. She dropped onto Rayshan's back and clung to the ridges.

The bronze trumpeted at them as she and Rayshan left the ledge.

He says thank you for saving him and his rider.

She crouched back down over Rayshan's neck. *We won't make first place.*

Rayshan snorted. *Maybe we can. Do you trust me?*

With my life.

Then tie the rest of the rope to your wrist. Is there enough for that?

She did as he asked, her numb fingers clumsy. *We can't possibly outfly them.*

I didn't say we would.

They pierced the cloud cover, and Jin spotted the glimmer of black scales beneath them as Madu glided down the mountain. Rayshan sped up, but instead of following Madu, he flew straight ahead, away from the mountain.

Where are you going?

To the landing area.

Jin peered ahead and renewed her grip until they were directly above the landing circle. Below, Jin discerned the speck of cleared dirt that must have been where they had taken off.

I'll have to hold you. Climb down onto my front claws.

What? Why?

You'll see, but there's no time to argue.

She pushed down her fear and lowered herself off his back, sliding awkwardly over his shoulder, which was pumping to keep them aloft.

Hurry!

I'm trying!

This was impossible with him moving, and it was a long drop past his side and to his claws. Her foot slid, and she was about to hurtle into open air when his claws closed around her arm. He pulled her in with both claws until she was close to his belly.

Now what?

Now we dive.

CHAPTER 20

Jin didn't have time to ask what Rayshan meant. He flipped head over tail, taking her with him, and then his wings wrapped around them both like some cocoon over a silkworm. The nauseating sense of falling gripped her. They were hurtling down toward the ground, headfirst, like an arrow.

Instead of pumping his wings for speed, Rayshan had turned them into a missile. Through their bond, Jin heard Rayshan's blood roaring in his veins, the air rushing by them, followed by intense pressure on her ears. She screamed and heard a sickening pop.

And then the wings unfolded from her, snapping upward as Rayshan caught the air and stopped his freefall. The earth rushed toward them, too fast. Rayshan's wing clipped the ground, and she experienced, as her own, the pain in him. They tumbled, Jin catapulting forward into the dirt, which scraped her hands and face.

She rolled onto her side, still holding the branch, and then stood and stumbled to Rayshan, who was shaking his head and testing his wing. The ground shook, and Jin looked up to see Madu and his dragon land, Madu's face incredulous. They stood in the center of the Oval, spent, while Emar and the others rushed to greet them, clearly stunned by the dragon's drop from the sky.

Are you alright? Jin asked Rayshan.

Never better. He hummed in triumph, glowing with pride at their stunt.

Jin wished she felt the same. She thought she might collapse upon hitting the ground, for nausea still washed over her in unpredictable waves. Her hearing was muted in her right ear, as if someone had tipped water in. She touched the warm fluid there. Blood. Everything was a little off balance. She gripped her branch and stumbled forward.

She knelt, partly out of ceremony and partly out of exhaustion, and held out the snowfire flower.

Emar hesitated, then took it from her. His lips moved, but she had to wait for him to repeat himself, louder, before she understood. "Who taught you that move, to dive?"

"No one, Master Emar. It was Rayshan's idea."

Emar looked over at Rayshan, brow furrowed.

Madu gave her a venomous glare before kneeling next to her and holding out his branch to Emar.

"Well done, Madu," Emar said, seemingly still preoccupied with Rayshan. "It seems like we have some very worthy students in the group this year. You have done us proud before our guests."

It was only then that Jin noticed the new figures on the sidelines. A tall man all in rich black stood with his furred hood, his dark eyes stony in a waxy face that looked practiced at betraying nothing. He had simple clothes, but finely made, that showed stature and taste. The minister of war stood next to him, looking distinctly displeased as he gazed over at Jin.

Jin did not know who the hooded man was, but she saw him gesture to an assistant standing nearby. The assistant quickly noted something on a scroll.

"Come, help our students recover from their first test." Emar motioned his own assistants forward, and several hurried to help Jin and Madu to their feet. Others went to their dragons, rubbing them down with great wool blankets and bringing warm water to drink.

As she left the Oval, Jin glanced back. The minister of war was saying something to the man in the robe, at which the robed man nodded. The minister then stood and strode off. She wasn't sure why, but the sight left her uneasy.

Emar's assistants escorted them to a nearby tent, where cups of tea and hot flatbread were pushed into their hands. Jin took hers gratefully and gulped, noticing with a grimace that her head had settled from spinning to a dull throbbing headache. Madu gave her one last glare before stalking from the tent, taking his food and tea outside.

"You'll be fine soon," an attendant said to Jin, mistaking her grimace at Madu for physical discomfort. "Just the effects of the heights." He glanced at her ear. "The healer will be here shortly, but I suspect it's simply a tear of the drum membrane. Happened to me once."

She put the bread aside, feeling too ill to even digest that. Soon, other students stumbled in, with the attendants sitting them down and giving them cups of tea. Aadan entered and grinned at her before he sat down.

He said something, but she didn't hear it. Seeing her bloodied ear, he leaned forward. "Is your ear alright?"

She shrugged. "I think it will be. You passed?"

He nodded and glanced outside. She saw him watching the man in black.

"Who is that man?" she asked.

He leaned in close so he didn't have to speak loudly for her to hear. His nearness made her breath flutter, but his next words stilled it. "Marquis Sanchin. Head of the Royal Veil."

Jin blanched. Every thief knew about the Royal Veil, or the secret police, the empire's formidable network of eyes and ears. She had heard enough stories of their methods. They amputated some, drowned others in vats of excrement, and boiled those they took a particular shine to. This head of the Royal Veil, Sanchin, had more gruesome stories to his credit than a street dog had fleas. The most ominous was the rumor of how he got his name: when he was done with a victim, only *san chin*, or three pounds, was left of the person.

"What's he doing here?"

"He always comes to the tests," Aadan said. "He recruits from the best here. No doubt many will be vying for his attention." She noticed his gaze drift to Madu, who reentered, grabbed another piece of flatbread, and left, tearing it with his teeth.

"Is it an honor to join the Veil?" Jin asked once he was gone.

"Officially? Yes. Unofficially, it's not an honor everyone wants."

Jin certainly understood that. She didn't fancy working anywhere near the Royal Veil.

"That was an amazing feat, winning with no saddle," Aadan said. "You certainly showed Madu."

But she had little time to bask in his congratulations, for soon a brusque healer with a groomed mustache and stern eyes had entered the tent, demanding to check her and Aadan for any injuries. He looked over the Persian and cleared him, but then spent a good time over Jin's ear, using a mirror to reflect candlelight into her canal. He confirmed she had indeed torn her drum membrane.

"It will heal on its own, but try not to get water in it." He took out two small balls of wax and slipped them into the pocket of her jacket, which lay on the table. "If you bathe or go near water, put these in your ears first."

He then left to attend to the other students. Jin rose and stepped to the tent entrance, where she had a view of the students who had newly landed, and their squadron leaders, who were gathering them and their dragons to return to the palace. Panshalar, Jao, and Ezho were congratulating each other, the large Mongolian making some comment that had even Jao grinning.

She spotted the dragons standing to one side, grooms checking them for injuries. One of them was trying to examine Rayshan's wing, but with little success. Jin walked over, soothing him for the groom.

"Thank you," the man said, relieved.

Where did you learn that move? To dive? Emar's question came back to her.

I saw it in the Firesong.

Something in his tone made her suspect Rayshan was hiding something. *Who did you see perform a dive?* He looked away. *It was Baikalan, wasn't it? Mengkhis Lai's dragon?*

It was a happier memory, Rayshan said, almost defensive. *He looked younger, less scarred. It felt like a memory from just after they bonded.*

She was about to press further, but then Bo Tan jogged up to her and gave a deep bow.

"My humble thanks, classmate Jin," he said.

"You would have done the same for me."

He flushed. "I've failed twice before. To fail three times would have brought unbearable shame upon my family. So . . . thank you. I am indebted."

Without waiting for an answer, Bo Tan hurried off, clearly awkward with apologies.

She turned and remounted Rayshan, patting his neck.

You've won an ally, the dragon said.

Good. After Madu's attempt to kill her, she was realizing just how much she needed allies.

CHAPTER 21

They flew back at a leisurely pace, giving the tired dragons a chance to recover, and returned to their quarters by dusk. For the first time, Jin was grateful for her luxurious rooms. She parted with Rayshan and made straight for Meipin's quarters, wanting nothing but a bed and sleep.

When she got there, however, Meipin was waiting. Her ears and hair dripped with pearls, and she wore a peach gown over a scandalously low green bodice that flattered her plump figure.

"The palace is abuzz with news that you came in first," Meipin beamed like a child on New Year's Day. Her excited voice meant Jin's injured ear had no trouble hearing her. "Rumor even has it that the Royal Veil was so impressed he wants to recruit you!"

Jin's stomach knotted. She had hoped the Royal Veil

was a traditionalist and hated women like the minister of war did. That would keep her safe.

"Meipin, I just want a bath and then sleep."

"But you can't!" Meipin protested. "There's a Dragon Class ceremony tonight, and all the initiates will be there."

Jin groaned inwardly. She had forgotten. Refusing to attend would be unthinkable. All she longed for right now, though, was a bath to take off the grime of the day —not to mention to have a few moments to herself.

She noticed Meipin bowing low just then and heard muted footfalls behind her.

"Your Highness, we are humbled."

She turned to find Prince Tai standing there in the doorway, and muffling a curse to herself, she bent to one knee. What a contrast she must be to Meipin, she thought. Bloodied and dirt caked.

Tai motioned for them to rise. "I am not callous enough to make the champion of the day kneel."

Both of them stood, and Jin couldn't read Tai's expression. Curiosity? Admiration? Disgust at her ripped clothes?

"Congratulations on your coming in first, student Jin. You certainly know how to stage a great upset."

She bowed her head. She had to admit she was glad to have defeated Madu. "I simply did my best."

"Yes, and I'm here to pay my debt as the loser in the bet with Lady Meipin."

Though she knew the bet was silly, part of her reveled in having made him lose.

"Your Highness clearly didn't know who he was betting against!" Meipin said, rapping Tai playfully on the arm with her peach-colored fan.

Tai smiled and gave Jin a sideways glance. "I have been guilty of repeatedly underestimating Jin, it's true."

"Aren't you going to ask what I want as my prize?" Meipin asked.

"Of course," Prince Tai said. "A dog? A new polo horse, perhaps?"

Meipin pouted. "I was thinking more of a day with Prince Tai at the summer palace lake."

Prince Tai bowed low. "But what a coincidence, that was the very prize I was going to ask for if I won!"

Meipin laughed. "Then it's settled."

The prince turned to Jin. "We should invite the champion to join us, since she's the reason we had the bet."

"You honor me, Your Highness, but I don't think I have any days off."

"Well then, as winner, let me at least offer you a similar prize to what I'm offering Meipin." He spread his hands. "A gift of your choosing."

What game was he playing? Was he simply trying to be a gentleman in front of Meipin? Jin bowed. "Winning was enough of a gift for me." At least her court manners were improving.

"I thought you might say that, so I took the liberty of preparing something," Tai said. "I hope this is of use."

This made Jin look up, and Prince Tai looked pleased at her surprise. "I heard you were short of a saddle this morning. So I thought I'd buy you a new one, as it seems you'll be continuing your training with Dragon Class. I've ordered the best saddle maker in the city to tailor you one."

He motioned to servants standing at the door, and they disappeared out the doorway. They returned with an ornate, large saddle. She was no expert in dragon saddles, but the thing was clearly tailored to perfection with top-quality leather and felt, inlaid with gold thread but nothing too ornate that would weigh Rayshan down as Madu's saddle had with his dragon.

"This is clearly too large," Tai said. "But will something like this do?"

"This rider is unworthy," Jin said.

"Or too modest, perhaps." Tai paused. "That was an incredible stunt you pulled to arrive in first place."

Jin bowed. "It was all Rayshan's skill."

"I'm sure everyone is curious what other skills he's hiding."

Jin glanced up. "There is no hiding, Your Highness. I think neither of us knew until today that he was capable of such a thing."

She sensed skepticism in his smile. "Of course. Forgive my poor choice of words. I didn't mean to suggest otherwise. Enjoy your new saddle when it arrives, and do keep our old ministers on guard. It's worth losing these bets just to see the looks on their faces. Peace upon your evenings, both."

And with that, he left. Jin went to run a hand over the saddle while Meipin closed the doors behind the prince and came back to admire the gift.

"I suspect he finds you fascinating."

Jin looked at her, unsure of Meipin's meaning. "Little boys are fascinated by bugs. Right before they crush them underfoot."

Meipin laughed. "I don't think he sees you as a bug. Don't worry, I don't mind, truth be told."

Jin cast her a curious look. "But you two are always so—"

"Flirtatious?" Meipin smiled. "It's all part of court manners, and Tai is a master of such things. My uncle wants me to be his bride, which will be good for my family, but that's simply politics."

"Regardless, I think you're mistaken," Jin said.

Meipin made a derisive noise. "You don't survive at court without having some useful knowledge about men and women, my friend. I'll have Ahlu bring some wine and a light dinner. And then it's time for the Dragon Class celebration."

She moved away to find her favorite maid, leaving Jin to continue admiring the saddle. To have one in Rayshan's size would be useful, and despite herself, she turned over Meipin's words about Tai. But Meipin didn't know she had punched the prince, and the more she thought about it, the more convinced she became that Meipin was wrong.

For now, though, she needed a bath. She drew her own, still unused to having servants wait on her, and received a beseeching look from the maid.

"You'll put us out of jobs," the girl said, taking the jug from Jin and heading off to fill it.

The maids were all Meipin's, but the noblewoman had insisted Jin allow three of them to serve her. Jin let the maid fill the tub and fetch the soaps and cloths, then stripped her filthy shirt and pants and leathers, along with her boots, and climbed in, wincing at the movement in her bruised ribs where the rope had broken her fall. She let the steam and smell envelop her, then noticed the girl was still standing in the room.

"I can bathe myself," Jin said. "Go, take the night off."

The maid flushed and lowered her eyes. "I—I just wanted you to know, dragonrider Jin, it is an honor to serve you."

Jin didn't know what to say. This only seemed to fluster the girl further, and she whispered, "You can fight like the men, you ride a dragon, you do things none of us would dream of doing. And some say that if you succeed, they will start allowing women into Dragon Class. And that would be . . ."

Jin searched for words but found none. The silence seemed too much for the girl, and she hastily bowed out of the room.

Jin leaned back into the tub, confused. She didn't know what to make of this awkward admiration. Jin was just trying to survive. How were others watching her, much less admiring her? She took the cloth hanging on the tub edge and scrubbed her skin until it tingled, hoping to clear her mind and body. When she was satisfied all the grit had come out of her nails and hair, she dug into her jacket pocket to retrieve the wax balls the healer had given her, put them in, and submerged herself, head and all, counting heartbeats. Underwater, the world didn't exist. Sounds, smells, and sights all faded until they were a safe distance away.

Only when her lungs screamed in protest did she come up for air and go to grab her towel. And that's when she saw him.

A figure sitting on the bench in the corner.

Jin froze, tense as a cat.

"Who are you?"

The man—for he was clearly male—had his face covered and wore a loose tunic of blue and black. She hadn't heard him come in, and shouting now wouldn't bring anyone in time. The man was close enough to have a dagger under her chin within heartbeats.

"A friend. Or a foe. Depending on the choice you make now."

The man sounded older than she, but young enough to do physical harm. She pulled a robe over and covered herself in the bath. "What do you want?"

"Your cooperation." The man let a pause fall, then

continued. "I have five gold bars here for you if you leave Dragon Class, and Rayshan."

She felt Rayshan stirring, alerted to her danger. He sensed across their bond that there was an intruder in her room, but he was cave bound. She could almost hear him growling.

"Why?" she asked.

"The why doesn't matter. All that matters is that there is ten times this amount for you, as long as you quit the trials and leave."

"What if I stay?"

The man shifted on his stool as if he had expected this. "I highly suggest taking the gold."

"I will consider it."

The man looked at her appraisingly, as if surprised at her boldness. "You have until tomorrow. Wear a red scarf to the Blood Oval if you agree to leave."

He stood, revealing a stack of gold bars, each the size of her index finger, on the stool.

"Choose wisely, girl."

He left on silent feet out the bathroom doors. Jin stood on shaky legs, stepping out of the high tub and walking over to the gold bars. A pool of water gathered at her feet as she touched them. They were real, and worth more than anything she had stolen in her life.

Well, almost.

I'm pretty sure dragons are worth more than this. You're certainly worth more than this.

The dragon huffed, as if to say this was obvious. *What will you do?*

I will stay.

He hummed his approval. *You are not afraid? Opening gambits of honey are usually followed by poison.*

She considered his words. *I'll take my chances. Besides, I've been a thief long enough to know that if someone offers ten gold bars, he really has twenty. He'll likely make another offer before he really shows his claws.*

CHAPTER 22

Jin attended the Dragon Class ceremony that night, glad for a chance to be in the company of her classmates rather than alone in Meipin's quarters.

And though Madu wore a sour expression throughout the ritual, especially when the winner's medal was announced and presented, no one else seemed at all hostile. Even the war minister kept a stony, noncommittal face amongst the select gathering of nobles as Prince Tai came forward and pinned the ivory medal to her chest.

"Congratulations, initiate," he said, stepping back.

She bowed three times, as Emar had instructed her when she arrived, and then stayed through the long-winded speeches and obligatory prayers to Buddha for a clear mind and heart. She had then retired to her quarters and checked every corner for intruders, before asking a maid to fetch her a bag of roasted chestnuts. After shelling these and carefully piling the pale flesh in a bowl, she set a vase before her bedroom door and scattered the crushed shells on the floorboards about her bed.

No one disturbed her sleep that night, nor the next —even though she had deliberately not worn a red scarf to training. After a week of no further threats appearing, she began to wonder if her enemy had changed his or her mind. Either that, or their threats carried no weight. At classes, she discreetly observed those around her, seeking hints as to who might have threatened her and who would note that she hadn't worn a scarf after the intruder's offer. But no one seemed to pay her any mind, and the gold bars remained wedged where she had hidden them, between the slats of her bed and the mattress.

She debated telling Aadan about it, but then decided against it. The offer might have been all bravado, in which case there was no threat. And if there was a threat, she didn't see the point of endangering him. She certainly would not tell Emar or the empress, for she had a feeling that would involve the Royal Veil, a scenario that chilled her more than her encounter with the intruder.

The only day when she momentarily forgot her problems was when her new saddle arrived. To her eyes, it was even more beautiful than the model one Tai had shown her, and she delighted in how it fit Rayshan perfectly. She made sure to send the prince a thank-you note, which she wrote and rewrote to ensure the strokes were as crisp and flowing as she could manage.

A fortnight after the intruder tried to bribe her, she woke at her usual time, then dressed and made her way to the Blood Oval. But even before she reached the training grounds, she heard the whispers from passing servants, and clearly talk was spreading through the court like wildfire: the king of Khitan was only a day's ride away, and speculation was rife as to what was happening. Kings did not arrive unannounced, yet the king of Khitan had only sent word when he was almost upon the city walls.

Jin joined the training with her classmates as usual, but the surrounding talk was all about the king. She couldn't shake the uneasy feeling that his arrival was connected to her. Did the intruder have something to do with this? But if so, what? As training wound down for the day and no one summoned her, she hoped she was wrong.

They had barely hung their saddles and put away tack when a frazzled messenger arrived at the Blood Oval and bowed low before Emar. When Emar glanced over at Jin, she steeled herself. She had been right after all. The king of Khitan was here because of her.

Emar motioned for her to follow him. They mounted horses that had been prepared for them, and then passed through the Imperial City walls, through the vast outer courtyards. As they entered the central square that connected the palaces to Dragon City and the training grounds, they passed a group of grooms leading a dragon by a chain attached to its metal collar. A bear insignia was emblazoned on the collar, and as the dragon walked by, Jin involuntarily recoiled.

The dragon was unlike those in Dragon Class—though well-fed, he bore scars on his hide that no young dragon should have. Whip and burn marks dotted his back and wings, but what was most disturbing to Jin was the dragon's eyes. They looked dead, too unaware to even be described as haunted. The dragon was a mere shell of what the dragons in Dragon Class were, as if the soul had bled from him.

"What insignia is that?" Jin asked, though part of her knew the answer.

"It's the family crest of the king of Khitan," Emar said.

She digested this. "Was that the dragon they sent in place of Rayshan?"

Emar didn't reply, which confirmed her hunch. A knot of anger formed in her. She was no stranger to cruelty. But somehow the sight of a creature so mighty brought so low disturbed her, and a shiver rippled through the bond with Rayshan. She hadn't met the king of Khitan, but she already despised him.

"And the empress allows the king of Khitan to treat dragons like this?"

"Some prices must be paid," Emar said quietly. "Even if one doesn't want to pay them."

Something didn't make sense to Jin. "Is the king not bonded to the dragon?"

"He is."

"Then why does he mistreat him? The dragon's death will mean his own."

Emar turned to look at her, brushing hair back from his white eye. "His last one died, which was why we were taking Rayshan to him in the first place."

Jin shuddered. "But how does he not—"

"Suffer the white death? His is a forced bond. A bond made of magic, not of souls." Emar paused, his expression morose. "A dragon's bond is like love. Forced love is never the same as love given freely. It carries less of the pain, but also none of the pure joy."

They dismounted at the palace gates. Grooms came forward, taking their horses, and Jin walked at Emar's side as a guard escorted them to the ceremonial offices of the palace.

A herald announced them as having entered the reception hall of Gilded Clouds before retreating. Inside, low tables lined the walls on both sides, where clerks sat, recording proceedings. At the far side of the room was the imperial throne, and even at this distance the empress blazed in gold: gold robes; a gold headdress that rose above her raven black hair, coiled into elaborate wreaths held by gold hairpins; and gold beads hanging off either side of her headpiece. The dragon throne reflected the sun in a halo, making the empress look as if she sat on a cloud of light.

A group of men stood before the empire's ruler, and as Emar and Jin knelt, she recognized the minister of war, Prince Tai, and the head of the Royal Veil. A man she didn't recognize, however, was a broad-shouldered giant dressed in furs and boots. A thick beard helped hide cheeks florid from drinking, and his dark eyes brimmed with malice.

"This is the thief?"

His voice was as flinty as his eyes. He looked her up and down, taking in her leathers, her tightly tied hair, and her face. Jin felt as if he would strip her and look into her private spaces if he could.

"This is the dragonrider initiate, Wang Kwei Jin," the empress said.

The stranger grunted in disgust. "A girl dragonrider. What shall we have next, monkeys?"

"I appreciate you're upset, King Ulagan," the empress replied sharply. "But you asked to see the girl, and you've seen her. She exists, and she is bonded to the dragon. Now I propose a solution to our problem."

Again the stranger grunted. "She still stole an imperial dragon, Your Highness— dragon that not only belonged to you but also belonged to me. We had an agreement, and if you're going to break that agreement, then I'm no longer bound to guard the prison of Baikalan."

At this there was a flurry of brushes on paper behind Jin as the official recordkeepers wrote this down.

"If ever the magic should fail, that dragon will tear through Khitan first," Ulagan growled. "Don't think I don't know why we have the so-called honor of hosting the worst threat this empire has seen. A single dragon is a paltry price for such risk."

"Calm yourself, King Ulagan, and hear my proposal," the empress said. "You are right, I promised you a dragon, though I might add that you were never promised a specific dragon. And I have already replaced it with another."

"A paltry gold one, Your Highness," the king protested. "A Jade was on its way to me, and I'll have the Jade. Execute this thief and bring the mages to bond her dragon to me."

"You do not command me, King Ulagan," the empress said, cold. "And though circumstances did not go as planned, a forced unbonding and rebonding would leave you with a very damaged Jade. Perhaps worthless. But you're right, this girl stole from you, and therefore we shall compensate you."

Jin's heart thudded. She didn't know where this was going, but she already didn't like it. Especially as Tai's expression looked grim. She had recovered from the shock of hearing the king demand she be executed and Rayshan be forcibly bonded, but now what the empress had to propose didn't sound promising either.

"In repayment for your having not received a Jade dragon, you will receive another dragon from our hatchery, in addition to the one we already gave you."

The scribes wrote furiously at this, and Jin saw shocked expressions everywhere. A dragon was priceless. Two dragons were unthinkable. Even Tai's usual gracious expression cracked for a second.

"You will have your pick," the empress continued.

"Any one I choose?" the king asked slowly.

"Yes."

Jin tried to shut out the image of the golden dragon she had seen, with its haunted eyes and lacerated body. The thought of this man doing the same to another dragon made her furious. But she had no say over her own life, much less another's.

She noticed the king was watching her, and when he saw her gaze, he broke into a smile.

"Since the girl took my dragon, Your Highness, I want her to choose my new one."

Jin's gut twisted. Tai and his mother both looked surprised.

"You do not wish to choose your own?" the empress asked.

The king shook his head. "In the North, our law is that whoever steals must pay with the lash or return something of equal value to show repentance. I am guessing you won't want to whip your precious dragonrider, but I think you can honor me and my customs by having the girl present me with my new dragon."

Jin roiled inside. The man seemed to know that her choosing a dragon for him was the more painful option.

"I choose the lash, Your Highness." She had received Haitao's wrath many a time. This would no doubt be worse, but she also couldn't stomach dooming a dragon to a beast such as this, especially as that dragon was paying the price for her having bonded with Rayshan.

Emar regarded her in shock. Everyone stole looks at Ulagan, to gauge his reaction.

The king's eyes bore into her. "I don't believe you were given that choice, girl." He looked at the empress. "I accept your proposal of a new dragon. But only if the thief chooses the egg."

The empress nodded. "Very well. Wang Kway Jin will choose your egg, and our treaty will remain intact."

The king clasped one hand over his other fist and bowed. "I accept. Our treaty is intact."

The recordkeepers scrambled to record this.

"Prince Tai," the empress said, "as head of Dragon Class, you will escort Jin to the hatchery so she may choose the king's new dragon."

Jin felt sickened. She again saw that golden dragon, those empty eyes that seemed to not care if he lived or died, much less flew.

"Your Highness, may I—"

"You may not," the empress said immediately. The king of Khitan looked smug. "You stole Rayshan; therefore you will help solve this diplomatic issue."

"Your Highness is wise and merciful in all things,"

Emar intoned, glancing at Jin. He was feeding her her lines.

She bowed, the words scraping up her throat. "Your Highness is wise and merciful in all things," she whispered while her heart screamed inside her.

CHAPTER 23

"This was not my idea, if you were wondering."

Prince Tai and Jin were walking to the hatchery, the king of Khitan following with his attendants. Tai glanced back to make sure the King hadn't heard, but the man seemed engrossed in talking to his companions about the new dragon.

"It doesn't matter whose idea it was, Your Highness," Jin replied flatly. "But clearly you and the empress think this best."

"Best? It's brilliant, given the circumstances."

Her look was almost hateful, and he dropped his voice to a whisper. "You're lucky you're not dead. First for stealing the dragon and second for stealing from the king of Khitan. He was raging like a bull when he arrived."

The sting of King Ulagan's tongue was still fresh in

Tai's mind, for the king had made no effort to disguise his rage at the prince blatantly lying to him during his official visit. Tai still didn't know how, but the king had discovered the dragon meant for him was a Jade and had left for Changan the same day. It was a diplomatic nightmare, just as Gao had predicted, and the situation had left the empress and Tai in an unenviable position. "It took all my mother's persuasion to make him not run out to the Blood Oval to kill you."

The girl scowled. "She has the power to decide who lives and who dies. He wouldn't be brazen enough to just kill me if she forbade it, Your Highness."

He sighed inwardly in frustration, wishing he could make her see. "You have no understanding of politics!" He saw from her expression that his tone had been harsh, but he pushed on, needing her to understand how much he and his mother had fought for her. "He might have been out of line, but my mother must step carefully with him. Having an offended king on your border is reckless at best and fatal at worst. Sending him home without him feeling like a lucky man who walked into a gambling house and cleared the coffers would have created a long, festering resentment that would have just grown and bitten us later. So my mother was being protective of you. Show some respect at least, if you can't show any political sense."

Her face crumpled before she regained her composure, and he bit his lip. Curse it. Why in Buddha's name did he care about hurting her feelings? She had punched him in the face, stolen a Jade, and stoked his nightmares about Mengkhis Lai. She also had an idiot's grasp of court dynamics, with no respect for how diplomacy worked.

And that, he thought in frustration, was probably why he was strangely and inexplicably drawn to her. Everyone else knew this game backward and forward; it was all they played day in and day out. All anyone cared about was this tiny chessboard called the Tang court. Jin was the first person he had ever met who had no desire to even learn the game, much less win it.

"I don't want to do this."

"You have to. There's no other way." He discreetly put a hand on her elbow, taking her around a corner to buy them some privacy from the king's party. "You don't want them to unbond you from Rayshan, do you?"

He could almost hear her heart cracking at the prospect and knew that he had struck her weakest spot. Jin would pay any price, suffer any lash, to stay with Rayshan. He wondered briefly what it would be like to feel that way about someone, but he dismissed the unexpected thought.

Jin followed him without a word after that, and he welcomed the silence.

They arrived at a set of ornate doors, decorated in carved dragons flying out of open eggs, painted in gold and red and black. Jin waited as Tai nodded to a group of guards, who ushered them and the king's entourage into an anteroom. Here the walls depicted murals of flying dragons, fire-breathing dragons, and dragons resting on clouds. Each one was painted differently, with differing expressions. Jin tried to ignore their judging eyes that seemed to follow her every move.

Rayshan's insistent hum on the other end let her know he shared her distress.

It must be done, he said.

I wish there was another way, she screamed.

Sometimes, there is not. And you must do the painful deed.

Jin waited sullenly as the guards unlocked the second set of doors, these plain and smooth, before ushering them inside.

Jin followed Tai and King Ulagan and gazed at the eggs arrayed around them. Unlike the first time she had been in here, the sight filled her with dread at the task before her.

Master Lo hurried forward. "Your Highness! What a pleasure."

"We are here to choose a new dragon for the king of Khitan," Tai said, voice neutral.

"Ah!" Master Lo's cheerful expression slipped as he turned to the king, and Jin had a feeling Ulagan's reputation was well known. "Did the last one die as well?"

The king grunted. "No, but it's a sickly sort."

Tai added, "The empress has agreed to gift him another."

Master Lo looked pained, and Jin's anguish grew.

"And this one here who stole my dragon will choose my new one," the king said, casting a wicked smile at Jin.

Try to find one that will survive him, Rayshan suggested.

How?

A bronze will be strong, Rayshan said.

How do I tell by an egg whether he's a bronze?

The darker ones tend to be bronzes, he said. *Such a dragon might have the endurance to live with such a man.*

"Come now," the king gestured. "Choose me my dragon."

Jin swallowed. There was no way out of this. It was Rayshan, or one of these eggs. She looked around for a dark one and saw a smooth-faced mahogany-hued egg in the upper right corner, nestled in a bed of hay and rock.

"That one," she whispered, pointing.

Master Lo called out to another hatchery worker, "Number forty-one!"

Master Lo moved toward the nest, his boots sure-footed on the rock, and gently lifted the egg.

Jin's heart thudded, but Tai seemed relieved. The recordkeepers in the hatchery made several notes in various ledgers to record the choice, before a small wooden plaque with a number was placed in a carved box and then taken away to some unseen record room.

"Make sure it's healthy!" the king called out after them. He turned to Jin, smiling. "I accept your repentance and forgive you your crime."

Jin wished to strike him. As the last of the officials left the hatchery, Tai gave Jin a sympathetic glance.

"You did what you had to."

And though Jin tried to believe this, a little ball of hate took up residence inside her. Not for the king of Khitan, but for herself.

CHAPTER 24

She didn't sleep all that night, plagued by images of hatchlings having their heads cut off by invisible enemies. One after another, they fell to a faceless man, his swinging of the blade methodical and emotionless. There was blood everywhere, and her ears rang with the sounds of terrified hatchlings. When morning dawned, she reluctantly pulled herself from bed, hoping that the king of Khitan would leave that day and she wouldn't have to see the dragon.

But as if deliberately adding to her misery, the king stayed on to enjoy the sights of Changan, and on the sixth day Jin woke to Rayshan's subdued mental greeting.

The dragon egg has hatched.

She sank her face in her hands. *So the king will bond to it?*

Tomorrow, yes. With mages.

Jin didn't want to go, but her guilt compelled her. The next day, she headed toward the Blood Oval, where drums were sounding an ominous rhythm.

When she arrived, spectators already crowded the perimeter: students and teachers, riders and servants. Forced bondings were rare, as Bo Tan had told her, so everyone, it seemed, wanted to witness it. Heralds entered and announced Prince Tai and the empress, and servants ran in with silk-draped chairs they placed on the northern side of the Oval, in the place of honor. The empress and her son took their seats, and their officials flanked out behind them.

An assistant pulled a cart behind him bearing a metal box, accompanied by Master Lo. He and the assistant carefully opened the lid, and Master Lo reached in with gloved hands to pull out the hatchling. A noose circled the creature's neck, and his jaws were bound shut with red leather. Jin's heart went out to him as he tried to claw his way away from the waiting mages.

The king of Khitan strode in, blustery as usual, and his eyes raked over the dragon. "It's a bit scrawny, isn't it?"

His words reached her even at this distance, and her anger bubbled.

"It is of normal size for a new hatchling, Your Majesty," Master Lo said politely. "Perhaps your last one was slightly larger, but we have checked his heartbeat and all his vital signs, and he is in perfect condition. With good care he will be a fine and mighty dragon."

The king of Khitan strode forward and grasped the dragon's chin in his hands, lifting it to look at the creature's eyes. He grunted. "Very well. Let's get the ritual done."

Jin found herself frozen to the spot as mages in their purple robes came forward, holding bowls, knives, and vials of liquid.

The king of Khitan threw off his furs and sat where one mage indicated, in a square drawn out of a chalk-like substance. The assistants dragged the dragon, mewling and growling, to a matching chalk-drawn box, this one in red. They strapped a weighted chain around the hatchling's legs, keeping him from moving out of the circle. The beast tried to pull it, to no avail.

"Lady Jin, the empress requests you sit with her."

Jin turned to see a female servant at her elbow, bowing low. She recoiled but knew the invitation was a command. Throat tight, she followed the servant to the royal seats before the empress.

Jin bowed.

"Rise, and stand by me," the empress said.

Jin took her place next to the empress, on the opposite side of Tai.

"I salute your fortitude in watching this," the ruler said. "We must all do things we don't want to."

"Yes, Your Highness."

"Surely that's not a new lesson for you."

This was true. In Jin's life with Haitao, she had had to do many things she hated. And with each of those things, she had hated herself for them. It was like Haitao knew that the more he made her do things she despised, the more she whittled her own sense of self, which made her more pliant. She knew that a part of her was going to disappear with this dragon's freedom today.

"The king of Khitan views the dragon as a status symbol," the empress said. "For that alone, he will keep it alive."

Alive is not the same as living. Lu had said that often. "Does it hurt?"

The empress shrugged. "I cannot say. Would you like a refreshment?"

"No thank you, Your Highness," Jin said. The thought of this spectacle being some sort of entertainment sickened her.

The empress nodded and took a goblet of wine from a waiting servant. Jin noted that Prince Tai also refused to drink.

"Remember, young Jin, with power and responsibility comes the necessity of taking life, of making hard sacrifices. You must choose. You, or him. This is a lesson I also try to teach my son, as he too suffers from a soft heart."

Tai bowed his head with a taut smile. "I simply find

charm a more useful weapon than the sword. Generally less messy as well."

The empress made an impatient gesture with her head. "My son, as you can see, would benefit from having your steely exterior, Jin."

Jin felt anything but steely as a chanting rose from the Oval.

Jin watched, fists clenched, as the mages began the ritual. The king of Khitan let one mage hold a handful of incense before his face, and the King inhaled the scent. The mage nicked the king's ear with his knife, then moved to the dragon. He waved the incense sticks near the dragon's snout, making him squeal at the smell.

Don't watch, Jin. Rayshan's anxiety buzzed on the other end.

No. I did this. I must watch.

The mages nicked the dragon's foreleg, then mixed the knife in a bowl of liquid. The mage flicked the liquid into the dragon's circle before doing the same with the king's. One of them had a drum, which he began beating in time to the chant. The chanting increased in tempo, and though Jin sensed no physical change, the dragon hatchling screamed, as if the singing cut his flesh. It thrashed and squealed, trying to claw at the weight around its ankle, before the chanting reached a crescendo and then the bronze hatchling went limp on the ground.

"Did you kill it?" the king of Khitan snarled.

The mages did not answer, but one of them stepped forward to remove the red leather muzzle around the hatchling's jaws.

They dribbled some water on the dragon, and slowly his eyes opened, but his stance was different. His head drooped, the fight drained from him.

The mages untied the muzzle and brought the dragon to the king of Khitan. The king ran his hands over the dragon, and the creature quivered but did not resist. There was no mewling, no struggle. No spirit. Something in the dragon had been snuffed, and seeing it twisted Jin's insides.

I'm sorry, she whispered to the dragon, then turned and left, ignoring Prince Tai, who was calling her name.

Fly with me, Rayshan said, and she broke into a run, then a sprint. She wanted to outrun the guilt, the shame, the anger.

She didn't even bother to saddle Rayshan, instead climbing onto his ridges and pressing herself tight against his back.

They flew for the rest of that day, saying nothing to each other. Jin tried to forget the image of that dragon, its struggle, and its eyes opening, dull and colorless, but she found it impossible.

The empress said that with choice come hard sacrifices.

She is not wrong. You cannot blame yourself forever.

She wished she could draw comfort from the dragon's assurance. First she had stolen Rayshan, and now she had condemned a new dragon. What if she was ripping the very fabric of all around her, destroying innocents along the way?

Like Mengkhis Lai did. The thought surfaced unbidden, and once there it would not leave.

CHAPTER 25

*A*adan hit the floor with a resounding crash, his opponent's forearm pressed against his windpipe in a solid lock move.

Tai eased off, then stood and held out a hand, which Aadan took. Both of them wore wide cotton pants that ended just below the knees. Sweat ran freely down their bare backs, despite the winter snow outside the royal training hall.

"Good moves and concentration, Your Highness," Aadan said, taking a ladle of water from the drinking jar. He held the ladle out to Tai, but at the prince's gesture served himself first.

The prince took the ladle when Aadan was done and helped himself. "Thanks to your teaching."

Aadan was supposed to be instructing the prince in Farsi, per the empress's wishes, but Tai had insisted early on that he had no gift for languages, and Aadan had to agree. Tai's skills were more in martial arts and diplomacy, while his science and language skills were next to none. Rather than fight the prince's nature, Aadan had simply accepted Tai's plea that Aadan instead teach him *koshti*: the traditional Persian art of wrestling.

"I have news of your cousin," Tai said.

Aadan stood. "Has he mobilized?"

Tai nodded. "He's marching with a Persian force against Kamarja."

"I should join him," Aadan said. A taking of Kamarja might just weaken the Arabs enough to launch an offensive into Persia. This news would excite his father. "If the empress would give us even a thousand troops, we'd be able to bolster my cousin's forces and ensure victory."

"I'll speak to her," Tai promised. "Though it's Gao who needs convincing." Aadan had heard enough of the man to know that the minister of war preferred to let enemies weaken each other before sending China into the fray.

Aadan bowed. "I'd be grateful for any persuasion you could work on him."

Tai raised an eyebrow. "Making him join your cause, my friend, is almost as difficult as making him a supporter of women in Dragon Class. One more round?"

As they took their positions, Tai asked, "Speaking

of, how is the female dragonrider doing? Is she still upset about selecting King Ulagan's dragon?"

Aadan nodded. "I believe it was hard for her. She dislikes suffering."

After the forced bonding, Aadan had caught her a few times with red-rimmed eyes, and each time he had been tempted to fold her in his arms, to offer some sort of comfort other than the words he had already said.

Tai positioned himself at the outer ring and nodded to Aadan. They circled each other, arms out. Aadan darted forward and feinted, bringing one arm around Tai's waist before lifting and throwing. Tai fell, making several guards in attendance step forward, but Tai waved them back.

"I have a feeling she blames me and my mother for the decision. Has she talked about it?" Tai dusted off his hands and circled again, blowing hair out of his eyes.

"No, Your Highness."

Tai rushed him. Aadan bent his knees and pushed back, locking them both into a skirmish. He tried to wrench Tai's leg, but the prince anticipated the move, and with one deft grab and pull, Tai had the Persian's arm pinned to the ground. With a swift twist, Aadan broke free and leapt to his feet.

As the two resumed circling each other, Aadan considered Tai's words. Jin held her feelings close and seldom spoke of them, though he wished she would. Aadan sensed a profound isolation, as if she were an island. *Or,* he thought, *like a foreign prince exiled in the*

Middle Kingdom. The more time he spent with her, the more he found things in common with her that he'd never felt with another.

"What are her interests? What does she do in her spare time?"

Aadan gave a wry smile. "Dragon Class does not allow spare time, Your Highness." But Tai's question made Aadan wonder.

They continued sparring until a sweat-drenched Tai called an end. They sat down heavily on the side bench, several servants rushing over to offer warmed towels and refreshments. Aadan politely declined, amused at the difference between when the prince trained and when the rest of Dragon Class trained. He decided to face the mountain before the door, as the saying went.

"Is there another reason you wish me to continue watching her for you, Your Highness?"

Tai looked over, still panting. "What do you mean?"

Aadan shrugged, trying to sound casual. "You ordered her a very expensive saddle, I heard, despite her having done a dive that only Baikalan and your uncle have ever been able to perform. I would have thought that would worry you."

He couldn't tell whether Tai flushed, given they were both red in the face. "Even more reason to ensure she sees me as a friend rather than a foe."

Aadan glanced around, making sure they had privacy. "It may not be my place, Your Highness," he said. "But such gifts can start rumors. And such rumors can be dangerous."

Tai wiped his face with a towel. "You know how I feel about rumors. Start fearing those and you will see a snake in every shadow. What do you think would happen if I reacted to every rumor that I'm not my father's son? Or that my mother is a witch? Or my favorite, that I'm actually Mengkhis Lai's son?" His mouth twisted in distaste.

Rumors of illegitimacy, Aadan knew, were an age-old tactic by enemies who wished to undermine the throne. And to his credit, Tai had never allowed those poisonous suspicions to take root.

"But what of the danger to her?" Aadan countered. From his friend's expression, this hit a nerve. Aadan sighed inwardly. Tai, of all people, should know the dangers that came with a prince's favor.

"Peilah's death was an accident," Tai said, in a tone that Aadan knew better than to contradict.

"I'm not saying it wasn't," Aadan replied. "But that doesn't mean she had no enemies at court."

A frown of worry appeared. Aadan wasn't sure whether his friend was thinking of the past, or the whispers about Tai's interest in Jin had merit. Ever since the girl Peilah's unexpected death two years ago, Tai's dedication was to the throne. It was part of why Aadan respected Tai. The heir was what every royal family wanted in a crown prince: smart, decisive, putting duty above all. In a way, Aadan thought Tai was the ultimate dragonrider: only his dragon was the empire, and he was bound heart and soul to it. Tai's charm toward women was fueled purely by politics—save for that one girl. And it wasn't just women he charmed, for he had the ability to win over men of all stations as well. His diplomacy and innate charisma were perhaps some of the prince's greatest skills, ones Aadan's father had always urged him to emulate.

"I'm sure I am simply overthinking, as I always do," Aadan said. "But you may want to ensure no one imagines feelings that aren't there."

"Thank you for the warning," Tai said with one of his usual disarming smiles. "You are wise as always." The crown prince stood, throwing the towel over his neck. "I show interest because I want to ensure we don't have another Mengkhis Lai."

Aadan nodded, and the two of them left the hall for the baths. But even as they talked of other things, Aadan wondered whether the prince's attention toward Jin wasn't purely to do with Mengkhis Lai. And this suspicion chafed him, to the point where Wanli reached out, questioning.

He reassured his dragon that nothing was wrong. And it was true. He wanted to protect Jin from Tai purely because she was a fellow dragonrider, and he deliberately ignored Wanli's chuckle of disbelief.

CHAPTER 26

*J*in left the library and headed, as she usually did, toward the Blood Oval. After three months of lessons with Aadan, she could finally read and write simple things, including her own name, and words on the maps began to make sense. Distances, directions, place names, and more had stopped being meaningless drawings. She had found her home province of Kwannay and even pinpointed her home city. And pinpoint was an apt word: a tiny black dot on an expanse of paper. It had once been her entire world, reduced to an insignificant spot of ink in the vast empire.

This morning, she hadn't had time to eat breakfast, and her stomach was protesting. You're getting spoiled, she warned it. All these regular meals were undoing Haitao's years of training. Part of her reveled in discarding all of his rules, but the fearful part of her also balked at the unknown. What was she becoming? What would happen if she abandoned all her old habits and rules? Jin was learning to fly, learning to read. She was even earning her own money, saving her stipend each month. Haitao's warning about education came back to her: "It's for boys because it's dangerous." She'd known better than to point out that her life as a thief was dangerous, yet he never suggested she stop stealing.

When she arrived at the Oval, Emar took her aside. She noticed a servant was standing at a distance, waiting.

"The war minister has summoned you to his office."

At Jin's look of surprise, Emar shook his head. "I don't know what it's about, and it's not my place to ask. But I said I'd send you."

"And miss training?"

Emar's face tightened, but he nodded. "Go."

Jin followed the attendant to the western wings of the Imperial Palace. She had never visited this side of the complex, where the ministers had their offices.

The attendant led her down a long corridor lined with official guards, before showing her into a rich but tastefully decorated room with a long *kang* and a sweeping desk, along with several metal bookshelves that were so tall and wide they gave her the feeling of a fortress rather than a study. Several braziers full of coals kept the room warm, and long windows looked out onto a courtyard with manicured trees, gardens, and a pond dusted with snow.

"The minister will be in shortly." The attendant bowed and left, closing the doors behind him, and Jin looked around the room once more.

Even now, it was hard not to notice the exquisite items in the room and think of the price they'd fetch: a vase of fine porcelain, jade writing brushes with the finest-quality horsehair, and statues of war horses whose saddles were encrusted with jade, silver, and pearls the size of goji berries. A collection of swords hung on one wall, and in their reflection Jin noted the window shutters, which were closed. She turned around to better look at them and noticed they were unlike any she had seen before. They were made of metal.

She had only seen metal shutters on pawn shops and moneylenders. Those were thick pieces, designed to dissuade even the strongest of thieves. These were the width of her smallest finger, meaning they had not been built for strength.

Jin tentatively opened one and was surprised at its weight. A stinging breeze pushed its way in, and Jin heard paper from the desk scatter to the floor. She cursed and hastily closed the shutter with a hard push.

She turned to see numerous sheets of paper lying on the silk carpet beside the desk. She hurriedly bent to pick them up, tidying them into a pile. Jin had no idea what order they had been in, but there was nothing to be done.

Jin stood and replaced them on the desk, when she frowned. Sticking out of the pile was a folded paper the size of her palm with "Wang Kway Jin" written across one corner. Mere months ago she wouldn't have recognized it, but thanks to Aadan it was now as familiar as her own face. She was about to reach for it, when the sound of Gao's voice at the door made her jump away.

"It's a fine desk, isn't it? Used to be my father's, and his father's before him."

Jin sank to one knee as expected. "Minister."

The minister swept around her to the desk, not bothering to give her permission to rise. Only when he had sat down and opened and closed a drawer did he speak again.

"Come, girl, have a seat."

She rose and slowly walked to the opposite side of the desk, trying not to look at the pile of paper and the folded message peeking out. Haitao would never use her name; they only communicated via code. But if it had been intercepted and Aadan's friend had told Gao who sent the message, that might explain why her name was written on it.

"Please, sit down," Gao repeated.

Thankfully he seemed to think her inaction was due to the polite custom of declining twice before accepting. She sat, wary. He, in turn, took stock of her, as one would a problematic dog.

"You and I are very different. And I think we may therefore have had a bumpy start. That's why I thought we'd have a chat alone, to get to know each other better." The minister placed a pack of thin square cards on the table. "Do you know the game of *pai*?"

"I have never had the honor, Minister Gao," Jin replied truthfully. Cards were a new-fangled game and the purview of the rich. The games of the common tavern involved inexpensive bones and wood pieces, not expensive paper that only the government or merchants had in abundant supply. She chanced a quick look at the folded letter. Its corner was still visible.

"Let me teach you," the minister said, sweeping up the pile of cards. "I have all my generals play this game. It keeps the mind sharp."

Jin tried to focus.

"There are three suits—coins, coin strings, and numerals," the Minister said, his plump hands handling the cards with an unexpected dexterity. He fanned them out on the table, his right hand stopping within a hand's length of the folded paper with Jin's name on it.

He showed Jin the paper *pai*, each one slightly smaller than his palm and each one embossed in gold. "The goal is to make all your pai into sets of three, in numerical order."

The minister showed her, arranging the pai in various combinations. Jin tried to absorb the rules while observing the minister and keeping an eye on the folded letter. She tried to guess his motives in having her skip training to play games with him. Was this a test? Or a trap?

"The trick is to keep all the useful pai and get rid of the useless ones," the minister said, dealing them between her and Jin until they each had a pile. "Useful pai fit in. Useless ones are those unable to form strings with the others, which prevents you from winning. And once you discard one, you do not take it back." The hard paper clicked in his fingers as he laid them down, making snapping noises in the silence. "When all your pai make full combinations, you call out 'eat.'"

"Eat?"

The man's smile was wolfish. "To signal that you have eaten your enemy." He gathered the pai into his hands. "Now let's see how well you learn."

She picked up her pile of pai, wary.

The minister smiled. "Good, you instinctively know you should not let me see your hand."

Jin looked at what she held. At first they were a jumble of symbols, but as she focused she saw which ones matched, and rearranged them.

"What do you want from Dragon Class, Wang Kway Jin?"

She weighed her words. "I am hoping to be the best dragonrider I can be, Minister."

He smiled, as if humoring her. "We are alone here, so we can put aside all flowery lies." The minister laid down a pai. "I commend you; you are very strong for a girl, and you have come far. But no matter how good you become, you will never be as good as the others."

She bristled at this. "I came in first in the Ice Beard Mountain test."

"Yes," he said, voice lowering, "in a move made famous by another. Baikalan." This made her stay silent. "If you can't think of yourself, then think of Rayshan."

She did, instinctively reaching out for him. She frowned at the silence that greeted her, then noticed Gao's smile.

"When I said we are alone, I really meant we are alone." He gestured to the windows. "You needn't worry about Rayshan overhearing us."

Lead shutters. Jin glanced around and realized that the whole of the study must have been lined in lead. That's why Rayshan couldn't hear her. That's why the shutters were so heavy. Her skin prickled, realizing she hadn't noticed the absence of Rayshan's usual pulse, as she had been so absorbed by the room's contents. And the letter.

"Don't worry, I don't wish to harm either of you," the minister said. He laid down another pai. "Quite the opposite. I want what's best for you, and the empire. Can you guess what that is?"

Jin took one of the pai that the minister laid down and then selected one from her hand to discard. She waited for his answer.

"I cannot expect you to know what's best for the

empire. You're but a thief who happened to steal something very valuable." He made a move and then looked at her directly. "We have built Dragon Class into a fine institution, and fine institutions are founded on traditions. The Middle Kingdom is built on over three thousand years of tradition. Think of that, Student Jin. Three thousand years. It is our sacred duty to protect those traditions. Sudden change endangers everything."

"Confucius said that only the wisest and stupidest of men never change." Haitao had not valued her education beyond how it related to thievery, but he had been a stout Confucian who had passed on many of the sage's quotes. And right now she needed to ruffle the minister.

Gao glowered, and Jin was certain her impudence would see her punished.

"If you can't think about the collective good of the empire, of preserving our fine Dragon Class traditions, then think about Rayshan. He deserves a real rider. The best rider we have."

"But he's bonded to me."

"Only because you stole him," the minister said, exasperation surfacing. "Tell the empress you wish to quit Dragon Class. I will make sure you stay out of the slave mines and have a job of your choice, in a place of your choice."

She studied him. "You sent the man to threaten me that night."

"Make an offer, not threaten," he replied smoothly.

"I may be the minister of war, but believe me when I say I prefer peaceful means to resolve problems. I'm hoping you'll accept my offer, now that I'm making it in person and I've explained what's at stake."

"But the unbonding will harm Rayshan?" Jin argued, holding the minister's gaze as she picked up a pai she had discarded.

He laid out another pai. "Have you considered that Rayshan's power has not shown itself not because he's a Jade and blooms late, but because you are a woman?"

She forced herself to stay composed.

"You've caused more ripples than you can imagine. You've lost us a bronze dragon, thereby weakening Dragon Class. I'm asking you to do what's best for all, because you're playing a game you know nothing about." He laid his pai out, face up on the desk between them. A neat line of patterns in ascending order confronted Jin. "Eat."

Jin paused, then gathered her pai and stood. "Is there such a thing as a tie in this game?"

At his frown, she carefully leaned over the desk and laid out her pai one by one, from right to left.

The minister looked at Jin's hand, then at her. "It seems there is." His voice grew quiet. "But in real life there is no tie, Jin. Leave Dragon Class, before it's too late."

She swept her pai up in one swift motion and sat back down with them. "What happens then? You'll kill me?"

The minister sat back and shook his head. "You're like the proverbial frog looking up from a well and only seeing a limited circle of sky, whereas I see the whole picture. I see the most powerful dragon the empire has being paired with an ignorant street thief. The last Jade we had was Baikalan, and even though Mengkhis Lai was our star rider, he used Baikalan to plunge the empire into dark times."

The minister had struck a nerve, though she tried her best to keep her face neutral. "I have no intention of becoming a Mengkhis Lai, or in creating chaos."

Gao sighed. "It's not about intention. Your very presence creates chaos, Jin. Don't let that chaos grow until it destroys us all, including you." He stood. "I am asking you politely, leave Dragon Class voluntarily."

Jin drew every ounce of courage she had. "No."

The minister's eyes narrowed. "Is that your final answer?"

"Yes," she said, standing and placing the pai back on the desk. "Thank you for teaching me your game, Minister. I should get back to my training."

The minister barked for an attendant to come. "Take the initiate Jin back to Dragon City." He leveled a cold stare at her. "Remember, the blade of grass that grows taller than the others is the first to be cut down." He paused, unsmiling. "Peace upon your afternoon, Initiate."

CHAPTER 27

*O*nly when she was safely in Rayshan's cave did she pull out the folded piece of paper from inside her shirt sleeve.

What is that? Rayshan asked, sniffing.

I don't know. She told him how she had been summoned to Gao's office and how the room was lined in lead. Rayshan growled.

She unfolded the piece of paper, eager and yet dreading the coded message within. But when she opened it, she frowned in confusion.

What's wrong?

It's not a message from Haitao. She struggled over many of the words but realized from the numerous boxes on the paper that she was looking at some type of form. An official document, for there was a faded seal on the bottom right corner.

What does it say?

She saw numbers and started there. *The fifth day of the fifth month . . . twenty-sixth year of . . . Kaizhong's . . . reign.*

It's the year.

She frowned. *Wasn't that the year Emperor Kaizhong died?*

And the year the empress ascended the throne, Rayshan added.

It says something about a baby, and a woman named . . . Lan Ming, I think. Her thoughts swirled. *What did any of this have to do with her?*

What does the seal say? Rayshan prompted her. *Usually seals are associated with various departments of the government.*

Of course. That made sense. She studied the round, black designs with the tightly packed, official-looking script, and her blood chilled. *It's the seal of the royal police.*

She redoubled her efforts and soon had pieced enough information together to realize what this was. *It's a birth record. A child born in the imperial jails to a woman named Lan Ming.*

Rayshan shifted in his cave, making the chain scrape. *Does it say whether the child was—*

A girl, Jin replied, feeling sick. *It was a girl. It's the same year I was born.* She reread the parts that said "huren," "execution for killing her husband," and "sale price: twenty fei." *Gao thinks I'm this child, this child born in a prison and sold before her mother's execution.*

Rayshan growled. *Why would he think a girl from Kwannay would be this same girl?*

I don't know, Jin admitted, but a little voice in her began clamoring that it was true. Haitao had told her he'd found her, abandoned and starving, on the roads of Kashgar. But had he actually bought her? A memory surfaced of a night when she and Lu had brought back a particularly lucrative haul from the annual lantern festival, and Haitao had been deep in his cups. He had pinched her chin and told her she was the best decision he'd made in Changan. She had blamed it on the wine and not bothered to contradict him. Why sour his good mood?

Now, doubt fluttered in her stomach. What if that had been the time he'd told the truth and not the lie? What if he'd bought her from the imperial jails and taken her to Kwannay? Knowing Haitao, he might have very well concocted the story of saving her just to make her feel indebted.

"What if I'm the daughter of a murderer?" Jin whispered. A part of her wished she had never found this paper. She hadn't realized how hard she had clung to the fantasy of her parents being loving, respectable people who had led a good life. This paper, flimsy as it was, had pricked a hole in that fantasy. Though she didn't know what had led Gao to this record and to thinking she was this girl, he had the empire's resources at his disposal. She didn't think he'd believe it without good reason.

You don't know that, Rayshan insisted. *Gao might just be trying to discredit you with rumors about your birth and searching through records to find something that vaguely fits. But even if all this is true and you are that child, that doesn't make you a lesser woman.* He lowered his head so his right eye was directly before hers. *In life, we cannot choose where our journey begins, but we can try to choose where we end up.*

In the days that followed, Jin tried to find comfort in Rayshan's words. It wasn't an easy task. Jin was on a constant watch for anyone lunging at her from the shadows, for despite the minister's insistence that he was peace loving, she didn't doubt he'd knife her if he thought he might get away with it. But no one seemed to pay her more mind than usual, and Rayshan agreed that the only option was to keep training and maintain a watchful eye for any threats. Jin decided not to tell Emar or the empress about her conversation with Gao, much less the birth record that she kept inside one of her cushion covers. Emar and the empress had made clear they didn't want her creating more trouble. And riling the war minister before stealing documents from his office sounded like trouble.

As the days turned into a week, Jin grew increasingly high-strung, until she realized she had to stop thinking about Lan Ming and the minister. She wasn't ready to face the possibility that her mother might have been executed for the murder of her father, and there was only one thing she could do to protect herself from Gao.

It makes me uneasy when the enemy doesn't show his hand, she said to Rayshan.

True, he agreed. *The unseen knife is more deadly than the visible one.*

If we knew your power, we'd have an edge.

The only way to hasten a power's manifestation is to blood bond, Rayshan said, whipping his tail. *And I won't do that.*

She knew better than to argue, but also wondered if she could afford to wait.

THE MAP SNAPPED OPEN, revealing a detailed diagram of reds, greens, and browns with veins of cyan through it.

Emar stood at the head of the class and pointed. "Familiarize yourself with every town, every river and stream. Your knowledge of the empire and its mountains will dictate your survival during your next test, the geography trial, so pay attention."

Jin sat at her desk, fiddling with her ink brush. She rolled it absently while observing those around her.

"Student Jin!"

Her eyes snapped back to the front of the room.

"Coming in first in the trials doesn't mean you don't have to learn geography," the big man growled. "Did you hear what your next test is?"

This, at least, she knew. "Finding our way back from a remote location within the empire, Master Emar. Without the benefit of a compass."

"And?"

"With only a limited supply of water, food, and tools. We are not to bring money or valuables to trade for food and help."

He nodded. "And so tell me, which region here borders the northern Anxi province?"

She looked at where he was pointing. She had never had to learn the lands beyond the province where Haitao operated. There had never been any need. "Mongolia."

Jin silently thanked Aadan for his lessons, and even now saw his questioning look, asking what was wrong. He had noticed her distraction.

"Good," Emar said. "Keep paying attention, or you'll fail your written geography exam before you even get to the real one. Now, the river along this border . . ."

She looked away. Would Aadan still help her if he believed she was the child of a murderer? The thought he might shun her was surprisingly painful. No, best not to tell him. And what if her background had something to do with why she couldn't find Rayshan's power?

Jin tried to focus on the geography class but couldn't. All she could think of was Mengkhis Lai and how to make Rayshan manifest his power, for both their sakes.

* * *

"THIS IS CLEARLY BORING YOU," Aadan said, exasperated. "You haven't been yourself. What is wrong?"

Jin came back from her thoughts and realized she had paused mid-page while reading aloud. The library was mostly deserted at this time of morning, when students had finished breakfast and were seeing to errands or prayers, depending on their faith.

She thought again of telling him about the birth record, but decided against it. "Nothing." She looked down at the page before her. "I suppose I don't find poetry very exciting. Who reads this kind of thing?"

Aadan looked amused. "Li Bai's a master, actually. But if you don't want to read this, why don't you choose something you are interested in?"

He pushed a pile of books toward her, but after glancing over them, she stood. "Not these."

She searched the shelves for a few moments before returning empty-handed.

"Where can I find books on Mengkhis Lai?"

Aadan regarded her. "You can't. There aren't any."

She frowned. "None?"

"Well, none here. They are kept in the restricted section, and you need permission to access them."

"How do I get permission?"

Aadan hesitated. "From the head of Dragon Class."

"Prince Tai?" Jin didn't fancy her chances of convincing the prince.

"Why do you want to study Mengkhis Lai?"

"It's obvious, isn't it? He's the last Jade dragon the empire had. I ride a Jade. Not to mention he was a huren, wasn't he?"

She couldn't gauge whether her knowledge surprised him or he was simply reluctant to talk about Mengkhis Lai. "Yes. He was the emperor's step-brother."

"So a brother through a concubine?"

"Of sorts. Mengkhis Lai's mother was originally a Rus princess captured when the emperor's father, Tai's grandfather, waged his campaigns against the North. She became one of his favorites, and Tai's grandfather gave Mengkhis Lai a more local name and raised him as his own. He grew up like a twin to Tai's father."

"Then why did Mengkhis Lai turn on his own father and brother?"

"Why does anyone do so?" Aadan asked. "Power. Perhaps you'd do the same."

Jin glanced at him. Did others fear her becoming another Mengkhis Lai? She shivered at her own fear of the man in Rayshan's Firesong. "I never knew my family. I would want to keep them rather than destroy them."

Jin looked about, then headed down a different row of bookshelves and returned to the table with a thick tome.

Aadan raised his eyebrows when he saw the title. "*Myths of Blood Bonding?*"

Jin turned the pages, struggling with the script but determined to find what she was looking for. "At least it's not about nobles and wine and moon gazing." Aadan looked offended, but Jin pressed on. "I'll start here. 'Blood bonding is rumored to cause all sorts of side effects: madness, wasting disease, cruelty, fits of strength, and . . .'" She struggled, until Aadan leaned over and looked at the page.

"Death."

Jin looked at him. "Did anyone besides Mengkhis Lai ever blood bond?"

Aadan shook his head. "It's all just myth and conjecture. No one knows for certain what happens. But the power clearly drove Mengkhis to madness. Blood bonding made a monster of him." Aadan looked thoughtful. "Those who are more philosophical think that taking on the powers of dragons breaks a man. I hope you're not considering it."

She gave him a look. "Of course not. I just want to find out Rayshan's ability, and I thought—"

"I mean it, Jin." Aadan's expression was more serious than she had ever seen him. "Many of the empire's rules are unfair—not allowing women into Dragon Class, for instance. But the rule against blood bonding was decreed by the Dragon Queen herself and was never meant to be broken."

Jin nodded, though a question still gnawed at her. Why would Mengkhis Lai blood bond if he knew it was so dangerous? Had he really been so power hungry that he was willing to risk his life and lose his soul? This led to another question.

"If Mengkhis Lai was so dangerous, why didn't the empress kill him? Why is he buried at the opposite end of the empire from his dragon?"

Aadan seemed hesitant, but then reached forward and pulled the book to him, flipping until he found what he was looking for. He turned the book around and pushed it back across the table.

"Second paragraph."

Jin looked down and read the section Aadan indicated. "One of the few known facts about blood-bonded riders is that they cannot be killed, except by another blood-bonded rider." She digested this, realization sinking in. "So Mengkhis Lai and his dragon are immortal?"

Aadan nodded. "They are held by very strong magic. But they cannot be killed."

When Jin returned to her quarters that evening, she found Meipin waiting for her in their shared foyer, beaming.

"Peace upon your evening! I thought you would never get back, you were taking so long!"

Jin frowned. "Was I meant to be back sooner?"

"This came in for you," Meipin said, pulling out a golden envelope and holding it out to Jin. "I already know what's inside."

"You read my mail?" she asked, wary.

"No, you silly melon," Meipin said. "All the nobles and most of the dragonriders received one. It's an invitation to the prince's spring festival ball. Everyone's going, and you'll need a dress. A proper one. You're welcome to any of mine." She frowned, looking over at Jin. "Though we'll have to make adjustments. I've already pulled out some possibilities," Meipin said, "and left them on the hanger over there. We can go through them together, and I'm sure the seamstress will be more than happy to make adjustments. Now, for the face." Meipin led her to a seat. "I know you don't like taking advice, but I'm here to help. I can handle your makeup, because you won't be going as a dragonrider, will you?"

"I'm not going."

"Of course you are," Meipin said. "It's the year's most important event. Don't worry, I can do your makeup on the day."

"I know how to do my own."

Meipin's brow arched. "You do?" At Jin's expression, she shrugged, conciliatory. "You just never wear any."

"It doesn't matter, as I'm not going." She spotted a bowl of lychees on the table and chose one, peeling it. They were luxurious imports from the South, a reminder of how different a life she now led.

Meipin grinned, undeterred. "Show me what you know."

"Why do you care so much?"

At this, Meipin's smile stiffened, and Jin realized the girl was nervous. "Because we haven't had a chance to talk. Truly talk. You're so busy, and when you're not, you're avoiding me."

"I'm not used to female company," she admitted.

Meipin smiled. "Of course. I hadn't realized. I'm not offended. Well, maybe a little. I'll go get the paints."

Meipin came back carrying a tray of lacquered

boxes full of small pots and jars. She also had a container of brushes, some thick, some thin, and she laid all these out on a long side table with an exaggerated flair. "Very well, Lady Jin, show me your art."

Jin reluctantly put away the lychees. She took the warm cloth Meipin held out to her, wiped and dried her face, and then sat down before all the instruments. The sight gave her a bittersweet pang. It had been so long since she had painted her face, but she remembered those days as clear as her own reflection in the mirror ...

HAITAO HAD SENT her to Lady Yang's once a week for her "woman" lessons.

Haitao had decided early on, though Jin wasn't sure exactly when, that Jin would be a different thief from the rest of his gang. Jin was his key to "moving up," he said, though she didn't know what this meant until he had taken her to Lady Yang's. When they arrived at one of the most notorious brothels in the city, Jin had nearly run away. She'd been convinced that contrary to all his promises, Haitao was now going to sell her to the singing house. She would be painted, made to dance, made to sing, and made to do all those things that were whispered about. Haitao gave her a hard slap across the face, shaking her twelve-year-old shoulders until her teeth had nearly fallen out.

"Be still! Or I'll skin you myself," he hissed. When he had her calmed down enough, he said gruffly, "It's not what you think. Lady Yang is the mistress of a brothel, true. But I'll have you know she used to be high born, from a renowned family. She knows their ways, and she knows beauty. She will make a phoenix out of you, my little sparrow. And phoenixes get to fly with other phoenixes, which is what you must do. What I want you to do." He looked her in the eye. "Now, go with Lady Yang and do what she tells you to do, and if I hear of any disobedience, I will whip you something good. Do you understand?"

Jin nodded, fear constricting her. She prayed to Buddha that Lady Yang wasn't going to make her join the singing house. She would kill herself before doing that. Haitao pushed her forward, and she stumbled into the three-story building as Lady Yang closed the door.

"Let's make a lady of you, little sparrow" . . .

Jin finished plucking her eyebrows and checked her work in the mirror as Meipin looked on.

"A swan brow," Meipin said, smiling. "A little traditional, but it does suit you. I have an idea for color. Wait here."

Meipin left Jin staring at herself in the mirror. The face looking back at her was lined, even more hardened than the one Lady Yang had worked on, and Jin drifted back to the past again . . .

* * *

Lady Yang ushered her into the heart of the singing house, to a private room. Along the way Jin tried not to look at the girls lounging in various boudoirs, men laughing with them. One lady in a rich silk dress of rose and cream slipping off her shoulders slammed the door on Jin when she accidentally peered in.

"In here," Lady Yang said, ushering her into a dressing room. "Now you will stand in the corner with this steamer basket on your head."

Jin stared at her. Was this some sort of trick? But, no, Lady Yang insisted, placing a large empty wooden steamer basket on her head. Jin stood for an hour like that and had to retrieve the dropped basket six times before Lady Yang said she was done and sent her home. Jin was more than confused, but her lessons continued, until one day Jin stood for her hour without the basket falling once. Lady Yang seemed pleased.

"You now stand like a lady, not like some stray dog wanting a bone," she said. "And now that you stand like a lady, we can dress you like a lady."

She had taken out several gowns and held them against Jin. "You have skin that's not quite the same shade as most. You'll need something that contrasts well with how pale you are. It's perhaps the one thing going for you." She smiled. "I don't mean that unkindly. Everyone has gifts. You just have to know what they are and learn how to use them. You are thin as a mantis, so don't wear or do anything that brings attention to that. Instead, lean into your strengths—you have interesting-colored hair, which will match certain combs nicely. And you'll be able to wear colors that other girls avoid, which will help you stand out when and if you want to."

Lady Yang had her try on several dresses, grimacing at some and tapping her fingers against her chin at others. "Not that one," she said when Jin reached for a brown robe. "Do you know why? Its sleeves don't suit thin arms, and brown simply blends into your hair. You need something that contrasts but complements. Here, try something in green, or red. That's better."

Lady Yang checked the sleeves of the dresses. "These sleeves will hide things you'll steal. Here's how you will do it and how you will make it look natural. Also, because you have such a skinny waist, you'll want to pad it more. No one will think twice that you have such a thick sash, which also helps to hide stolen objects. Here, try my comb, for instance."

Jin slid this in, and then another. Lady Yang was right. A woman's sash was a brilliant place to hide stolen items.

"Now, for your face," Lady Yang said, clapping her hands together in a businesslike way. "I will tell you how to make yourself attractive. Though not too attractive, for I doubt Haitao wants you to draw too much attention. But back in the day, I used to prepare young girls for marriage. Noble girls." Her face looked wistful, but when she caught Jin looking at her, she smiled, back to business. "You, Jin, will need to appear a lady. No one suspects a lady of stealing. Now, the art of this is to be subtle, to know your shades, and not overpaint until you look like a botched thousand-color cake. That's what unskilled peasant girls do. But ladies know how to make this an art. And I will teach you."

She laid out a confusing array of powders, paints, brushes, tweezers, thread, creams, and rouges. Jin looked at them all as if they were some wizardry.

"You've used none of this before?"

Jin shook her head. Lady Yang nodded, as if she had expected this but had hoped for better. "We have powders for the face, rouges, eye colors, eyebrow ink, and lip paint. Now, beauty practices change, but one rule remains: do what makes you radiant. Now take a good long look at your face in the mirror, because I want you to see what change we can work with art."

And Lady Yang had showed her. She had outlined her eyes, using a fine brush dipped in moistened black ink, then taken a lush vermillion paint and carefully colored in the center section of her lips, powdering the outer edges to make her mouth look smaller and more petal-like. She had shown her how to pluck her eyebrows if she wanted, while painting them back on to give them a bushier look for when she was in the streets and needed to look like an urchin again. By the end, it amazed Jin what Lady Yang could do. She was a magician of sorts, and she could make Jin into anything: a well-bred lady, a courtesan, a shopgirl, a maid, a nun, a street rat. Jin learned what her face could become and how to do it herself. On the surface, at least, she could be anybody she wanted, even if just for a night.

"And now, my girl," Lady Yang said after many moons of practice, "you are ready to go steal the immortal peach from the Jade Emperor in Heaven if you so choose."

* * *

JIN LAID down the brush and looked in the mirror, turning her face to make sure the powder was even. Meipin stared.

"I am impressed," Meipin said after a moment. "Who taught you to do your makeup?"

"A noblewoman," Jin said. "But you didn't just want to talk to me about face paints and eyebrow styles, did you?"

"No." Meipin took up a hairbrush and gestured. "May I?" She seemed to take Jin's silence as assent and moved behind Jin to pull out the strip of cloth holding her hair. "You likely see me as some painted bird at court, with my greatest dream being to become empress, am I right?" Meipin tucked a stray strand of hair back in place and smiled. "Don't deny it and don't feel bad. I work very hard to make sure everyone sees me that way, including Prince Tai. But now that we're alone, I'd like to ask for your help."

"Help? With what?"

Meipin worked at a knot in Jin's hair, making Jin's eyes water. "You know my uncle is the minister of laws? I've been trying to convince him to hold a vote on allowing women to join Dragon Class."

Jin frowned. "You want to join Dragon Class?"

Meipin laughed. "Heavens and all below, no. But I think women should be allowed to ride dragons, work in government, choose any job, really. If I was a man, my uncle would be able to get me a position in the secretariat." She sighed. "But it's not done, as all those in power keep saying. Just like having a girl in Dragon Class isn't done." She smiled wickedly. "But you did it. Despite girls being barred from entering the hatchery, you somehow showed the entire empire that dragons can bond with girls. This is a chance to change the laws, Jin, change the empire. Do you have any idea the power you have?"

Meipin's voice had risen, and Jin instinctively glanced about. Her maid Ahlu was sewing stitchwork in the next room while another swept the outer courtyard.

"Don't worry, they are my most loyal maids." Meipin leaned in close, pulling the brush through Jin's thick hair. "You can do what none of us can. You can change things for all women."

"I'm not here to change things."

Meipin smiled. "That's why you're perfect. Men fear the woman who wants change, but if you make them think it's their idea, they will champion it with their sword if need be. Come to the ball and speak to my uncle. Let him see that you have no agenda to let women join, that you're here purely out of service to the empire or to your dragon or whatever spurs you, and he'll hold a vote."

"Surely you can simply ask your uncle to speak to the empress. She's a woman. She'd be sympathetic."

Meipin snorted, then grew serious. "Just because she's a woman in power doesn't mean she wants to see other women in power." She leaned close to Jin's ear, so close that Jin's skin prickled. Meipin's voice was a whisper, even though they were the only ones in the room. "Be careful of her, Jin. Even when she's your ally, she may still burn you."

A sliver of fear crawled down Jin's spine. She had thought the war minister was acting alone, but what if the empress shared his views? But the empress could simply get rid of Jin, and no one would question her. No, Jin decided, the empress had an interest in seeing her succeed. But Meipin was right that even allies might sting when it suited them.

Meipin smiled brightly, as if they had been discussing nothing but makeup. "So will you come? After all, there will be at least one prince who will be very disappointed if you don't show!"

Jin's cheeks heated at that. A part of Jin wanted to go—it had been so long since she'd worn a luxurious dress, transformed herself into elegance. But she couldn't afford to. She needed every spare minute she had to find Rayshan's power. Then a thought occurred to her.

"Is this why you agreed to take me in on my first day? You wanted me to help influence your uncle?"

"Of course not!" Meipin's brows wrinkled. "Is that what you think?"

"No one offers kindness without expecting something in return."

Meipin looked astounded, then, to Jin's surprise, pitying. "It must be very lonely," she said softly, "to live life thinking there's no such thing as friendship."

The words threw Jin, leaving her unsure how to reply.

"I won't push you to do anything you don't want to," Meipin continued, gathering her pots and brushes. "But if you change your mind, let me know. There is more to life than just Dragon Class."

Jin went to Rayshan's cave, her feet taking her there almost of their own accord. He seemed to sense her pensive mood when she arrived and simply stretched his wings to suggest they fly.

She was only too happy to agree. She slipped his reins from his collar and saddled him with Tai's gift. After what happened at Ice Beard Mountain, she kept all her tack and saddle gear in Rayshan's cave, on a series of hooks she had struck into the rock. Anyone wanting to shred her saddle would have to fight Rayshan. She cinched the gear into place, making sure Rayshan was comfortable, and then pulled herself onto his back.

He stepped out on the ledge and spread his wings, then leapt, and she was soaring. She would never tire of this, she knew, no matter if she lived to be a hundred with white hair and no teeth. She would never, ever give this up. No matter how many gold bars Gao offered or how many threats he made.

Rayshan dipped before pumping his wings, stretching them out and relishing the freedom. He climbed into the sky, pushing himself with all his being until he leveled out and glided over the imperial walls and out over the people's city. She sensed the eyes, the tens of thousands of citizens who saw dragons every day and yet still gazed at the heavens, at the symbol of their empire's power.

Rayshan took her over the city wards, divided into neat grids by avenues and rows of trees, over the marketplaces where shops were closing for the day and carriages were hurrying home. Taverns, song houses, and game dens were opening their doors to nighttime business, and she heard stringed instruments beckoning patrons from every teahouse on every corner. She drank in the sights and scents, happy to soar above it all here, where time seemed to thicken and the horrors and trials of the world were safely earthbound below.

Dragon and rider said nothing for a while, enjoying the cocoon of their togetherness, before Rayshan banked and headed south, passing the Great Wild Goose Pagoda on the southeastern corner and over the outer city walls toward Splendid Jade Mountain.

Rayshan perched on an outcropping overlooking the placid water of one of the mountain's main lakes, and Jin climbed off, sitting with him as they gazed at the impossibly large, sprawling city in the distance. They sat in silence for a while, cold on the outside but warmed by on the inside from the thrill of flying.

Feeling better?

Yes, thank you.

What troubles you? the dragon asked.

I don't know. She paused. *How do you even know I am troubled?*

I am getting to know you more and more. I can sense these things, like colors that radiate from you.

What color am I now?

Brown. Muddied. You are confused.

She supposed he was right. Meipin's words had unsettled her, almost more than the war minister's. A part of her ability to defy Gao was her insistence that she wasn't changing anything, that her mere presence in Dragon Class wasn't a threat to the powers he represented. But Meipin's plea for her to speak to her uncle reinforced Gao's point that not everyone shared that view. Not only was Jin's presence emboldening people like Meipin, but if she actually convinced Minister Wei to hold a vote, then she was certainly taking an ax to tradition. And she had no doubt the minister would take an ax to her if that happened.

And what of Meipin's words about living without friendships? Mistrust was a strength that Haitao had meticulously cultivated in her. It was a strength to be sharpened. It had never occurred to her that it might be a weakness.

She watched the winter pleasure boats drift across the lake, some clearly private vessels of the rich, others floating tea or song houses, judging by the bright colors on their roofs, visible in flashes from their lanterns, which swung with the water's movement.

Rayshan, what will happen to you if I die?

Rayshan shifted, but looked at her with an unblinking eye. *That depends. My understanding from the other dragons is that most do not survive the grief. They lose a part of themselves and usually die alone somewhere.*

You mean . . . they kill themselves?

They don't have to. Rayshan curled his tail around her. *We die slowly from the inside out. Our hearts and minds fade into nothingness.*

Like how Emar is slowly turning to marble.

Yes, Rayshan answered.

I don't want to die, or lose you.

She looked toward the city, where a million lanterns glittered in the deepening dusk. She couldn't just leave Dragon Class. But there was also no doubt that time was short—the war minister would think of a way to get rid of them. The only way to fight back was to discover Rayshan's power and make them indispensable. *Do you think there's anything in your memories that will show how we can find out your power?*

He didn't answer immediately. *I don't know.*

We could try. At his lack of response, she asked, *What's wrong?*

I sometimes don't like using the Firesong. It shows disturbing things.

I know, she said, placing a hand on his scaled neck. *But we have to try.*

He blew air through his nostrils, his eyes closing. *Each dragon has collective memory, but our strongest memories are from those of our color who came before.*

So your strongest memories are from those of other Jades? Of Mengkhis Lai's dragon?

He turned to look at her, his eyes full of trepidation, his ears flat. She realized she had never seen him fearful. It made her both tremble and yet want to protect him, as ludicrous as that thought was, since he was now several times her size.

They are just memories, nothing more, she said, putting a hand on his neck. *Both Mengkhis and Baikalan are secured by magic far away.*

The dragon dipped his head and took a breath. *Yes. That is true. Yet somehow memories and visions can be strong.*

Rayshan, Minister Gao wants us gone. But if you find your power, we'll be that much more able to fight back if he makes a move.

The dragon closed his eyes. *Let us try.*

A cold seeped into Jin, making the blood in her veins slow. The world around her faded, slowly at first, then faster and faster, until a tunnel of white engulfed her. Indistinct shapes loomed at her, like she was a disembodied ghost floating through fog. But when she reached out with her mind, she felt Rayshan's presence, his life force a comforting ribbon of warmth in this world of cold.

She let him take his time, knowing his instincts would be far greater than hers here. His pulse steadied, his life force focused into a solid, tangible point, and then she was struggling through the white abyss around her. Something was ahead—the glow of coals. She made her way toward it, pulled by Rayshan. As she approached, she made out a carpet with intricate lotus designs, drifting bed curtains. And through the bed curtains was a large four-poster bed, each post carved with the imperial symbol of intertwined dragons and phoenixes.

On the bed, a young woman lay cradling a swaddled baby whose face was still blotchy from birth. Despite the disheveled hair, the unpowdered face, Jin recognized the empress—or at least a younger version of the empress. The woman crooned to her child, touching its cheek and hands. "Precious child," she whispered.

A figure came through the door, though Jin couldn't make out who it was. "He's on his way. He wants to see the prince."

The empress's face contorted in terror, anger, and grief. And in that moment it seemed the empress's emotions cut through Jin like a physical sword. Something propelled her back through the cold white cloud of Rayshan's memory, with snippets of images and half-choked sobs sounding in her ears. She shivered and then gasped as light exploded against her eyes and she felt the ground beneath her again. She threw out an arm and connected with Rayshan's reassuring bulk.

She didn't know why Rayshan had taken her to that memory.

Can you control what you see in the Firesong?

Rayshan shook out his wings as if trying to rid himself of the last of the image. *Not all the time. And Baikalan's memories are strong, like a magnet. They are all full of pain, anger, and overwhelming hate.* He paused. *And, no, I do not know what, if anything, that memory has to do with finding my powers.*

Jin had endless questions, but she knew Rayshan was exhausted. *That's enough for today. Come, let's get back.*

The Firesong was proving limited in pinpointing Rayshan's power and seemed to only exhaust him.

It was time to try her fallback plan.

usic poured from the banquet hall. Sogdian dancers in brilliant costumes twirled to heart-pounding beats. Platters of food crowded the tables, and lanterns of gold, red, and purple hung from every roof, turning the imperial city courtyards into a glittering array of light and color.

Meipin and Jin stepped through the main entrance, where servants bowed low and greeted them with empty goblets.

Meipin took two, and at Jin's expression nudged her in the ribs. "It's a feast. You must drink."

Jin took the goblet. She could use a little wine to ease her nerves. Meipin had been overjoyed when Jin informed her she would attend, even when Jin said she would not try to persuade Minister Wei one way or another. But the girl seemed convinced that just speaking to Jin would sway her uncle. Jin reached out to Rayshan and felt the comforting hum of his being in his cave. He was contentedly sleeping after she had taken him for a feed at the hunting grounds.

"We fill our cups there!" Meipin pointed.

In the middle of the courtyard was what looked like an iron mountain, higher than Jin's head, sitting in a moat of water. Guests were placing their goblets on lotus leaf–shaped platforms that folded out on hinges from the mountain. Above the leaf platforms, dragonhead spouts poured dark liquid. Meipin pulled her closer, and Jin now saw that the liquid was wine, flowing from the dragon's open jaws. When the cup was mostly full, the liquid would trickle to a stop.

"Is it magic?" Jin asked, as admiring as she was apprehensive.

Meipin laughed as she placed her goblet on one of the lotus leaves, and the dragonhead tap above it flowed with wine. "No. It's powered by a pump which draws the wine from below, and a series of weights and counterbalances makes the wine flow and stop."

Jin glanced at her, impressed.

Meipin brushed it off. "My father's an imperial engineer." She handed Jin her goblet, then raised her own. "To your advancing in Dragon Class!" Then, in a softer voice, "And charming my uncle." At her expression, Meipin added, "I'm glad you changed your mind. Tonight will be fun, I promise."

Jin took a sip from her goblet and scanned the room. She had her own quarry tonight.

She noticed people staring, and it took her a while to understand that she was the cause, not Meipin. People parted and murmured behind their fans.

"Why the looks?" she murmured.

Meipin smiled behind her peach-colored fan. "I think everyone's surprised that underneath the hawk is a genuine, elegant swan."

Jin flushed, unused to the attention despite all the time training with Lady Yang. Lady Yang had taught her to highlight her features, yes, but only in order to blend in. Tonight, coming here in silks and powder, she felt as if she would have stood out less if she had danced naked on the rooftops. She spied Madu and his friends across the floor, dressed in finery. At the sight of her, the rider smirked and nudged his friends, but she turned her back on them.

"Oh, look who's there," Meipin whispered, touching her elbow.

Jin looked where Meipin indicated. Prince Tai stood surrounded by a group of noblemen and women, exuding natural charm and magnetism—like his mother. Something he said elicited peals of laughter.

Jin drew a breath. "Shall we pay our respects?"

Meipin gave her a surprised look but followed. As they approached and Tai caught sight of them, his laughter faded to puzzlement, then to recognition.

"Lady Meipin, and . . . Lady Jin, I presume?" He cocked his head and squinted. "I presume that's you, since you're the only one not smiling at a feast. Other-wise, I wouldn't have recognized you."

Of course. She had momentarily forgotten Lady Yang's training. She summoned what she hoped was a radiant smile. "I thought a special occasion calls for a special dress." She looked at the twirling dancers around them, their robes spinning in a dizzying water-fall of color to the rhythm of the musicians. She gath-ered her courage. "Does Your Highness care to dance?"

There were titters amongst the prince's compan-ions, and he himself looked taken aback. Women did not ask men to dance, and certainly not the crown prince. Meipin watched shrewdly while Jin's throat went dry.

What are you doing? Rayshan asked from his cave. Clearly he had woken at her increased heartbeat.

You'll see.

Just when she thought he would publicly humiliate her with a refusal, the prince smiled. "It would be a pleasure."

He held out his hand, and she took it, knowing tongues were wagging already. He turned to Meipin with one of his most disarming smiles. "Will you excuse us, Lady Meipin? I hope you will be free later, as I always save the best dancer for last."

"You flatter me, as always, Your Highness," Meipin said, bowing. "Your ask is ever my command." Meipin glanced around, seemingly in search of her uncle. "But if I may beg Your Highness, I need her back soon." She gave Jin an expectant look before bowing and melting into the crowd.

"Do you know how to dance?" Tai asked.

"A little."

The court had the best Sogdian and Persian musicians, many sent as tribute from distant sultans and kings. Lady Yang had taught Jin the basics, again in order to fit in at parties, but Jin was certainly no expert.

He spun her, his feet flying out in a brisk rhythm that she matched. They drew apart, then glided together as the music grew faster and slower in turns.

"You lied," he said lightly. "You dance very well."

"As do you, Your Highness."

He had a way of sounding sincere in all he said. In another life, Jin realized, he would have made an excellent thief. One of Haitao's favorite sayings was that a pleasant face and a smooth tongue were worth more than a thousand keys. Jin folded her arms and swept around the prince in a knot move, surprised at how she remembered these things, how she had even enjoyed some of it, when she had forgotten she was meant to lift an item for Haitao.

"So, I sense you want something," Tai said as they circled each other in a figure eight. "Or did you ask me to dance solely for my dance skills?"

She drew a breath, then said, "I'd like to access the restricted library."

His steps faltered for half a heartbeat. "How do you know about it?"

"Aadan," she admitted. "I want to know if there's a way to manifest Rayshan's power." She was panting now, for her limbs were more used to riding than dancing.

"I can tell you how Mengkhis Lai's dragon manifested, if that's what you want to know," he said. "But I doubt it will help you."

She pivoted away, then back, in time to the music. "Why not?"

"Because," Tai said, slowing down with the music to draw her in and put his lips near her ear, "Baikalan found his power through a near-death experience."

The music grew frenzied, and they broke apart, the flutes rising to a shrill crescendo before dropping to a close. The dancers applauded the musicians, who bowed. Other dancers were already drenched in sweat.

"What kind of near-death experience?" Not all of her breathlessness was from the dancing.

He didn't immediately answer. "It's said he was ambushed one night while in the city. A group of drunken guards who disliked huren chose him for their evening entertainment, not knowing who he was. They beat him senseless, until Baikalan broke free of his cave and rescued him. And that's when his power manifested."

"I'd still like access to the library so I can read for myself. If you don't mind, Your Highness?"

He regarded her, thoughtful. "I'll consider it. Shall we dance one more?"

Jin glanced around, seeing the furtive glances behind fans. She caught sight of the empress at a high table on the dais, watching them. "I'm not sure. Your mother might have me killed for it."

A haunted look crossed his face, and she wondered uneasily at what truth she had hit. He bowed, stiff. "Peace upon your evening."

"On second thought, I would be honored, Your Highness."

The musicians had started another tune, this one slower. She raised her hand, and after a moment's hesitation he did as well, mirroring her. As they began a circular dance around each other, she tried to ignore the renewed whispers and stares. She didn't need more enemies, and this dance was making her more by the second. But he had looked so stricken in that moment.

"I apologize if I said something wrong, Your Highness."

He smiled, though it was dimmer than usual. "You didn't. I gather you aren't familiar with popular court rumors."

She shook her head. "Training leaves little time for that."

She spotted Aadan standing near a pillar speaking with another rider. He stopped mid-sentence and stared, his manners clearly forgotten. The other rider turned and squinted, and Jin recognized Bo Tan.

Aadan's surprise turned into a frown. Perhaps he thought dancing with a royal was inappropriate, and she supposed he was right. She had been audacious in approaching the prince.

"Are you and Aadan good friends?"

Thrown by the question, she concentrated on making a tight circle with her dance. "I don't have friends. Besides Rayshan."

"That must be hard."

She decided the conversation was going into uncomfortable territory and steered it away. "I realized I never said thank you."

"For the saddle? You did thank me." They whirled another circle, the prince taking her by the arm and leading her in a spin toward an adjoining moon gate. The music climbed to a dizzying close, and when they stopped, Jin realized they were on a mostly deserted side balcony with terraced steps leading down to a garden. He took a moment to catch his breath, and one hand smoothed back his hair.

She tucked an escaped strand of her own behind one ear. "Not for the saddle, though I am grateful for that. I mean thank you for what you and your mother did with King Ulagan. I didn't like the outcome, but you were right. I am ignorant of politics. I was ungrateful for your intervention, and I'm sorry." And she realized it was true. She had been so engrossed in her own feelings, she hadn't considered what the consequences had been for the empire.

"Your mother gave up a dragon for me. So thank you."

"It was worth it."

She couldn't tell whether that was charm or sincerity. "Because Rayshan is so powerful?"

"That. But you yourself were worth that price. More."

"If only I wasn't a girl, you mean," Jin added.

Tai gave an impatient shake of his head. "No, that's not what I mean. Not everyone views girls the way Gao does. Certainly not my mother." He paused. "I actually think my being a boy was a great disappointment to her."

At this, Jin choked on a laugh. He looked offended, and she studied him, incredulous. "Your Highness, no one in this empire prefers girls to boys. Least of all an empress."

His tone was wry. "Perhaps you haven't noticed, but my mother's not like most empresses. Or anyone else."

He was right. Tai put on a very confident appearance, but how much of that was to win his mother's favor? How much of that was a survival technique, as she had learned to be quiet, small, and obedient in Haitao's service?

"What makes you think she'd have preferred a girl?"

Tai regarded her before speaking, as if momentarily regretting his candor. "She talks often of what she would do if she had a daughter. I see a wistfulness in her face when she looks at you."

A memory of a rug, a brazier, and a newborn rose in her mind.

"Your mother loves you dearly."

He looked puzzled. "You sound very sure for someone who doesn't know her well."

"Do you know what the Firesong is?"

"I know of it, of course. Never experienced it."

"It's hard to explain, but . . ." She paused, remembering. "I saw your mother holding you, and the joy she felt was as real as I'm standing here now."

"That is . . . good of you to tell me." He seemed to grapple with this information.

"Though it seemed something terrible was happening at the same time," Jin added.

"The palace was under siege, so things were very unhappy and perilous then."

She recalled the fear, the sounds of sobs she heard as she drifted through the memory fog. "What happened?"

Tai's expression darkened. "I only know the story as I've heard it from my mother and Marquis Sanchin, and Emar. My uncle, Mengkhis Lai, had advanced on the capital, and broke down the palace gates on the day of my birth. My mother saved me from him, but she couldn't save my father. Mengkhis killed him."

"I am sorry," Jin said. Though her situation differed greatly from Tai's, she, of all people, knew what it was like to have never known a parent. She, at least, didn't have a family that killed one another. Without realizing it, she rubbed his arm in a gesture of comfort like Lu used to do when she was particularly low.

Tai looked down at her hand, and Jin realized, as he must have, the audacity of her touching a royal person uninvited. She pulled away. "I am sorry, Your Highness. That was presumptuous."

"I prefer it to being punched in the face," he said lightly.

A sharp cough made them step apart. Two figures stood at the entrance to the balcony. The minister of war's face was taut with disapproval. An elegant girl of about eighteen glided next to Minister Gao, her hair pinned in an ornate weave and her clothes marking her as one of the highest noble families. She gave Jin a false smile before following the minister of war right up to Prince Tai.

"Your Highness, have you met my daughter, Lady Gao? She is a fine dancer and can play all the latest Sogdian songs. She also shares some of your other interests. Your mother said I should introduce you two." He gave Jin a pointed look. "You are dismissed, Initiate Jin."

Jin bowed and stepped back, even as Prince Tai shot her a regretful look. She steeled herself, then turned to rejoin the crowd in the main hall. No doubt the war minister disapproved of her even more now. She'd have to watch her step.

"There you are!" Meipin's hand landed on Jin's arm as she pulled Jin around. "Come, my uncle is free and wants to talk to you. This is our chance." Meipin sighed at her expression. "I know you don't care about changing the rules, but I'm not asking you to argue that. Just be yourself. Show my uncle you're a credit to Dragon Class, that you're not trying to wreak havoc on all under heaven. Please."

Jin followed Meipin through the crowds of nobles and up a staircase to a raised dais where a horseshoe of banquet tables had been set out. On an even higher dais was the imperial table, where the empress sat at the center of a similar horseshoe arrangement. Nobles and court officials were dining, drinking, and laughing as they lounged on cushions by the tables. Many were toasting the huren dancers twirling and spinning on the dance floor, their breasts visible through their sheer silk gowns.

Minister Wei sat with a group of other ministers she didn't recognize. As Meipin presented her, Jin bowed low.

"Ah! Dragonrider Wang Kway Jin," Minister Wei said, standing and putting one hand over his other fist in greeting. "Meipin speaks of you often."

Jin darted a look at Meipin, who smiled widely. "It is natural to speak of one's roommate. Jin has been keeping me company since Aunt left."

Her uncle nodded. "And how are you finding Dragon Class? It must be hard being a woman on an all-male team."

Jin bowed again, unsure what to say.

"Meipin and some others seem to think that Dragon Class should allow women. What do you think?"

"I am but a lowly rider," Jin replied, "and know nothing of laws. I leave that for those more educated than I."

She sensed a deep approval from the minister, but wasn't sure whether that helped or hindered Meipin's cause.

"So you do not wish to change Dragon Class law?"

"No, Minister Wei. I am now a law follower now, not a lawbreaker."

He nodded, satisfied. "That is good to hear. Meipin could do with some of your thinking. Thank you, Jin."

Jin was about to take leave, when she saw Gao approaching with his daughter. The minister came to Wei's table and cast Jin a blistering look while Lady Gao gave her a smile so condescending it made Jin's fist ache with restraint.

Jin turned back to Meipin's uncle. "If you would indulge me, Minister Wei. When I was a thief, my master had a saying: 'What does it matter if the thief be Han or huren, as long as they can cut a purse?'"

"Initiate Jin," the war minister said in an oily voice, "you are saying Dragon Class is thieving?"

"Never, Minister Gao," Jin replied. "But my master always said he became head of the richest clan around because he took apprentices for their merit, and not their skin color."

"Your master sounds like an interesting man," Gao said. Something in his tone made Jin feel as if a snake had slithered over her. Gao turned back to Wei. "Certainly a female in Dragon Class has created no end of talk and speculation. But I urge you to not act too hastily. After all, am I right that Rayshan's power has not manifested?"

"Not yet," Jin admitted, tensing.

Gao nodded sympathetically. "We do not know for certain whether bonding with a woman diminishes the dragon. It would be premature to open Dragon Class to women."

"A good point, though perhaps we should let other ministers have a say," Wei replied. "My niece suggests I formally propose a vote."

Gao's eyes narrowed as he looked from Meipin to Jin.

"It seems the womenfolk have been busy behind closed doors. And once they enter Dragon Class, the sky's the limit, is it not?" Gao glanced at Jin coldly. "Peace upon your evening, Minister Wei."

And as he left with his daughter, Jin knew she had moved even higher, if that were possible, on his blacklist.

Jin wove through the crowd, heading for an open banquet table that was piled high with carved melons, iced pears, lychees, candied apples, and plums. But Jin only had eyes for the oranges.

She was sliding a third orange into her sash when a voice interrupted her.

"That's a clever use for a waistband."

She whirled to see Aadan behind her.

"It's for Rayshan," she said.

"I guessed." He took in her dress, her hair, and her shoes, suddenly making her self-conscious. "Dance?"

This was the last thing she had expected him to say. She hadn't been to a ball for such a long time, and despite the encounter with Gao, Meipin was right: this was the event of the year, and she might as well enjoy it. "Why not?"

Jin remembered what was in her sash. She pulled them out and replaced them on the table, then took Aadan's hand. The music slowed to a deep, leisurely tune, and they moved in time.

"Your dancing is excellent," he said.

"Yours isn't," she replied truthfully. She mentally berated herself. Why had she said that? His nearness was clouding her thinking. "I'm sorry, that was rude."

"I don't dance often," Aadan admitted, smiling. "Where did you learn?"

In a song house. "I took lessons."

"You dance well and fight like a beast," he said. "I have a new respect for thieves."

"I have a new respect for princes," she replied. "I thought all they did was sit about and look regal all day."

Aadan frowned. "Prince Tai is very talented in many things."

Jin shook her head. "I meant you, not Tai."

He looked surprised, pleased even. Just then the music stopped, and they did as well, bowing to each other.

Aadan motioned toward the fruit table. "Did you still want those oranges?"

She shot him a questioning look. "Will you report me?"

He grinned. "Frankly, I doubt the imperial larder will miss a few fruits."

She gathered six oranges and slid them into her

sash, and was surprised to see Aadan pick up several as well.

"I'll go with you. Wanli will be jealous if Rayshan gets a taste and he doesn't."

They left the party then, walking out the courtyard gates and into the cool quiet of the imperial city. A part of her was loath to leave the music and excitement, but at the same time, it was a relief to escape all the sharp looks and sharper tongues.

"You didn't wish to stay longer?"

"I think I was making more enemies there than on the Blood Oval."

"You didn't look like you were making enemies," he retorted, tossing an orange and catching it. "Sorry. Perhaps I'm overstepping, but you should be careful with Tai."

"Why? Besides the fact that his mother is empress?"

"Prince Tai is a model crown prince."

"Meaning?"

Aadan hesitated, clearly choosing his words carefully. "Meaning he cares about the dragon throne above anything—or anyone—else."

She sensed his meaning and flushed. Did he think she was foolish enough to imagine Tai had any feelings for her? Or equally ridiculous, that she had feelings for Tai? She heard a thrum of inquiry from him as Rayshan sensed her confusion.

It's nothing, Jin reassured him. *I have a surprise for you.* She turned back to Aadan, following him as he turned down an avenue toward Dragon City. "Thanks for the warning."

They arrived at Dragon City and showed their passes to the guards before crossing the yard and climbing to the caves. They sat in companionable silence outside Rayshan and Wanli's caves, watching the dragons devour the oranges in ecstatic bites.

Can you get more? Rayshan asked, licking the last wedge of orange peel from his teeth.

She batted him. *Next you'll ask me to plant you a grove of them.*

As she gathered her things, she noticed Aadan waiting in the cave mouth.

"I'll walk back to the palace with you."

Ah, a perfect end to the evening, Rayshan hummed.

She batted Rayshan across the muzzle. She stepped out and started down the path with Aadan, trying not to let Rayshan's teasing unsettle her.

"What banner would you like to join when you become a dragonrider?"

His question made her realize she hadn't given it much thought. "Let's see if I pass the trials first."

"You will."

She wondered at his confidence in her, when she scarcely saw beyond surviving the next day. "Do we get a choice?"

"No. But everyone has their preference. What's yours?"

She thought on it. "Messenger. I'd get to see

different lands, spend most of my time flying." The thought of having only the responsibility of carrying messages while spending vast amounts of time alone with Rayshan appealed to her. "How about you?"

"Don't laugh. But Wanli and I hope to join the Banner of Agriculture."

She looked at him, surprised. "Why would I laugh?"

"Everyone thinks the warrior banner best. Especially for a prince who has lost his kingdom."

"Well, you do need an army to regain a kingdom, don't you?"

"I do," he said, thoughtful. "But grain is the backbone of any army, any civilization." His voice grew animated as he launched into a topic he had clearly thought through. "Control the food and water supply, and you control the land. You can lay siege to your enemy without lifting a sword."

She thought about this. "That's . . . brilliant."

It was his turn to look surprised. But she meant it. Haitao had, for all his ruthlessness, discouraged violence during their jobs, as that usually forced the police to take greater action. "The best theft is where there is no theft. The target hands you their purse of their own accord."

He studied her. "Did that happen often?"

They stopped, for they had reached the great eastern gate that led back into the imperial city. Meipin's quarters lay within to the west, while the barracks and Aadan's dorms were to the far east of the city.

"Never for me," she said. "I don't have the charm for it."

"That's not true. You can be charming when you wish, in your own manner."

"Was that a compliment?" His praise both warmed her and embarrassed her.

"You sound surprised."

"I don't hear compliments often."

"Spend more time with me and you will," he said quietly.

At this, the distance seemed to shrink between them, and she noticed his scent, a pleasant mix of sandalwood and orange that felt familiar yet exotic. And then he was leaning forward, his eyes on hers, and she held a breath as he neared.

When his lips touched hers, the night seemed to melt and rearrange itself around them, like an embrace. She put a hand on his shoulder to bring him closer, but just then a bell pealed nearby, marking the curfew hour.

Aadan pulled away, smiling. "I'm pretty sure we just broke a Dragon Class rule."

She wasn't sure she wanted to follow that rule, but she nodded, her emotions in a happy turmoil. She thought back to her training in the song houses, how she had never understood the appeal between men and women, for all she ever saw of it was a monetary transaction. Any pleasure seemed feigned. But this was different. The kiss was like a new, intoxicating tide.

"I'll see you tomorrow at the Oval," he said, brushing her fingers with his before striding away.

"Aadan?" she called after him. He turned. "You're not such a bad dancer."

He grinned. "And you're a good liar."

It was her turn to grin. She thought again of Meipin's words: that the world was a melancholy place without trust and friendships. Jin was beginning to understand what she meant.

The gong for the hour sounded, and she hastened her steps, her feet still light from Aadan's kiss.

She was nearing the outer wall of Meipin's quarters, finding her way by the lanterns that hung from stone pillars at regular intervals. She tinkered with the idea of suggesting a flight to the mountains with Wanli and Aadan the next day, when she heard hushed voices.

Jin hesitated at the corner of the lane, listening. She heard a man speak, and frowned when she recognized Tai's voice. She instinctively pressed herself into the shadows against the wall, where the pools of lantern light didn't reach.

". . . misunderstand."

"I have eyes, my son. And so do other people."

Jin tensed. Was that the empress? The voice was too soft to tell.

"I assure you, you are seeing things that are not

there. Everything I do, I do for the benefit of the throne."

"Then use other people. Do not come to her quarters yourself late at night after you've behaved abysmally toward the noblewomen at court."

"I danced with everyone we agreed on," Tai protested. "How is that behaving abysmally?"

"We can debate that later," the empress said. Jin now knew without a doubt it was the empress. She heard footsteps and realized they were walking her way. She needed to disappear, for shadowed or not, when they came around this corner, she would be visible. She looked around in panic. The only option was the pillar next to her, its curved arm an elaborate dragon holding a lantern in its jaws.

She took a running leap and grabbed hold of the dragon's lower tail. Her dance slippers made climbing difficult, so she compensated with her arms, pulling herself up and onto the curved top of the dragon.

Just as she managed to find a secure position, Tai and the empress came around the corner. They still seemed to be in hot debate, despite the hushed tones.

". . . rumors about you being infatuated with this girl."

"You, of all people, know better than to listen to rumors."

"Don't change the subject. When you neglect your duties at the feast, and then I see you disappearing from the hall and I find you here, what am I to think?"

"My befriending her will make sure we don't have another Mengkhis Lai on our hands," Tai said.

Jin stiffened. So that's why the prince had gifted her the saddle and agreed to dance with her. And why he had avoided her request to access the restricted library.

"I think you are a little too involved," the empress said. "I can ask Meipin to report back to us."

Tai scoffed. "Meipin covets the title of empress. She'd likely find something to report just to win your favor. But if it comforts you to know, I arranged for Prince Aadan to be our inside man. He's reliable and has been keeping me informed."

Jin's knuckles whitened on the lantern arm, and she felt the air go out of her, as if she'd been struck.

The empress made a noise of approval. "A good choice. Of course, he simply wants an army from you, my son. But that does keep him loyal."

Her heart clenched. The reading lessons, the walk to Rayshan's cave, the offers to fly with her—all had been at the prince's behest. Aadan didn't care about her; he simply wanted an army so he could achieve his dream of retaking Persia.

The two figures were nearly at the end of the lane, and she lost the next few words, but she managed to catch the end.

"I'm glad to hear it, my son. Rumors of your interest in a lowborn thief will only hurt the throne. Not to mention the dangers if those rumors were actually true."

There was an expectant pause before Tai replied.

"Of course not. I have no interest in the girl beyond her being one of the empire's more valuable assets. Throne above all."

Jin stayed motionless on the lantern pole until Tai and his mother had disappeared and even their footfalls had gone. Then she silently lowered herself to the ground, her limbs shaking less from the physical exertion and more from the anger and hurt gripping her. Her lips where Aadan had kissed her now burned with shame. She made her silent way back to Mei's quarters and into her own rooms.

Jin dismissed the maid who had been waiting up for her, then sat before the mirror and scrubbed away the makeup on her face until her cheeks and lips grew red.

She thought over the evening, Tai's words tainting everything. She would have laughed at herself if she had the strength. The two princes had, like the expert nobles they were, been playing her like Lady Yang's song girls played their clients. Tai and Aadan had only been trying to pry into her mind, spy on her every move because they feared she would become the monster Mengkhis Lai had been. She would have expected such tactics from the war minister, and even the crown prince. But that Aadan, too, had done it cut Jin more than she expected.

She looked at herself in the mirror, taking in the unadorned features of Jin the thief. A sudden rage made her ball up the multi-colored cloth in her hand that held the smudged face of Lady Jin. She angrily threw it, knocking the mirror to the floor. The sharp crack of shattering glass was strangely satisfying, and when Rayshan reached out to her with a worried hum, she reassured him back to an uneasy slumber. There was no point troubling him with her emotions.

Haitao had been right. He had always been right. She had been a fool to trust anyone, much less the nobility. They were here to keep people like her down, and if she wanted to survive, she had to trust no one. No one but Rayshan.

$\mathcal{J}$in was almost too happy to throw herself into her training over the next week, as physical exertion, riding with Rayshan, and studying for her written tests were all preferable to thinking about Tai, the birth record, or, worst of all, Aadan.

Jin silently balled her resentment and hurt within her, telling no one but Rayshan, who had taken her flying and offered silence rather than words. Meipin, on the other hand, seemed to be happy as a cat on a warm kang. She told Jin the day after the ball that Minister Wei had decided to put forward a vote to the Ministry of Laws, on whether women should be allowed in Dragon Class. As a gesture of thanks, Meipin presented her with an exquisite ink painting of Gaozho, Jin's home city, complete with a depiction of the Green Cloud Pagoda, but the sight of it only made

Jin's heart ache. For all its faults, she missed parts of her former life and its familiar, if harsh, rules.

Jin had told herself she would try to remain civil with Aadan, but this conviction melted away the first time she saw him after overhearing Tai's conversation. When Aadan approached her after morning exercises for their usual reading lesson, his broad grin faded at her expression.

"Is something wrong?"

She glowered, raging against the tears she had to blink back. "I think I've had enough of your help." At his confusion, she said, "I know you report everything I do to Tai."

He flinched but didn't contradict her, which burned the last scrap of hope she'd been nurturing that Tai had lied. "Jin, it's not that simple, I—"

She rounded on him, fierce. "Yes it is that simple. You want to raise an army for your kingdom, so you need Tai's favor. And you played me from the beginning."

He flushed. "That is not true. Believe me when I say—"

"That's the problem," she said coldly. "I can't believe you, can I?"

"You're right about Tai," he said, voice strained, "but that doesn't mean that everything—that last night— wasn't real."

She shook her head. "You said I was a good liar, but you're clearly the best here."

Jin left before he could say anything else, and ignored him from then on, until he at last stopped attempting to speak to her and gave a convincing show of depression instead.

A fortnight after the ball, a frowning Emar halted training and gathered them around the Blood Oval. From his expression, Jin knew he was about to relate unwelcome news.

"We have been ordered to bring the geography test forward, to three days from now."

There were gasps and protests at this, but Emar raised a hand, and silence dropped immediately. "Trust me, I have argued and done all I can to stop this, but it's orders from the ministry. We are conducting the test at the half-moon and not at the full. So we will make sure all saddles are readied and supplies are checked, and all of you must be fit to fly early. Your written test will be tomorrow."

Orders from the ministry. So the minister of war must have sanctioned it, perhaps even suggested it. This was odd. Jin wondered why the man would break tradition when he was such a stickler for it. She noticed Aadan looking at her, concerned, but she deliberately ignored him.

Emar continued, "I don't know the why, so I can't give it to you. But orders are orders. Now go prepare. Training is over until after the geography test."

Still in shock like the rest of her classmates, she

replaced her weapons and tried to shake her foreboding.

We are to do the geography test in three days, she told Rayshan.

The dragon growled, flicking his tail, but only said, *We will be ready.*

She asked him for a ride, just to clear her mind. He stretched and lay down for her to saddle him, and she ran her hands down the fine embroidery, the gift reminding her of Tai and his words to his mother. She almost wanted to throw the thing out now, but she was a rider and she needed a saddle.

They lifted off into the late afternoon sky, the cold air welcome against Jin's face after all the sweat of the day. She folded herself against Rayshan's neck and looked at the sea of roof tiles and winding laneways beneath them as they rose to the point where she could smell the clouds and sense rain on her skin.

They flew, dusk deepening around them. Here, the stars were almost painfully vivid. She gazed skyward into the frozen swirl of the River of Milk, where legend said that doves formed a bridge once a year so the cowherd and his love could be together. Up here, everything was simple, pure. She didn't want to go back to where everything seemed convoluted and shrouded in intrigue, where love like the cowherd's was a story told to naïve children.

Only when the moon had climbed to a great height

and her fingers were numb did she tell Rayshan they should head back. He obediently swept around, pivoting in a perfect circle and dropping down so they skimmed above the city. During the day they could not fly so low, as the streets were full of people and the likelihood of accidents increased. But at night the streets were mostly deserted, and Jin felt a thrill as they passed within sight of windows and balconies, where the occasional child or family craned their necks and pointed at her.

By the time she had hung her saddle and brushed Rayshan down, the curfew bell had rung. She made her way back to her and Meipin's quarters, ready for a deep sleep in her large four-poster bed and fresh sheets to wipe away the day.

Jin was approaching the main gates of the mansion when she paused. She knew each and every one of the guards who patrolled this area, but even in the dim light she didn't recognize the build and walk of these two. And that was another thing. They weren't walking as they usually did, but instead seemed on the lookout for something. Or someone.

Just as her instincts kicked in and she began backing away the way she came, two hands grabbed her arms. She spun, about to fight, but then recognized the face. It was the man who had threatened her in her bath.

"The minister wants a word with you." He indicated the roofs of the adjoining buildings, where two archers stepped out of the shadows. "We don't want to use force."

What's happening? Rayshan's voice roared in her head. At first she thought he had heard her distress, but then she sensed the panic in him was firsthand, a panic arising from something happening there. *Jin! Jin!*

Rayshan!

They're putting a headpiece on me!

Before she could reply, the imposter guards had swept in to help her attackers, their swords at the ready. She was trapped.

She called out to Rayshan again, but only silence greeted her this time. This scared her more than the danger to herself, and she screamed within her mind until she had to admit that whatever had happened to Rayshan, the bond had been broken. There was nothing to do but go with the minister's men. Whatever came next would not be a battle of blades, but of wits.

CHAPTER 33

Instead of the minister's quarters, her captors took Jin to a section she had never visited. Here they pulled her roughly from the horse they had put her on, and fear gripped her anew. Rising before her were high stone walls, with towers flanking each side. Iron-studded gates painted gray led inside, with an individual smaller door. They led her through this opening when it slid open on iron bolts, and Jin tried not to let the sound of it clanging shut fan her fear.

They took her through a barren courtyard lit by torches, past a row of offices, and then into a room with straw on the floor, and an unadorned chair and table.

"Wait, when will—"

They closed the door before she had finished her sentence, leaving her in the dark. The lock scraped shut. She went to the door's tiny grille and tried to peer out, but saw nothing except more stone walls and a desolate courtyard beyond. She decided shouting might only bring a beating, and so she paced, exploring the cell by feel. However, she knew there was no point escaping, for where would she go? Especially as she still couldn't hear Rayshan when she called to him.

Jin bit her lip and tried to keep her frustration at bay. She had no idea what Gao's plan was, and the not knowing would unravel her if she let it.

It must have been an hour before she heard steady footfalls outside and the lock scraped again. Jin stood as Minister Gao entered with a lantern.

"Jin," he said, placing the lantern on the table, "I am very sorry we have to have this conversation here."

Jin stayed silent, gauging.

He looked around the room in distaste. "That building opposite holds the tea rooms. You've heard of the tea rooms, I am sure? Where prisoners are . . . well, we're beyond euphemisms now, aren't we?" He smiled. "Where prisoners are tortured. And the courtyard outside is the execution ground. You wouldn't think it, would you? Marquis Sanjin loves cleanliness and insists it's scrubbed of all blood after every beheading."

Jin swallowed. His talk of the tea rooms was meant to unnerve her, she knew. But it was working. "Why did you bring me here?"

"I felt like we have been failing to understand each other. So I thought a change of scene might help you listen to what I am trying to say." He paused. "How can I best explain this to you? A sheep cannot become a shepherd, which is why we have the rules we have. We cannot allow women and common folk into Dragon Class, and the sooner you understand that, the sooner you stop harming the empire." Gao regarded her. "I've kept trying to teach you this, but you are a very obstinate woman. And I've come across some very obstinate women in my time." She knew he was referring to the empress. He dusted off the chair and then sat on it. "Do you know this is where they keep murderers before execution?"

"Am I to be executed?"

"No. But you know someone else who will be executed here."

Jin stared at him.

"Oh, child," he said with exasperation. "Did you really think you could enter Dragon Class and we wouldn't look into your background?" His smile could have frozen fire. "All students are thoroughly checked. Usually it's an easy matter, as only nobles with meticulously documented lineage are allowed in. Your background, of course, was as murky as your bloodline, but I would be remiss if I didn't look into it. I had my people ask questions around the area where you stole Rayshan, and I heard about a mixed-race girl thief."

Everyone already knew she was a thief. This was not news. So what was Gao getting at? She thought of the birth record she had found. He couldn't believe that she'd agree to leave just because of her supposed origins?

"Thankfully, we found the Iron Hawks clan very willing to tell us everything they knew about this girl thief, this girl thief raised by the Red Crows."

No. No, no, no . . . she hoped her face didn't betray her horror.

Gao gave a regretful smile. "I am sorry your reunion has to be this way."

Jin heard metal hinges somewhere outside, and shouts, then a shuffling. She went to the grille as if she was going to her own execution, her stomach in such a knot that she had difficulty breathing.

In the courtyard outside, a prisoner was being dragged into the middle of the flagstones. Even in his bloodied and broken state, with his soiled hair and face swollen from broken bones, Jin would have recognized him.

"Master Haitao!" she breathed. The chief of the Red Crows. The brutal disciplinarian who had made her who she was. The one who had saved her life but also dealt her a harsh existence.

"He was a very tough man to crack," Gao said, not bothering to stand from his table. "Much tougher than all the other thieves in his little clan. One was called Mukang, I believe? We gave him a quick death due to his age."

Mukang was only a boy. The thought that they were dead and that they suffered in the tea rooms before they died nauseated her.

"All of them broke by the second day," Gao said. "But this one, we had to smash every bone in his hands —twice, actually—before he admitted to knowing you and telling us where he found you and how." He paused. "You took the birth record from my desk, didn't you?" At her look, he nodded. "It's no matter. Every record ever made has three copies stored in separate places. You'll not erase the truth so easily."

"That child could be anyone," she protested. "Not necessarily me."

"True," Gao admitted. "But when Haitao broke, he said he bought you from a prison guard, right here." He let this sink in before adding, "Why do you think I began searching the prison records?"

Her mind reeled as the implications hit her. "How long has he been here?" she whispered. No wonder Haitao hadn't answered her message. He and the whole Red Crow clan had been arrested and taken to Changan before her letter had arrived.

"Long enough for me to know everything about him," Gao replied. "And you."

The questions pressed on her until she felt like she simply wanted to curl into a ball and seal off the world. But she couldn't take her eyes off what was happening in the courtyard, couldn't shut out the infuriating help-lessness in her.

The figure being forced to kneel out in the court-yard was no longer the man Haitao. He was a flesh-

and-blood embodiment of pain, but she found herself pleading for his scrap of life anyway.

"Please. Spare him."

Gao spread his hands. "I'm afraid I can't."

She screamed as the sword rose, and Haitao looked over, recognition flickering in the eyes that had nearly disappeared in his swollen face. Their gazes locked, and then the sword was coming down, and Haitao's eyes widened. His head fell to the paving stones, and his body followed, like a sack of rice. Jin shut her eyes against the sight of Haitao's dirtied face lying on the ground. She leaned her head against the door and bit her knuckles.

"I see that distressed you," Gao said, "but I had to show you I have teeth, since you always seem to doubt that I'll bite. You didn't give up after I had Madu slash your saddle. You didn't take the bribe I so generously offered. So I informed the king of Khitan that you had stolen his Jade, but instead of executing you as she should have, the empress simply gave away another dragon."

She wasn't sure what was spinning more—her head or her stomach.

Gao leaned in close. "Now I hope you are paying attention. Are you? Good. Because you couldn't save Haitao, but—are you listening? Do listen, because this is very important." He paused. "You do have the chance to save another."

Jin looked at him, trying to grasp his meaning. The

sound of another door opening across the courtyard drew Jin's attention, and this time the man coming out was instantly recognizable.

"Lu!" Jin shouted.

His hands were bound behind his back, a gag was in his mouth, and chains hobbled his ankles, but otherwise he looked unharmed.

"I left him untouched especially for today," Gao said.

Lu looked in her direction, and when he caught sight of her, his eyes watered.

"He's a fine man, Lu," Gao said, "intelligent and capable. I don't want to kill him, but I will if I have to."

"Why don't you just kill me?" Jin said, trying and failing to keep the desperation from her voice. "Let Lu go. Leave everyone else out of this!"

The minister smiled. "It's not that simple. It's illegal to kill a dragon or a rider. Your death comes with consequences and questions that insignificant thieves like Haitao or Lu don't. And when possible, I prefer peaceful methods, remember?"

"Then what do you want?"

"Do the geography test, as everyone expects you to. But don't come back." He paused. "Don't come back, and Lu lives."

She looked out at Lu. "How do I know you'll keep your word?"

Gao sighed. "You don't. But you're also out of

choices, as you repeatedly ignored my other offers, I might add. So what's it to be?"

Jin looked outside. The guards had forced Lu to kneel and held the blade ready. He looked over at her and blinked rapidly: twice, then twice more. Her heart cracked. It was their code for "leave me."

"I agree to your terms," Jin said. "Spare him, and I'll do what you ask."

Gao nodded and gestured out the window grille. The guards pulled Lu to his feet and pushed him back to the door where he'd come from. Jin watched him as he tried to look back at her, watched until he had disappeared, before she turned to face Gao. She had never hated another person so much, never thought that the eight levels of hell were eight hundred too few.

"I'm glad we've come to an agreement," Gao said. "I'll keep him for another two weeks, just to make sure you don't go back on your promise or tell anyone of our arrangement today."

"You give your word you'll free Lu?"

"Of course."

"I want to speak to him."

"I think not," Gao said. "I can't chance you two plotting some wild escape."

Jin pushed down the urge to punch him. "Then tell him to meet me at the rat seller's after you free him," she said. "He'll know what I mean." They had always called a popular tavern in Gaozho the "rat seller" ever since they caught the cook trapping and dicing rats to serve customers.

Gao raised an eyebrow. "I'll be sure to."

"And if he's not there by the full moon after the test," she said, keeping her voice even, "I will return with Rayshan and make you regret lying to me."

Gao looked amused. "Are you threatening me?"

"Absolutely."

"Very well. If he isn't at your meeting spot at the right time, it won't be because of me." He picked up the lantern and signaled the guard outside. "I'm delighted we had this talk and could understand each other. Good day, Rider Jin. May you, Lu, and Rayshan enjoy a long and anonymous future. Far from the capital."

CHAPTER 34

After Gao released her, Jin went straight to Dragon City.

All along the way she called out to Rayshan but heard only silence. She swore she would tear Gao limb from limb if Rayshan was harmed. She reached Dragon City by dawn, breath ragged in her throat, but despite the burn in her body, she took the snaking path up the cliff face at a sprint.

She nearly cried when she saw Rayshan, shackled in his cave so that he could barely move from a crouch. A hammered lead covering left only his snout free to breathe. His eyes and ears had been covered, and Jin's heart ached to know that he had spent the last hours blind and unable to communicate with her, chafing his neck raw on the chains holding him in place.

When she pulled out the metal pins under his chin securing his headpiece, she threw them to the ground and wrapped her arms around Rayshan's head. His eyes flew open, then winced at the dawn light.

Where were you? What happened?

The thoughts spilled from her in a messy outpouring, and it took a while for her to explain everything to him. When she had finished, he roared, making the caves reverberate, but Jin pressed a hand on him and urged him to calm.

We're still together. But I have to save Lu, she said.

It's not fair. Rayshan's mood was white hot.

No, it's not, but it's never been fair. I was wrong to think I could change my fate, be anything other than a thief in the streets.

She cried then. Her tears ran in a salty, bitter flood for the Red Crows, even for Haitao. She sobbed for Rayshan and the unfairness of the few choices open to them. But if she kept her promise and Gao kept his, she and Lu would keep their lives. And Rayshan.

* * *

WHEN SHE ENTERED the apartment courtyards, she was surprised to see Meipin already dressed and feeding the koi in the ponds.

"Peace upon your . . . !" Meipin's smile faded into shock. "What happened? You look like the polo field after a long game."

"I didn't sleep well," Jin muttered. "Nerves about the trial."

"I'd say you didn't sleep at all," Meipin replied with a critical eye, looking her over. She started toward their rooms. "I was about to go to the temple to offer prayers for tomorrow, but I think you need food and a bath first. I'll arrange something."

Jin was too tired to argue and sat down at the foyer dining table while the maids brought steamers with pork buns and bowls of congee speckled with dried fish. Jin held her chopsticks but simply stared at the food, unable to stomach the thought of eating.

"Something happened," Meipin said. "Maybe I can help."

"No," Jin said curtly. The girl's silks and fans, makeup and lifestyle, all seemed unbearably obscene after her encounter with Gao and the blood spilled in the courtyard. Only saving Lu mattered. She forced everything from her mind but that one goal. Leave and save Lu.

Jin stood abruptly. "Thank you for breakfast, but I am not feeling well. I'm going to rest for tomorrow's trial." She had clearly stung Meipin with the rejection, but Jin didn't have the energy for better tact.

"I know you will do spectacularly in the trial tomorrow," Meipin said gently. "And when the ministers see you as an example of a girl dragonrider, it'll change Dragon Class and the futures of so many girls. Don't worry."

The words were like a branding iron on flesh, and she rounded on Meipin, vicious. "Stop. Please stop. If you want to dream of walking where no woman has, then do so, but do not use me to do it, or expect me to be your tool of change."

Meipin's face slackened in shock, before she gathered herself and drew on her best court smile. "Very well. I shall pray to Buddha for your safe return, regardless."

Jin bowed her head, stiff, and left the room. Something Lu had once said echoed wickedly in her mind: *Since when has Buddha ever smiled upon thieves?*

* * *

THE DAY of the test dawned clear, the air crisp with the promise of snow and the frost sparkling cheerfully in contrast to the dark in Jin's heart.

Jin rose early, dressed herself carefully, and double-checked all the supplies in the single pack initiates were allowed, for she was going on a much longer journey than the others.

Jin took in deep breaths of the morning air as she wove through the palace toward the Blood Oval, looking around her one last time at surroundings she would never see again. But this was her one chance to save Lu, and she wasn't going to risk losing that chance.

She arrived as the first assistants were preparing the day's ritual. The mages were circling a path around the Oval, sprinkling holy water on the grounds and chanting mantras to bless the riders. A silk pavilion for officials and recordkeepers stood along one side, with tables and chairs. A few riders were checking their weapons and readying their saddles. Jin spied pallets being laid out in a circle in the middle, with large canvases put in place to lift the dragons as well. Emar had briefed them: each dragon had to be drugged and carried to an unknown location, which would mean a team of four dragons would accompany each apprentice dragon, flying them in shifts of two.

"Are you alright?"

She turned to see Aadan standing next to her. She stiffened. "I am well enough."

He looked unconvinced. "I know you're still angry, but forget that for now. You don't look yourself. Are you sure you—?"

Her throat tightened. "I don't need your minding or your help."

He nodded, looking hurt. "Good luck then."

She watched him walk to his assigned spot, firmly snuffing out the flicker of regret that this was the last image she would ever have of him.

A bugle sounded, and the initiates lined up before Emar, who wore new robes and all his official Dragon Class seals, the ivory and gold striking against his dark robes. The viewing pavilion had filled with clerks, Dragon Class administrators, and various nobles, Tai and Gao amongst them.

"Initiates!" Emar called out. "Hail your prince and

commander, first in Dragon Class, His Highness Wu Tai Shen!"

Everyone bowed low as Prince Tai approached. He wore a robe with the silver-and-scarlet colors of Dragon Class, with an official black headscarf wrapping his usually uncovered hair.

He moved down the line of initiates, starting with Madu. A purple-robed mage moved with him, holding a bowl of holy water, and with each initiate Tai murmured words of encouragement before dipping his fingers in the bowl and sprinkling the initiate's bowed head in blessing.

Jin was last in line, heart and mind numb. It took her a moment to realize that Tai had reached her, and she bowed her head, wooden.

"May Buddha bless you with his ability to endure the hardships of the body and the wants of the mind," the prince murmured as drops of water landed on her hair.

When she stood, she found the prince had not moved, but was instead standing before her.

"Are you alright, Initiate Jin?"

"Yes, Your Highness." At his dubious expression, she added, "Simply nervous about the trials."

He hesitated, then stepped forward, as if to adjust something on her collar. As he leaned in, he spoke low so the others couldn't hear.

"Promise you'll come back."

Her heart dropped. Did he know about the minister's threats? Gao said no one was to know. "No one can promise that, Your Highness."

"Nevertheless, make sure you return." He held her gaze. "The empire needs you back."

Her disappearance with a Jade would worry him and his mother, make them think she'd gone rogue, or worse. But Lu's life was at stake, and at this point crossing over into a foreign kingdom sounded truly appealing.

Another bugle sounded, breaking any opportunity for speaking. Retainers led the dragons into the Oval. Jin spied Rayshan and tried to draw on the usual comfort of knowing that at least he and she would be together. But even that comfort seemed hollow. She was dooming him as well with her actions.

I'd rather exile with you than glory here as a forcibly bonded slave, he reminded her.

Each student took their place next to their dragons. Emar came forward once more to take Prince Tai's place.

"Students! Welcome to your second and final test. Today, you will be dropped off in a remote location with your dragon. From there, you both must make your way back to the capital, unaided. You'll have your supplies of food and water, but you are allowed no compasses, no maps, no money or valuables. You will rely on your and your dragon's ability to chart the stars, the sun, and other directions, as well as your knowledge of the empire's geography."

He paused, scanning them. "The assistants will be offering milk of the poppy and to search your packs to make sure no one's cheating by taking compasses or other forbidden tools. Take the poppy, and when you wake, we simply expect you to make it back alive. We look forward to welcoming you back and inducting you into the Dragon Class. Good luck."

Jin stepped forward and took her stand next to her pallet. She noticed a figure standing amongst the spectators, and her blood ran hot.

Minister Gao.

He nodded to her, a broad smile on his face.

It's not too late to change your mind. Tell everyone what Gao is doing, that he is making you fail this test.

She wished she could share Rayshan's view. *No, he'll kill Lu. And who would believe me anyway?*

Prince Tai would. So would Aadan, despite their initial suspicions.

She shook her head. *I am done with trusting or relying on others. I must leave. If there was a way to unbond you without harming you, I would.*

I would never choose that, Rayshan growled, *even if the process left me intact.*

The assistants in their white robes approached with trays, each bearing a cup of water, a plate of pills, and a sticky resin-like substance. They put these down and then began systematically searching each student's prepared supply pack, making sure there were no compasses or valuables they could trade for assistance.

The assistant assigned to Jin finished searching her pack, satisfied. He held out a hand to Rayshan to show him he meant him no harm, then bent and took up the ball of resin. He pushed five of the small pills into it and held it out on his flat palm.

Rayshan sniffed at it, then looked to Jin, eyes questioning her once last time. There was no point delaying the inevitable. She nodded, and Rayshan pulled it into his mouth with his long tongue. The thing was the size of a fist, and Rayshan swallowed it almost without trying. Jin cradled his head as his inner eyelid blinked rapidly, then slowed. Her heart lurched as his head grew heavier and heavier in her hands, until he had gone limp and was lying, tongue lolling, on the stretch of canvas staked under him.

"Do not worry, your dragon is fine," the man in white said, his kind face split in a smile. He motioned to her own pallet. "Now it is your turn. Are you ready?"

Her heart thudded. She looked around. Aadan had just put Wanli's claw onto the canvas and patted him reassuringly. She saw Jao and Panshalar each lying down on their pallets, ready to take the medicine.

She sat down on her own pallet. It would, like Rayshan's, fold up, and then she'd be transported to who knew where. And from there, she and Rayshan would disappear.

The man in white prepared a smaller lump of resin, pushing only one pill into it this time. She watched him knead it until it was a smooth ball, before he offered it to her. She looked over one last time at Gao, who was watching her intently from the pavilion. He turned and motioned to someone behind him, and a figure in servant's clothes stepped forward. Jin immediately recognized Lu. By the way he stood and moved, Jin knew he was under guard and could be seized and taken away at a moment's notice. No one would fault Minister Gao for disciplining an unruly servant trying to run away.

Throat tight, she took the sticky globe and put it in her mouth, then accepted the cup of water the man offered her. She nearly choked as the large ball of poppy resin struggled down. Gao looked triumphant.

The man smiled. "Now lie back."

He helped ease her down, and as darkness creeped in at the edges of her vision, he leaned in close to tuck her hair behind her ear.

"Minister Gao wishes you a good sleep."

She tried to grip his arm and sit up, but nothing happened. Her limbs wouldn't obey, and fear snaked through her. As blackness closed in, she thought she saw Lu's face, shouting something she couldn't hear.

CHAPTER 35

old. She felt nothing but a cold that made her teeth ache and her mind numb.

Jin!

Rayshan . . .

Wake up! You must wake up! His voice sounded faint in her head, as if it was coming through layers of blankets.

Sleep . . . I just want to sleep a while longer . . .

No! You must wake up!

Something struck her, making her howl in pain. Her head spun, and then waves of nausea were rippling through her, beading her skin with sweat.

It hurts.

I'm about to make it worse.

She tried to scream at him to stop, but something punched her in the gut. Once, twice. Then warm fluid rushed up her throat, and she was retching.

Jin lay, not knowing whether she was in her own filth, and struggled to sit up. Though her limbs were still sluggish, at least they obeyed. The cold seeped from her, and suddenly she was warm. Much too warm. And thirsty. Her throat felt stuck together.

She forced her eyes open and through the blur made out blinding light. Grit scraped in her eyes, and she tried to rub it away, but her hands were too weak.

Rayshan, where are you?

The comforting bulk of his tail wrapped around her.

We are in the desert. And you were given a much too heavy dose of poppy resin.

Her eyes adjusted enough for her to just make out Rayshan's outline standing over her. Nothing but sand stretched into the distance.

Where's my pack? She needed water. Rayshan probably needed water.

At Rayshan's silence, she looked up at him, shading her eyes from the merciless sun.

Realization fell. *There is no pack, is there?*

Minister Gao wasn't going to risk their coming back. He had given her a paralyzing dose of poppy and then made sure they were stuck in a desert with no food or even water. Which meant . . . She tried to scream, but she didn't have the strength. If Gao had lied to her, then he had almost certainly lied about sparing Lu. She cursed herself for her naivete. Haitao would have whipped her if he'd found out she had been so foolish. And she would deserve it. She would take any punishment now, for having doomed Lu.

Rayshan's tail lashed across her arm, and she held up a defensive hand.

Mistakes will bring you down, but self-pity will keep you there.

What would you have me do? It's over, we'll die here, and Lu's probably already dead. I am sorry, Rayshan, I am so sorry . . .

You are a survivor, Jin. Remember? So survive.

How? We are lost with no food or water. I'm too weak to ride.

Rayshan brought his great head close to hers. His large amber eyes made the panic in her ebb just enough for her to focus. *You must. You can.*

I was born a thief, and I'll die a thief.

You are Jin, dragonrider of Dragon Class, winner of the Ice Beard Mountain test, and a Jade rider. You will never die a thief even if you breathe your last right here, right now.

She sank to the sands. *But in the end, none of that makes a difference . . .* She saw again the dungeon where Haitao had been beheaded, heard Gao's words.

It's over, Rayshan, she said bitterly. *Gao was right. Perhaps my being female has stifled your power. I cannot help you now . . . I cannot . . .*

Rayshan's anguished roar rang in her ears as she sank her face into the sand, shutting her eyes and willing her heart to stop, if only to escape the pain and guilt and despair for just a moment.

* * *

"You're not listening."

The empress's long nails, painted their usual gold, tapped his hand sharply. Tai looked over at his mother. "I am. The agenda has space for the grain tax to be discussed."

Empress Wu pursed her lips and finished pressing one of her dragon seals to a scroll of paper, transforming some order into an imperial decree. "That was five minutes ago." She pushed the scroll aside and looked out where Tai had been gazing. Through the floor-to-ceiling windows of the empress's office, one had a clear view of the highest turrets on the outer walls of the palace.

"It's not time to lose all hope, but you must consider that they are dead, my son," Empress Wu said. "Those in Dragon Class die all the time."

Usually a rider that didn't make it back had encountered someone along the way, been spotted somewhere, and therefore been identified and found. Occasionally a rider had died, but that was rare. This was the only time in Tai's memory that a rider and a dragon had been gone for over a week. Some had been found weeks later, injured or confused from dehydration, but Jin, he somehow knew, was too capable and tough for that.

There was also the possibility that she had simply fled. And though he'd be relieved that she was alive, her fleeing to another kingdom would be a political and military nightmare.

He remembered that day last week, when the initiates had been sent off for their geography trial. Something in Jin's expression had thrown him—her usual defiance had been dimmed, to the point where she looked ill. He had reluctantly accepted her explanation about nerves, but now he wondered. The toughest rider he had ever met had seemed spooked, defeated.

The thought that she might not return filled him with more disappointment than he expected.

He had taken up the habit of walking along the outer walls during the day, hoping to sight a returning rider. Madu had been first to return, which made Tai wonder about whether he'd bribed the Dragon Class administrators to pick an easy location near Changan for him. Tai would have to look into that. But for now his thoughts revolved around the returning riders. Every time one had appeared on the horizon and the guards beat the great drums on the watchtowers, his heart filled with hope. But all the other riders had returned within days of the send-off, save Aadan and Jin.

"You take particular interest in the tests this year," the empress said, taking another scroll from her desk and scanning it.

"It's natural for the head of Dragon Class to want the riders safely home."

"And is it Aadan or Jin you worry about most?"

He refused to take the bait. "Both. Aadan is a friend, and Jin rides a Jade."

His mother's face puckered as she pressed her imperial seal into the ink and then stamped the scroll before her. "Well, I for one am more concerned that Jin returns. If she doesn't, it will be a loss of face for me and the throne. Not to mention the loss of a Jade." Her brow furrowed. "Another ill omen our enemies will pin to my being a female ruler." She eyed him. "You had no hints she might be disloyal?"

Tai shook his head. "None. And Aadan said repeatedly she wasn't hiding anything. He has sound judgment when it comes to character."

His mother gave him a look he knew well. "Let's hope so. And please try to stop pacing the watchtowers so often. If the nobles think you're lovesick over some street rat, you'll be the laughingstock of Changan."

He was about to snap back that he didn't give two turds what the nobles thought, but held his tongue, for it wouldn't help his argument. "Taking my Dragon Class duties seriously and being concerned for the riders' welfare is hardly lovesick."

She gave him a sideways glance. "I didn't say it was true; I simply said what the nobles will think."

"If that's all for now, I need to see to arrangements for the Dragon Class swearing-in ceremony."

His mother's lips tightened, but she nodded and turned back to her pile of unstamped scrolls.

Tai bowed before striding out of the audience

chamber and toward the Hall of Rites. There, the Head of Imperial Ceremonies, a short balding man with a face as round as a moon cake, hurried to greet the prince and lay out various plans for the swearing in of new dragonriders, with a rundown of who should give speeches and when. Tai buried himself in the myriad details, trying to stay busy enough so that his mind wouldn't keep circling to Aadan and Jin and his eyes wouldn't keep going to the windows.

He was about to take leave when a horn sounded from one of the outer towers. He managed to make a polite exit from the head's office. As soon as he stepped out, he mounted his bay horse and galloped toward the training grounds, where he knew returning riders had landed.

He kept his eyes on the sky as he rode, trying to see whether the returning dragon was silver or green. If it was Jin, he could stop worrying about the implications for his mother—and Jin's safety. If it was Aadan, then the chances of Jin being dead or a traitor increased.

Crowds of congratulatory dragonriders were already gathered in the Oval when he arrived, including Emar. Through the throngs he saw Wanli's silver spiked head arced high, jaws open and panting from exhaustion.

Relief that Aadan was safe flooded Tai. But a hard knot formed at the thought that Jin was still missing.

The crowd parted for the prince, and he strode to

Aadan, all broad smiles. "Welcome back, Dragonrider," Tai said, clapping him on the shoulder.

Aadan grinned through his dust-caked face. Despite his good spirits, he had circles under his eyes and his voice came out hoarse. "It's good to see you, Your Highness." Tai caught his friend's quick scan of the crowd, the frown.

"Master Emar!" Tai called out. The man turned from his conversation with the grooms removing Wanli's saddle. "May I borrow this rider?"

Emar gave him a curious look but nodded.

"The grooms will see to Wanli," Tai said to Aadan. "Come." He drew Aadan to the side as he motioned at one of the servants to bring water.

The servant hurried back with a goblet for Aadan, and the rider took all of its contents in one go. He looked about the Oval. "Am I the last one back?"

Tai shook his head. "There is one more."

At his tone, Aadan shot him a look. "Jin?"

"Yes." Tai paused. "Where were you dropped?"

"Outside Kashgar," Aadan replied.

Tai nodded. "About as far as the geography rules allow. Jin should be back soon if you're here."

"If she's not, things get complicated," Aadan said.

That's putting it simply, Tai thought. "Did Jin seem a little strange to you that day of the geography test?"

Aadan glanced down. Tai knew this meant he was debating something.

"Tell me. Is there something you know?"

Aadan drew a breath. "She found out that you had me keeping an eye on her."

Curse it. "So she was angry?"

"Very. I'd say she felt betrayed."

Just what they needed. Guilt stabbed him, but the prince in him realized that a Jade rider feeling betrayed was a dangerous thing, possibly ruinous, as history had proven. "Do you think it's possible she has fled the empire?"

Aadan again looked down, face unreadable. "I wouldn't rule it out."

"Just tell me what you know, Aadan!"

The dragonrider took a breath. "She had been very interested in Mengkhis Lai beforehand. She wanted to access the restricted library."

"She asked me about that. Anything else she wanted to know?"

"How the dragon Baikalan discovered his powers." Aadan paused, hesitant. "She read books on blood bonding and learned Mengkhis Lai was immortal and buried in the South."

Tai digested this. No doubt a very heated discussion with his mother would follow. If Jin had decided to go to another kingdom, and there were many who would welcome a dragonrider and her dragon with open arms, then they had a thorny military and diplomatic problem on their hands. And if she had decided she wished to be immortal like Mengkhis and seek him out

. . .

"Why didn't you tell me this before?" Tai's tone was sharper than he'd ever been with Aadan, but part of him felt his friend deserved it.

"I . . . was worried she'd be taken to the tea rooms," Aadan replied. "I thought . . . I thought you or the empress might take extreme measures."

Tai caught the brief flash of protectiveness in Aadan's expression. How had he not seen it before? His friend cared for Jin, and he briefly wondered if Jin felt the same toward Aadan.

"What will you tell the empress?"

What would he tell her, indeed? If Jin made it to another kingdom, she'd be alive. But if she were caught within the empire's borders while trying to escape, she'd be sentenced to death for treason, dragonrider or no. It was the only crime for which a dragon and his rider could be killed.

Tai turned on his heel and walked away.

"I didn't think she'd disappear!" Aadan called out. "I'm sorry, Your Highness!"

Tai paused. "I am too. Let's hope she returns of her own accord." He continued walking, his chest tight.

* * *

TAI RUSHED to his mother's offices, practicing what he would say. But when he arrived, he realized he was too late. Minister Gao was already there, giving Tai no chance to speak privately with the empress.

"Ah, Your Highness," Gao said, "I was just sharing the fortuitous news with your royal mother that another dragonrider has returned. I know you and the foreign prince Aadan are good friends, Your Highness. Though I'm afraid his return does only stress our need to consider the possibility that Jin has perished."

Tai wrestled down his annoyance. Despite Gao's best attempts, the man couldn't hide his pleasure at the prospect of Jin's death.

"I wouldn't give up hope," Tai said.

"Of course," Gao replied. "But I wonder whether we should nevertheless arrange a search party for Wang Kway Jin and her dragon."

Tai kept his expression neutral. The man was already ahead of him, putting out a hunting party before Tai could speak to the empress.

"Very well. Find out from the Dragon Class exam organizers where she was taken and send a party of four riders," the empress said.

Gao nodded but made no move to leave. "Your Highness, may I suggest something a little more ... precautionary."

Tai frowned. What was Gao getting at?

"As we are dealing with a Jade," Gao continued, "we must be certain as to its whereabouts and whether it's still alive. No doubt Jin is honorable, but we cannot ignore the possibility that she decided to . . . seek other patrons."

"Do you have evidence of that, Minister?" Tai asked, sharp.

"Of course not," Gao said, placating. "But I am sure you'll agree it doesn't hurt to play a conservative hand."

"What are you suggesting we do?" the empress asked.

Gao didn't look at Tai. "I suggest we send a large search party. And not just to the area she was dropped off, but elsewhere too. Because if she decided to seek our enemies, or worse, Mengkhis Lai, then she could be anywhere by now."

His mother stiffened, and he didn't blame her. No doubt Gao was simply driving home the threat Jin now posed, and how this predicament was squarely the empress's fault. But the man did have a point. The kingdom of Silla, or their age-old enemy the island empires of Nihhon, the Turks—any of them would pay a mountain of gold for a dragon and its rider, much less a Jade.

"The sooner we find Jin," Gao said, "the sooner we can bring her back here. And, of course, the sooner we stop worrying about her falling into the wrong hands."

"How many do you propose sending?" Tai asked.

"Every last one of our Dragon Class riders," Gao replied.

"Is that wise?" the empress asked. "Our entire Dragon Class searching for this one girl?"

"A girl with a Jade," Gao countered. "I would say we cannot afford to leave any stone unturned. We need all wings and all riders so that we may find Rayshan and Jin quickly." The war minister looked from Tai to the empress. "But that is simply my advice. Your Highnesses must decide what you think best for the empire."

"We have dragons and riders stationed around the empire's perimeter. Let's send them instead," Tai pointed out.

Gao nodded. "We could. But then we'd be leaving the borders unprotected, and word might spread. The riders who serve the palace are all the most loyal. We can trust them to not just search but also keep the mission secret, which would avoid damaging gossip about why we have lost a Jade in the first place."

The empress was quiet before looking at Tai. "What say you, my son?"

She gazed at him, expectant. He didn't believe Jin would betray the empire, no matter how angry she was. Nor did he believe, deep down, that she had gone to seek Mengkhis Lai. But no matter what, Gao was right: they needed to find her, discreetly if possible. And they wouldn't do so through inaction or by dispatching a small search party. Once they had found her, then he would be able to help her, even if she had turned traitor or worse. "Throne above all, Mother. I will deploy the whole of Dragon Class, and they shall leave tonight."

Gao bowed. "As you wish, Your Highnesses. You are most wise."

But as Gao left, Tai felt anything but wise. His gaze drifted back to the towers outside, where the sun was making its last flamboyant display against the clouds before surrendering to night. *Where are you, Jin?*

CHAPTER 36

"Jin."

The voice sounded familiar, and close.

"Jin, it's time."

Wiping the grit from her eyes, she sat up. Rayshan was curled around her, protective even in restless sleep, though she sensed the erratic flurry of his dreams scuttling across his mind.

Jin looked around, seeking the voice. And then she saw him.

"Lu?"

The man walked forward and squatted down before her, his face split in that familiar grin, his bulky frame agile even while balancing on his haunches.

"How'd you get here?"

"Thief's secret," he replied, eyes twinkling.

She was about to make her usual face at his taunt, but frowned. His *pao* and shirt were pressed, and not a speck of sand or dust marring the cloth. She looked over at Rayshan, who hadn't stirred even though Lu was only an arm's length away from his snout.

This was not real.

"Am I dead?" she asked. Rayshan would have woken at the slightest smell of another person.

Lu shook his head. "Not yet. I'm here to save your skinny little carcass."

She laughed. She had missed his banter. Her laughter faded at the solemnity in his eyes.

"This is the last time, little sister."

She reached out to grasp his arm, but nothing except a cool breeze met her fingers. She was not the one dead.

He smiled.

Hot tears welled and her throat closed. "I'm sorry. I was so stupid."

Lu shook his head. "It was all meant to happen this way. You'll see. Listen to your dragon. You're a dragonrider now, not a thief. Go back to Changan and show Gao he cannot break you. The whole reason I suggested we rob the Dragon Class in the first place, Jin, was to make a new future. Don't give up the future you deserve just because Gao wants to crush you."

"I can't."

"Why not?"

"I have nothing left," she said, eyes stinging.

Lu looked at Rayshan. "You have Rayshan. You have a future, a good future, if you'll fight for it. Fight for it, and you will change the fates of so many across the empire. You have gone further than I ever dared dream for me, much less for you." He smiled. "The mightiest people in the land, the empress and Prince Tai, see you as a dragonrider. So now—" he shrugged "—there's just one question left."

Her voice cracked. "What?"

"Do *you* believe you are a dragonrider?" He let the question hang there, then stood. "It's time. Live well. And soar."

And with that her friend shimmered and collapsed, like ash on an incense stick grown too long.

She sat listening to the wind for a moment but knew he was gone. She whispered the words for the dead. "Walk well, Lu."

It took all her strength to grasp the bond with Rayshan, to muster her thoughts enough to cobble together her words.

Rayshan, wake up.

The dragon stirred, and one eye slid open. At the sight of her, he immediately shifted, concerned.

We will return to Changan. We will not let Gao win, even if it kills us.

Rayshan hummed in excited approval, then stood, stretching his wings and neck to shake off the sand. Jin struggled to her feet but then fell, her vision darkening.

You've lost too much water, and you still have poison in you, Rayshan said, concerned. *Can you ride?*

I have to.

Jin reached up with one arm, but her fingers didn't even have the strength to grip his wing to stand. She tried again, but each attempt only weakened her, until she slumped to the sand, without the energy to even raise her head.

I need a moment.

You are dying.

Even as he said it she knew it was true. The sun was leeching the life from her, making her muscles cramp and her thoughts hazy.

We must blood bond.

It's against the rules, Rayshan. You said—

Forget what I said. It's the only way, Jin. Dragon's blood will save you.

Images of Mengkhis Lai and his dragon flashed before her—destruction and bloodshed everywhere, cruelty and chaos rampant through the empire.

What if I become like him? What if they are right and I become a force of destruction?

We don't know that blood bonding makes you evil. Just because Mengkhis succumbed doesn't mean you will.

She closed her eyes. It was either accept the risk of becoming a monster like Mengkhis Lai or die here and let Gao win, let others like her be barred from Dragon Class. Was she doing this because she believed in her ability to resist the temptations that came with blood bonding, or was she simply too proud to let Gao beat her? Either way, she wasn't ready to die. Not yet. She nodded.

Rayshan twisted his neck and bit deep into his leg. He lay down with his wound close to her, the dark blood already trickling into the sand. She tamed her stomach, put her mouth to Rayshan's wound, and drank. It was not pleasant, but within seconds of his blood going down her throat, her mind began clearing and her pulse slowed from its earlier frenzy. She forced herself to keep drinking until she thought she would be sick. She pulled away, wiping the blood from her mouth, and took several halting breaths.

The world around her spun, then sharpened. The sands had a song, and she could smell everything the wind touched: scorched bone, dried shrubs, insects. The heat of the desert coursed into her, through her, and every scale on Rayshan's hide seemed clearly etched, every mote dancing in the shimmering air became visible. Her blood grew from an irregular rhythm, struggling to survive, to a steady beat that sang in her body.

How do you feel? Rayshan asked, concerned.

Alive.

But that was only partly true. For Jin the thief was dead. And Jin the dragonrider was just being born.

Let's fly, she said.

adan scanned the grassy hills skimming below Wanli's great wingbeats but saw no signs of Rayshan or Jin.

He had barely returned to the capital before the order came to fly once more. All fifty-five Dragon Class riders in the imperial city had been called to the search, with wings of five dragons each sent to various target points: south, where Mengkhis Lai was buried; north, to where Baikalan the dragon slept in a frozen magical sleep in the king of Khitan's domain; east to the seas which separated the empire from Silla and Nihhon, in case Jin had fled there; and west, in case she had gone to Persia or further. This seemed the least likely choice, but clearly the empress was taking no chances.

During the geography trial he had been able to focus on survival and lock away all guilt about Jin. She had repeatedly refused to give him a chance to explain, and he had stayed awake nights, haunted by the memory of the hurt on her face. Wanli had done his best to offer comfort, but Aadan had felt terrible all the same, and played out every way he could make things right.

But after returning to Changan and finding out she hadn't returned, he simply wanted to find her alive—even if she never spoke to him again.

Aadan heard Wanli's warning in his head and realized he had missed a signal from one of the other riders in his wing. He flew with Panshalar, Jao, and Ezho, along with one other rider, Ko, a tall older man with a birthmark on his neck. Ko had been one of the crew to drop Jin and her dragon and was leading them back to the site.

Aadan squinted and saw the signal repeated. Ko was motioning to land. Aadan told Wanli to bank and follow Ko's dragon, a large gold with a crooked spike on his back. Wanli huffed, and Aadan knew his dragon was grateful for a chance to rest. They landed in rolling grasslands, a distant herd of sheep bleating as they fled from the descending dragons.

Aadan dismounted and looked around. The place was unremarkable—remote and with no city within a day's horse ride, it was true, but certainly easy enough for someone like Jin to survive and navigate.

"This is where you dropped her?" Aadan asked Ko. The rider nodded and pointed. A strip of red cloth, tattered and dust caked, was staked into the ground, the words "Dragon Class: 20th Year of Empress Celestial Light" written in gold ink on it. These stakes, Aadan knew, were used to mark drop points specifically in case of searches like this.

"Prints should be easy to find," Ezho said, taking command. "Everyone spread out." The riders circled out obediently, their dragons happy to let the humans work while they carved out spaces for themselves to lie down.

"Rain's probably washed any prints away by now," Ko scoffed.

Aadan squatted to the ground. He doubted Ko's assessment. The soil didn't look terribly wet, and this year had been dry in the steppes. He heard the distant bleating of sheep and saw a figure on a hillock. Spotting the dragons, the man turned and disappeared over the other side.

Aadan called to Wanli, who growled in admonishment. He had only just settled himself. Aadan repeated his call, and Wanli rose. Aadan climbed on and instructed him to fly low.

They caught up to the shepherd within a few wingbeats, and the man cowered as they landed before him, his sheep scattering in terror at Wanli's presence. The man could have as easily been forty as eighty—a rough life in the pastures had carved a map of creases into his brows.

"Leave my sheep be! I haven't any extra to spare!" the shepherd cried angrily.

Aadan told Wanli to stop salivating at the sheep, then turned to the shepherd and spoke to him from astride Wanli. "Did you lose any of your sheep to another dragon recently?"

"No, but I pay my taxes! Please, I've lost five to blight already. I don't have any extra for feeding dragons!"

Aadan frowned. "Do you always graze here?"

The man eyed him, unsure where this was headed. "Yes. It's my land."

"But you've seen no Dragon Class rider these last two weeks? No rider asked you for a sheep or food?"

"You only just got here. No one's had time to ask me for anything, except you!" The shepherd protested. "Now please, leave us be. It'll take me until sunset to gather this flock now."

Aadan rummaged in his pao and pulled out a coin, which he tossed to the shepherd. "A contribution to your flock."

He spurred Wanli to the air before the man could properly thank him. When he returned to his companions, he found Ko drinking from a water gourd while Ezho and everyone else were still diligently combing the area.

Aadan dismounted from Wanli and strode up to Ko. "Where did you actually drop Jin?"

"What are you talking about?" Ko growled, stoppering his gourd and wiping his mouth.

"You didn't drop Jin here or anywhere near here," Aadan said, just struggling to keep his anger in check. Ezho had approached as well and listened to this, frowning.

"The marker's right there!" Ko protested.

Ezho looked at the marker, then at Aadan. "We haven't found prints."

Aadan nodded. "The marker's here, but you dropped Jin somewhere else. For the last time, where did you drop her?"

Ko held up his hands. "Look, I don't know why you think—"

Aadan's fist connected with Ko's jaw, sending the rider backward and spilling his water gourd. Ezho shouted, and from the corner of his eye Aadan saw Ko's gold dragon leap to his feet, roaring. But Aadan already had Ko down on the ground with an elbow against his windpipe in a lock move while Wanli blasted water over the gold's head as a warning. The two dragons lashed their tails, tense, while the other dragons watched with flattened ears and bared teeth.

Aadan leaned in closer. "Where? Where did you drop her?"

Ko gasped beneath him, and Aadan eased off just enough to allow the man to speak. Panshalar and Jao had all run back now and stood in wary silence around the two riders on the ground. "It wasn't my idea . . ." Ko rasped. "We were told . . . we were told we'd be paid if the girl was dropped in the Singing Sands."

By the Wise Lord. Aadan leaned back, mentally scanning the maps he had studied for countless hours. "That's double the distance allowed by the trial rules." Not to mention a vast stretch of sand with no water or food for hundreds of *li*. Even the hardiest of traders tried to skirt the desert rather than cross it, and if Jin had been left unconscious there, her chances of survival were next to none.

"Who paid you?"

Ko hesitated, then said, "Minister Gao."

Panshalar's eyes widened. "He would try to kill one of us? A dragonrider?"

"It was just a prank," Ko scowled. "Besides, she's not one of us, she's a girl."

Aadan felt like striking Ko again but refrained. They needed him to ride.

Ezho shook his head. "It's not right, breaking the test rules."

"If he was willing to kill her, he'd kill any of us," Jao muttered, looking like a child who had discovered his parents lying.

"Take us to where you dropped her," Aadan said.

The rider sat up, testing his throat with hesitant fingers. "It hurts to swallow," he protested. His dragon prowled to his side, snapping his jaws at Aadan before nudging Ko to his feet.

"Answering questions in the tea rooms about why

you took a bribe will hurt much more," Aadan snapped, "unless you help us."

As they mounted their dragons and took to the sky, he tried to fight the fear that they were too late and that Jin was already dead.

CHAPTER 38

Jin and Rayshan flew faster than they had ever flown before. Jin put this incredible speed down to the blood bond. But no power stood a chance against the vicious weather, and when a violent sandstorm swept down upon them, Jin tried to control her frustration as Rayshan insisted they stop. The dragon plunged his tail into the dunes, burrowing in it until he had dug out a space for himself and Jin. He kept a hollow free under his neck, and Jin crawled into the crude shelter while the wind made the sands roar like some giant beast. Jin was sure that anything wet on her, even her eyes, might freeze.

As soon as the winds had died down enough, Jin insisted they press on. She mounted Rayshan, and the great dragon shook the sand from his wings, then paused.

Rayshan?

What's that?

She looked where he indicated with his head, and frowned. *Are those . . . dragons?*

Rayshan growled. *Maybe they've come to finish the job.*

Jin knew they couldn't fight several dragons and their riders, even if every fiber in her being now sang with life and vigor. Best to hide.

Rayshan burrowed back into the dune they had used for cover, and Jin followed suit, the dragon using his tail to sweep the sands over them in an attempt at camouflage.

Jin peered at the approaching figures from beneath one of Rayshan's wings. Were these the riders who had dropped them off in the desert, drugged and without a drop of water? Anger burned in her. But as they approached, she recognized the silver dragon at the front and from Rayshan's humming knew that he had too.

Wanli!

She scrabbled out from under Rayshan's wing and shaded her eyes against the vicious sun. Wanli called out, and Rayshan answered, and then the wing was landing around her. She recognized Ezho, Jao, and Panshalar, though there was a sullen stranger with them on a gold. Aadan dismounted first and ran over.

"Jin!"

His betrayal still smarted, but she also couldn't deny the joy of seeing him. She stifled a sob of relief and held back the urge to hug him. Aadan, however, didn't hesitate and wordlessly crushed her to him for a moment before stepping back to look at her, concerned. There was so much to say, but scanning those behind him, she knew now was not the time.

"Why are you all here?"

"We were looking for you," Aadan said.

"The whole of Dragon Class is looking for you," Ezho said, sliding off his dragon's shoulder and coming forward.

Jin frowned. "The whole of Dragon Class?"

"Every rider in Changan, at least," Panshalar added.

"Does Minister Gao know you're out here?" she asked.

"He's the one who sent everyone to find you," Jao said, scowling. For the first time, she noted, his scowl was directed at someone other than her.

"I'm guessing they thought you'd—" Ezho stopped at Aadan's pointed look.

"But . . . that doesn't make sense," Jin said. If Gao thought she was dead—and he certainly had no reason to think she wasn't—why send the whole of Dragon Class after her?

Unless he wants all the dragons gone from Changan, Rayshan said.

"Jin, what's wrong?" Aadan asked.

"I don't know," Jin said, a terrible premonition growing in her. "I only know that something is. We have to return to Changan as quickly as possible."

* * *

RAIN DRUMMED on the roof tiles, sending the birds twittering as they rushed for cover in the ginkgo trees lining the palace boulevards.

As Tai let the servants dress him in his official court robes, he looked out the windows over the towers to the south. Aadan had traveled north, where the records showed Jin had been dropped. So far, the messages from all directions had been the same: no sign of the Jade or the rider.

The servant finished his sash, and Tai nodded his thanks. As he stepped into his boots, he noticed movement on the outer walls and watched as the guards changed shifts. As a child he had loved watching these moments: the discipline, the marching, the saluting, and the shouted "Hei!" as the guards changed over, drumming their spear butts against the ground. Today they had not just the spears but also long swords at their waists. Perhaps it was due to the vote.

Once his headscarf was tied in place and his ceremonial sword was buckled to his belt, he pulled the imperial seal marking him as heir to the throne over his neck and stepped out into the palace halls.

This vote to let women into Dragon Class, he knew, was likely to be little more than a charade. With Jin missing and the whole of Dragon Class taken from their usual duties to retrieve her, Gao would have little trouble persuading the ministers that women joining

Dragon Class had proven disruptive at best and disastrous at worst. Gao would no doubt rejoice in his win, and perhaps even try to push his advantage by calling for the laws to be rewritten to expressly ban women from all government departments, not just military ones. And from there, perhaps he'd even think of toppling the empress.

His attendants seemed to sense his gloomy mood and kept silent as they walked with him. As if conjured by his thoughts, the war minister himself appeared from an adjoining corridor just as Tai reached the courtyard before the Hall of Mandates, where the vote was to be held. Two lines of imperial guards stood at attention, forming a human corridor to the building.

"Ah! Your Highness," Gao said, bowing his head. "May I walk you to the hall?" He motioned to his servants, two of whom rushed forward with silk umbrellas. Tai knew it would be rude to refuse, so he waited as the umbrellas were opened and then stepped out with Gao under their covering. As they walked between the guards, Tai again noticed that they all had long swords at their waists.

"The guards have extra arms today," he commented.

Gao glanced at the men they passed. "The vote is contentious. The Department of the Household decided it best to take precautions." He held out a hand from under the umbrella. "A spring rain is a good omen, don't you think?"

"Perhaps a harbinger of new beginnings," Tai said, unable to resist goading Gao.

Gao smiled. "Perhaps. I have always welcomed the rain. It feels . . . cleansing."

Tai kept his expression neutral as they climbed the stairs and the heralds announced their arrival. No doubt Gao saw this vote as cleansing the Dragon Class of women and commoners. Not for the first time, Tai wished Jin would magically return, if only to see Gao's face.

Ministers and clerks filled the Hall already. Special teak boxes marked with the words "YES" and "NO" were placed on a long table at the front of the room, before a wide, golden dragon throne. His mother would arrive only when everyone else was settled, and as Tai murmured greetings to officials and clerks before finding his way to his seat, he noted there were many more guards present than usual, even for a formal vote.

The drums sounded, and a herald stepped to the center of the floor.

"Her Imperial Highness, Empress Wu Ze-Tian of the Celestial Light."

Everyone bent their heads and began kneeling the traditional three times. "May the empress live ten thousand years."

Tai said the familiar words but as crown prince did not have to kneel. And as his mother entered, her golden robes and headdress nearly blinding, he thought he caught a smile on Gao's face as the minister bent for the last bow.

It was the smile of someone who was about to shout "eat" at a game of pai.

* * *

THE SUN HAMMERED riders and dragons alike, drying them like the grapes that farmers in Kwannay spread on trellises. Jin leaned into Rayshan, covering her face and head as best she could with what clothing she had, urging him on.

She and her wing had ridden without stopping for the last day. They flew over the dry northern stretches of the empire, which gave way to plateaus before transforming into the sculpted loess plains surrounding Changan. Jin's legs were practically chafed raw, and her face was lacerated from the wind. But she held on, seeing that the others were even more tired than she, yet they didn't protest once.

I hope we're not too late.

Question is, too late for what?

Like Rayshan, she had no idea what Gao was up to —she just knew he was setting something terrible in motion.

A gentle rain began falling as they neared the capital. When Rayshan trumpeted at sighting the city's great walls, the other dragons all gave answering calls and flew faster.

Guards stationed along the outer perimeter spotted them. They shouted the message along the walls to other sentries, and Jin knew that runners would be riding to alert the empress.

She and the other riders banked, heading for the Blood Oval. There, a group of grooms awaited them, but Jin had no time for congratulations or welcomes.

"Where's Emar?" she demanded of the nearest groom.

The groom pointed, and Jin saw Emar emerge from one of the upper offices of the barracks. Jin ran toward the nearest staircase to meet him, rain splattering around her.

"Good to see you back, Jin!" he called out as he limped his way down the stairs.

"Where's the empress?" Jin panted, arriving under the shelter of the eaves.

"Is something wrong?"

Aadan had jogged over and joined them, leaving the other riders watching. "Gao dropped her off beyond the permitted zone, Master Emar. He intended for her and Rayshan to die and for the whole of Dragon Class to leave in search of Jin."

Emar absorbed this, face dark. "Are you sure? This is the minister of war you speak of."

Jin nodded. "He needed Dragon Class gone for some reason. Is the empress safe?"

The man's eyes narrowed. "She is in the Hall of Mandates, in the Legal Ministry. All the ministers are there today, for the vote on allowing women into Dragon Class."

All the ministers. Gathered in one place. With the mightiest faction of the army, the Dragon Class, far from the capital.

"By the Wise Lord," Aadan muttered, "he's planning a coup."

"Where's the Hall of Mandates?" Jin demanded.

"West side of the Imperial City," Emar growled. "There will be guards. It's a closed-session vote!"

But Jin was already running back to Rayshan and vaulted onto his wing and from there onto his back as Aadan followed, shouting to the other boys, "To the Hall of Mandates! Now!"

Please don't let us be too late, she prayed.

"*N*o!"

The clerk read out the paper in a booming voice, then put it into the teak box marked "NO." Three clerks dutifully recorded the vote in their ledgers.

"Minister Gao!" The clerk bowed and gestured for the minister to come forward with his vote. Tai's mother wore a dark look, and Tai knew his expression was likely no better. Though the clerks hadn't been counting the votes as they tallied, it was abundantly clear that all the ministers save a few had voted to keep the law barring women. Gao's vote would no doubt simply add to the mountain of naysayers and fan the ever-present murmurs about women being where they didn't belong.

Gao rose and bowed in the direction of the throne. "Before I cast my vote, I'd like to say a few words. Your Highness, this humble servant has always tried, to his best ability, to advise on what is best for the empire's army. For when an empire's army is strong, it fears no enemies. But when its army is weak, it falls with the slightest breeze." He paused, looking around him. "Today, my fellow ministers have clearly shared my view and voted to keep women out of Dragon Class. This will ensure the army stays strong and undiluted. But as your minister of war, Your Highness, I believe it is my sacred duty to make sure I am doing all I can to protect the empire from its enemies—" he paused "—especially if those enemies are within our borders, even within our palace."

The empress frowned. "And what enemies do you speak of?"

"You, Your Highness."

A gasp rippled through the ministers, and Tai shifted uneasily, but before he or his mother could respond, the guards at the entry barred the doors to the hall while those on the side drew their swords in a smooth, practiced motion.

At first he thought the guards were readying to arrest Gao, but then why bar the doors? The clerks and ministers darted nervous looks at the weapons.

"Guards! Stand down!" Tai commanded.

Gao smiled. "These soldiers do not listen to you, Tai, or your mother."

Tai stared at him, taken aback. Addressing the

prince by name, without his title, was a gross insult, almost more shocking than a physical blow.

"What game is this, Minister?" Empress Wu asked, her tone brittle.

Gao smiled as one would at a child. "If anyone has been playing a game, it is you. The late emperor would never have tolerated this affront to tradition and the natural order. A woman sitting on the Dragon Throne?"

"You forget yourself." Tai's mother leaned forward. Tai had never seen her face so tight with rage. "This empire has peace because of me. I ended the Year of Chaos."

Gao walked forward. "Your rule is simply another form of chaos. You're dismantling every tradition we hold dear by putting women in Dragon Class."

"Tread carefully, Minister!" the empress said, standing. The beads of her headdress clicked, the sound loud in the shocked silence, and her hands closed into fists.

But Gao continued, undaunted. "You were a mere concubine, no blood relation to the late emperor, and yet you dared wear royal robes and wield his seals of office when he died."

"He gave me his seals to protect the empire from the likes of you," the empress retorted.

"That's your version of events," Gao replied. "A convenient little lie. But I see through you: you're so power-hungry you won't even let the emperor's own son rule."

Tai flushed at this and made to speak, but Gao barked at him.

"Sit down, princeling!"

Another wave of horrified murmurs swept the room, and Gao pushed on.

"You won't select a wife amongst our daughters, choosing instead to drive wedges between the noble houses. How is that unifying the empire?" A rustling came from the nervous ministers, and Gao turned to them, scornful. "You all agree with me, even if none of you dare say it." He faced the throne once more. "You are a threat to the security of the empire. And as the minister of war, sworn to protect China, I must remove you from the Dragon Throne. Give me the dragon seals, and I will spare you and your son."

"You do not frighten me," the empress said, icy.

Gao motioned the guards closest to Tai, and they sprang for him. The prince leapt up and drew his ceremonial sword, wishing he had his usual battle-scarred one, but it was better than nothing. One guard brought his blade down from above while the other darted to Tai's right and cut low toward his legs. Tai blocked the first and kicked the second's weapon from his hand. But then the first soldier swung his spear in a vicious arc that caught Tai in the head and spun him.

He heard a scream. His mother's? Through the bright spots in his vision, he managed to ward off the second attacker, who lunged at him with his retrieved sword. Tai fought back, but then heard a crack and realized in horror that his own sword had snapped—it was an antique built to portray power rather than wield it. A hard kick in his ribs sent him sprawling to the floor, and then the two guards were on him, one holding his arms behind his back and the other with a blade pressed to his throat.

He saw his mother still standing on the dais, looking down at Gao in loathing. The minister approached Tai and the guards, then looked back at the empress.

"Your official seals, woman, or I kill your son."

The room seemed to narrow to just Tai's mother's face. To the lines around her eyes and the white of her knuckles as she gripped the royal pendants around her neck. Tai struggled against his captors, but the sword nicked his throat in response.

"What's your answer?" Gao snapped.

"You wouldn't dare kill the son of heaven."

Gao turned to the guards. "Finish him."

Tai's eyes met his mother's. He kept waiting for her to say stop, to say anything. But the silence stretched, interminable and heavier by the second.

Throne above all.

It had never occurred to him that "all" included Tai.

A thunderous crack split the air, and he wondered if that was death or the sound of his throat severing.

✳ ✳ ✳

THE DRAGONS HEADED west per Emar's directions. Jin expected to see smoke, clashing guards, or other signs of destruction, but when they sighted the Hall of Mandates, recognizable by the single-horned ram statues guarding the golden eaves, all seemed subdued and quiet. Even the rain had stopped.

Could she have been wrong? Perhaps Gao had not yet made a move. As they drew closer and circled to land, the soldiers in the courtyard looked up, and a shout rang out.

There were far too many guards for a normal closed session. Something was different.

Jao's dragon roared in pain, and Jin glanced over to see an arrow protruding from his great bronze wing. She looked down and saw two dozen soldiers had moved into formation, bows primed.

"Bank!" Jin screamed as a wave of arrows arced toward them. She heard more cries as some shafts found their targets, but then Rayshan was descending, crashing into the line of archers, snapping bows and sending men face down to the flagstones.

Jin leaped onto the ground as Aadan and Wanli landed next to Rayshan, and only then she realized she was unarmed against the remaining soldiers who were regrouping, shields and blades at the ready. She counted a dozen, with a few of the archers struggling to their feet.

"Aadan, I need a . . ." But her words hadn't finished before a wall of water scattered the soldiers across the courtyard. Jin looked behind her at Wanli, jaws open and water dripping. He had been absorbing the rainwater during the flight.

"... hand," she finished.

Go, Rayshan said. *We'll keep the soldiers here.*

Aadan gripped his bow and quiver as he ran up the rain-slicked stairs, lifting a fallen sword and tossing it to Jin. She caught it, then burst through the doors of the Hall of Mandates. Before her stretched a long corridor, at the end of which was another set of doors. Imperial guards stood barring the entrance while frightened shouts came from inside.

"Open the doors!" Jin shouted, running toward the guards.

The men rushed them, spears aimed at the dragonriders. Aadan nocked his bow and let fly, taking down the first guard, but the second guard reached Jin and tried to spear her through her middle. She dodged, then rolled as the soldier brought his sword into play. She brought her own up and parried several vicious blows before locking both her ankles around the guard's shin and yanking. The guard fell to the floor, and Aadan slammed the side of his head with the butt of his bow, knocking the man unconscious.

Jin ran to the hall door but found it wouldn't budge. She heard Gao's voice inside, then a shout and the clash of weapons.

"Help me!" Jin cried. Aadan pushed with her, but it was no use. They had barred the door from the inside.

Rayshan!

The dragon bounded into the hall, wings folded and tail thrashing. His bulk filled the entire hallway, and his spikes scraped the teak ceiling.

I need you to break down the door!

Stand back.

Jin pulled Aadan with her behind Rayshan's shoulder as the dragon opened his jaws and sent a wall of flame hitting the door. Fire rolled up its surface to the rafters and cracked its wood as if it were a stick and not solid teak a few hand spans thick. Rayshan gave the door a hard punch with his spiked head. The double doors shattered inward, spraying wood and flame. Shrieks erupted inside.

Jin ran in, Aadan close behind her, and froze at the sight before her. Ministers and clerks huddled amidst overturned tables and papers in the middle of the room. At the far end, the empress stood before the Dragon Throne, while at the foot of the dais Gao stood with two guards who held Tai down on his knees. One of them had a wicked-looking sword at Tai's throat, spots of blood dark against the metal.

"Stop!" Jin shouted.

The minister's head whipped around, his eyes narrowing at the sight of the intruders. An arrow flew from behind Jin, hitting the swordsman straight through the throat. The weapon clattered to the ground, and Tai, his throat bloodied, lunged for it, setting off a struggle with the remaining guard.

"Seize them!" Gao shouted.

Several imperial guards rushed toward Jin and Aadan but then froze, eyes fixed on something behind them.

Jin heard a growl and the crunch of wood and didn't have to look to know that Rayshan had entered the hall.

"You can't win this, Gao!" She moved warily toward the dais while Aadan held his sword at the ready. Tai, she saw, had grabbed the dropped blade and now stood at the ready. Blood smeared his throat, but judging by his stance and the strength in his arms, it hadn't gone deep. The guard was clearly torn now that power had shifted, and held back from attacking Tai.

"Rayshan will kill any of your men who don't surrender," Jin warned, looking at all the imperial soldiers in the room. Their eyes darted from Gao to the dragon, their resolve wavering.

"She's right," Tai said to Gao. "Submit now, and my mother will show leniency."

Gao laughed, the unexpected sound making Rayshan snarl. When the minister stopped laughing, he leveled a pitying gaze on Tai. "You still do not know your own mother, prince."

The minister pulled a dagger from his sash and lunged up the stairs two at a time to the throne, his speed surprising for a man of office. The empress made no move to dodge, instead staying frozen to her spot.

Gao's action seemed to spur Tai's attacker, and the man bore down on the prince with a war cry.

Jin didn't even know she was moving until she found herself behind Gao, her sword pressing clean through his back and out his abdomen. The empress sank onto the throne, her face ashen, as Jin pulled her blade free from Gao's body and held it ready, in case he attacked. Tai had felled his guard with a thrust through the leg and now moved to her side.

Blood wet the minister's robes and slicked the stairs beneath him. He turned over, grimacing, until he faced Jin. "You have no inkling what you are doing, what you are destroying."

"I know I am destroying you," Jin said. "This is for Lu." She pressed her sword to his neck but faltered at his smile.

"You are like your mother," he whispered, "nothing more than a common murderer."

"You know nothing of me," she hissed.

But Gao's eyes already had the unfocused stare of the dead, a hint of a smile still on his lips. She dropped her blade, enraged yet spent.

Hands gripped her shoulders, and she looked up into Tai's face. He seemed to have aged in the week she had been gone. The cut in his neck was not deep, she saw, but had bled enough to soak his collar and smear his jawline.

"You came back."

She was about to answer when the empress descended on them.

"Tai, my son, are you unharmed?"

"If you mean am I alive," Tai said, terse, "then, yes."

Jin frowned, confused at Tai's obvious anger, but the empress cut into her thoughts. "I owe you a great debt for saving my life. You have my eternal gratitude, and I will see that you are well rewarded."

"Gao's death is reward enough, Your Highness," Jin said, and realized it was both true and false. She was glad Gao was dead. But a thousand deaths would never save Lu, and no matter what power the empress wielded in this world, she had no power to bring people back from the next.

CHAPTER 40

In the days that followed, Jin's quarters flooded with gifts, letters, and people wanting to visit the dragonrider who had saved the empress and the empire.

Jin knew many of these were genuine outpourings of gratitude, while most stemmed from court nobles hoping to curry favor with the person who would surely now be one of the empress's favorites. Meipin drew great amusement from both Jin's discomfort with her new status and the sudden influx of attention to Meipin herself, since she was seen to be Jin's closest confidante.

Meipin had brushed Jin's apologies away with a very unladylike hug. "I'm just so glad you're safe," she had whispered. Meipin had pulled back and looked at her, serious. "No matter what you think, I consider you a friend." Jin had heard the truth in her voice and felt ashamed she had never given Meipin the benefit of the doubt.

"They're all asking me whether you intend to try to marry Prince Tai, you know," Meipin said now as they dressed in Meipin's rooms. Jin's own had become so full of offerings that the maids had trouble keeping pace with the unpacking, and Jin found she had no space to walk around.

"Ridiculous," Jin muttered in response.

"Oh, they're not asking directly," Meipin retorted, "but they're all dying of curiosity to see what lengths the empress will go to show you her favor."

Jin pulled on the loose ceremonial rider's robes the royal household had provided, the silver and scarlet bright against the black of the leathers beneath. "She's already granted me the favor I asked."

Meipin looked over from adjusting her short pao, eyebrows raised. "Oh? And what's that?"

"You'll see," Jin replied, and received a playful slap on the arm in response.

"You're being a tease!"

Jin allowed herself a smile. Meipin kept pestering her as they finished readying themselves, but Jin refused to give any more hints, even as they left in a two-person horse carriage for the inner palace grounds. Since the Hall of Mandates still hadn't been fully repaired after Gao's attempted coup, today's gathering of ministers and nobles was to be held in the Hall of Justice. By the time they arrived, the vast courtyard leading inside was already teeming with people, all eager to hear the proceedings, even if they weren't allowed into the hall itself.

Jin and Meipin stepped off the horse carriage. The crowds parted for them, for everyone recognized the famed dragonrider who had thwarted the coup. Jin tried her best to smile and seem responsive to the shouts and greetings all around, but inside, her stomach tensed at what she was about to do. She had survived the geography trials, fought Gao, and survived blood bonding. But what she was about to do today terrified her in a different way, and she had rehearsed the possibilities in her head all night.

They passed through the great carved double doors and into the teak-and-marble room beyond. The ministers all took their places at their assigned tables while clerks busied themselves over ink stones, brushes, and paper.

Jin and Meipin were led to seats close to the throne, a spot of honor. Jin scanned the room and saw dragonriders gathered in a row of seats on the far end, including Ezho, Jao, and Panshalar, who all nodded encouragement. Aadan sat amongst them and gave her a reassuring smile that doubled the fluttering in her stomach. Madu was conspicuously absent, having been taken to the tea rooms to be questioned over his involvement in the coup. Despite everything, Jin didn't wish the tea rooms on anyone and hoped he would be found innocent.

Emar sat next to Jin's wing mates, on the seat closest to the throne, dressed in his finest official leathers and with a black headscarf. He caught her eye, and the good side of his face broke into a wide smile.

The herald entered and beat nine times on the great bronze gong to announce the empress's arrival.

"Her Imperial Highness, Empress Wu Ze-Tian of Celestial Light!"

Jin knelt and spoke the words with everyone else. "May Your Highness live ten thousand years!"

A rustle of silk and beads announced the empress's presence before the woman herself ascended the dais, Prince Tai behind her. Everyone stood, and Jin saw Tai seated next to the Dragon Throne, settling his ornate silk robes.

The hall fell into such a deep hush of anticipation that Jin felt she could have heard snow fall.

"Today," the empress's musical voice cut in, "we gather to decide a very controversial matter, one that will tear us apart if we let it. We are here at the request of Minister Wei to determine whether we should change a tradition hundreds of years old and allow women to enter Dragon Class alongside men. This means they will be given the chance to bond to dragons and train as the men do, fight as the men do—" she paused "—and die as the men do."

The silence held.

"We will hear from our ministers shortly," the empress said. "In usual order. But first, I will break one other tradition today and invite dragonrider Jin to address the floor."

Meipin looked at Jin in shock. For no woman, save the empress, had ever been allowed to speak before a vote.

Jin rose. "Thank you, Your Highness. Given the vote involves letting other women into Dragon Class, I think the ministers should hear from the one woman in it."

Jin paused, gathering her courage, then turned to look at the gathered ministers, including Minister Wei.

"Respected ministers, you are here because Minister Wei put forward a radical idea, the idea Dragon Class might be open to merit rather than a certain class or sex. My dragon, a Jade, chose to bond with someone who wasn't a man or a noble, which is why I'm here. And, no, my Jade has not yet manifested his power, but we survived the Singing Sands and returned despite all Minister Gao's efforts. I have survived a greater trial than most who have entered Dragon Class." She paused. "I do not say this for praise or to boast of what I have achieved. I say this for the many dragonriders out there who are better than I—dragonriders ready to serve the empire, to protect what you all hold dear, but for the fact that they are low born or happen to be women." She paused. "A woman ended the Year of Chaos. A woman showed you dragons don't just bond to men." She glanced at Meipin. "A woman showed me that change is possible—not with force or violence as Minister Gao believed, but with patience, generosity, and friendship."

Meipin's mouth opened, but Jin knew that even if they hadn't been in a formal hall, Meipin was speechless. Jin smiled, pleased at surprising her housemate. She turned back to the waiting audience.

"Dragon Class can reach new heights, achieve great feats, but only if you undo the legal ropes that keep it tied to old rules and illogical traditions. And no woman has the power to do that. Only you do. Only you have the power to choose whether you stay the same or become the best you can be. I, too, once feared change. I feared it so much I preferred remaining a downtrodden thief rather than reaching for a better life. But I stand before you now a dragonrider. And if a thief can ride a Jade, then anyone can enter Dragon Class."

She bowed, spent. She couldn't recall ever speaking so much, and marveled that so many had listened. Looking up, she saw the empress wearing an enigmatic expression.

"Dragonrider Jin has spoken," the empress said. "Now it is time to vote, and I urge you to vote freely. No one will be punished for their choices. Minister Wei, as the one who called this vote, you may proceed first."

Minister Wei bowed his head, then raised a wooden plaque from his table.

"I vote yes. Let us change the law and allow women

who are chosen by dragons to be admitted into Dragon Class."

"Minister Wei votes yes!" a clerk's voice boomed out in the hall. Jin looked around, heart hammering. Then another minister reached for a wooden paddle and raised it.

"Minister Yao votes yes!"

"Minister Meng votes yes!"

One by one the other ministers began raising similar wooden plaques. Soon the row of ministers had all held up their plaques, almost every one voting yes. Murmurs of excitement swept the room, as the vote was clearly about to be unanimous. Meipin's fingers clasped Jin's.

When all the ministers had had a turn, the head clerk stood, an open scroll before him. "Voting for the law of allowing women into Dragon Class is now complete. The tally has been taken. Your Highness, may I read the tally?"

The empress waved assent.

"Twenty-eight vote yes to amending the law. Two abstained. One votes no." The clerk cleared his throat. "Let it be heard today, in the twenty-first year of Her Highness the Empress Wu's celestial reign, that the law banning women from Dragon Class shall be changed."

Meipin gave an unladylike whoop of joy, and the hall erupted into laughter. Jin caught Prince Tai's eyes on them, his right hand drumming on the throne's armrest in a show of support. She looked over at Aadan and the other riders, who were also beating their palms against the floor in approval. Since their discovery of Gao's treachery toward her and the throne, their hostility had turned to solidarity, if not outright friendship.

Heralds ordered for drums to be sounded. At this, the ministers and nobles knelt as the empress took her leave, and only when she had gone did the nobles stand and file out of the hall. Meipin was rapturous and squeezed Jin's hand.

"That was your favor?"

Jin nodded. "It's not getting you into the secretariat, but it's a start in opening doors."

Meipin grinned. "It most definitely is."

"Greetings, Lady Meipin, Dragonrider Jin."

They turned at the prince's voice. He wore a high collar, but from here Jin glimpsed the bandage covering the cut on his throat. She wondered if it would scar.

"Congratulations. You gave a fine speech, better than I could have done."

She bowed. "I doubt that, Your Highness."

"Lady Meipin, I was about to talk over some details of the dragonrider's swearing-in ceremony, but I'd hate to bore you."

Meipin noted his cue and bowed. "Please, do not delay such talks because of me. I must congratulate my uncle on today's vote, if you'll excuse me."

She bowed and left with her attendants, and Jin

found herself alone with Prince Tai. She glanced over to the dragonriders on the opposite side, who were also leaving with the nobles. Aadan was looking her way, frowning, but at a reassuring wave from her, he turned and left the building.

"I wanted to explain," Tai began.

"A prince need not explain," Jin said. "Besides, you were simply keeping track of your assets."

Tai winced. "I am sorry for the betrayal of trust, but . . . you should know that Aadan wasn't exactly willing to do my bidding, and I knew this."

He was speaking with large pauses, as if finding the words as he went. The prince with the silver tongue had, it seemed, lost his glibness.

"He did so only because he felt obligated, so try not to hold it against him." Tai paused. "And for what it's worth, I don't view you as simply an asset. I never believed you'd leave the empire or become another Mengkhis Lai."

Jin fell silent. She wasn't ready to tell anyone about her blood bonding—much less him or Aadan.

"Your Highness honors me with his trust," she managed to say.

"As I hope you'll honor me with yours," Tai said. He reached into his robe and pulled out what looked like a metal key.

"What is this?" she asked, taking it.

"The key to the restricted section of the library," Tai said. "I made you a copy. I trust you'll use it wisely."

Jin hesitated but then pushed aside her qualms. She had broken a taboo because she had to, but as long as she didn't follow Mengkhis Lai's path, she needn't share her secret. "I will. Thank you."

He smiled. "Welcome back, Dragonrider Jin."

*   *   *

SHE HAD ONLY JUST CHANGED out of her official garb and into comfortable trousers when a herald stepped in, bowing low. "Her Imperial Highness, Empress Wu, wishes to call upon you."

"Now?" Jin replied. Meipin was still at her uncle's, and Jin had been about to see to Rayshan's meal, but that would have to wait. She was about to suggest they meet in the foyer, as that space was not cluttered with boxes of silks and teas and other fine gifts, but the empress had already swept into the room, accompanied by her retinue of a dozen maids and valets. As always, her radiance both in personality and attire seemed to light up the room.

Jin knelt.

"You have many admirers, I see," the empress commented, taking in the gifts.

Jin couldn't think of a modest reply. "May I clear a chair for Your Highness?"

"Never mind," the empress said. "Walk with me."

The empress turned and glided out, her maids following, and Jin rose. She followed the empress, who strode into the gardens that lined Meipin's quarters. Here she slowed at a koi pond and waited for Jin to join her. When she had, the servants seemed to all pick up on some invisible signal and melted away until they were out of earshot.

"You impressed the ministers, Wang Kway Jin," the empress said, her eyes on the younger woman. Seeing that Jin wouldn't answer, Wu continued, "The power to sway people is a mighty one."

"I only spoke my truth, Your Highness."

"And it worked." The empress smiled. "You saved my life and by doing so saved the empire. Of course, this is all part of your duty as a Dragon Class rider protecting the realm, yet I still feel . . . fond of you. As a mother would for a daughter."

Jin didn't reply, unsure where this was headed.

"And if you were my daughter, I would advise you about life. About men." At Jin's confusion, the empress smiled patiently. "I think it best you spend less time with the crown prince."

Jin's ears burned. "Rest assured, Your Highness, there is nothing of that between me and the prince."

"Of course not. And I want to avoid any misunderstandings. You have exceeded the dreams of any woman in this empire. Just as I did." The empress's tone held admiration but also an edge. "I love two things in life: my empire and my son. And I will make sure I do what's best for both of them, no matter the cost. You are a beautiful and fascinating girl with a bright future ahead, but I cannot have the noble families think for a moment the crown prince would choose you over their daughters. You do understand?"

"Of course, Your Highness." Jin had never entertained the idea of a future with the crown prince, but somehow the empress made it seem like she had been deliberately luring Tai.

The empress smiled, the iciness disappearing like sugar in water. "Good. I look forward to the official swearing-in ceremony for all Dragon Class members, and I will present a special award for you. You're a great asset to the empire, and I am sure that your name, Dragonrider Jin, will be sung for centuries, along with other heroes like Oyang Kang."

***

JIN STOOD at the edges of the Blood Oval, saddling Rayshan, and watched a group of young rider hopefuls, all roughly fifteen to eighteen years old, file in. Over the past days a few such groups had come through—noble youths who took an introductory tour of the Dragon Class grounds to determine if they wanted to put their names forward and apply to enter the hatchery after the next harvest.

Jin counted only five girls amongst the thirty, but then again, when she had first arrived nearly a year ago as a wary thief with nowhere to run, the very idea of a woman putting her name forward was impossible.

The girls all noticed her immediately and stared, until Emar barked an order and they all hastily looked back to him.

"I think you're now as famous as the dragons."

She turned to see Aadan and Wanli next to them. Wanli was already saddled, while Jao, Panshalar, and Ezho were readying their dragons for the morning's flight drill. Amid training, rehearsals for the dragonrider swearing-in ceremony, and speculation over the new minister of war, they'd had little time for private conversations since Gao's coup.

"Hardly," she said, self-conscious.

"Have you heard the news about Madu?"

She stopped in the middle of fastening the last saddle buckle. She had heard of his release, but when he hadn't returned to training, she had assumed he'd retreated to his family home to avoid the scandal at court. Though Jin disliked him, she didn't wish for him to receive a criminal's end and had been dreading the news that he and Gao's sons might all be executed. Lady Gao, she knew, had been hastily married off to a minor duke, thereby effectively banished from court.

"He and his dragon will be sent to Gansu for a year as punishment for their relationship with a traitor."

Jin nodded, a weight lifting from her. Gansu was about as far away from Changan as possible. It would be good not to have to deal with Madu, though exile, along with the shame of his uncle's end, would likely only fan his hatred of her.

A comforting wave rippled across her mind, and she looked over at Wanli. The dragon huffed as he let her know that no matter what, she had the dragon's support.

"Thank you."

Rayshan whipped his tail in warning, and Aadan looked at her strangely. "For what?"

"For—" she stopped, realizing her slip.

I think only blood-bonded riders can hear other dragons, Jin, Rayshan said.

Aadan frowned. "You can hear Wanli?"

"I meant thank you for letting me know," Jin said, covering. "And also, the prince told me that you hadn't wanted to spy on me for him."

At this Aadan looked surprised. "He said that?"

"Why?" She glanced at him. "Is it not true?"

He shook his head. "It's true, I just—it doesn't matter. I'm sorry I didn't tell you." His brow knit for a moment. "That night after the ball—"

"You don't need to explain," she said quickly.

"My feelings were real."

"As were mine," she replied, sincere. The memory of his eyes, his smell, and the way he had made her feel were still vivid in her mind. "But you were right that night."

"About?"

Curse it, this was not easy. But she knew it had to be done.

"Dragon Class rules wouldn't allow it. No matter

what our feelings, we can't risk expulsion. Or worse."

He nodded. "I've thought about that too. There are no rules about this because there has never been a woman in Dragon Class. "

"And how will this look? The first female dragonrider 'corrupting' a fellow dragonrider just as women are allowed into Dragon Class?" At his expression of protest, she added, "Sometimes we must all do things we don't want to. I think this is the best. For now."

He looked pained, but nodded. "So . . . wing mates then?"

Wanli grumbled his disapproval, but she assured him this was the right thing.

"Always," she smiled.

Aadan studied her as if she was a puzzle to solve. "Something about you has changed since you came back from the Singing Sands."

Jin pulled the last buckle into place, then climbed onto Rayshan's back. "Everything's changed."

She still didn't know the extent of the powers the blood bond had given her and Rayshan, or what dangers those powers held. For now, she would simply take things a day at a time, which also meant keeping her and Rayshan's blood bonding secret. Would she become a monster like Mengkhis Lai? She didn't know. But one thing was certain: she had never felt so alive.

Jin signaled Rayshan, and he took to the air, his roar filling her heart with joy. The women apprentices all looked up, shading their eyes as they looked in equal measures of awe and fear at the great beast rising above the Blood Oval. Almost without thinking, Jin called to the other dragons using her mind—and as one they craned their necks into the air, then bellowed to the rider in the sky.

As she and Rayshan ascended, they passed a gold dragon landing, and Jin recognized Mao in the saddle. She watched him as he landed and leapt down to Emar, and wondered what news he brought.

She was too far away to hear Mao's words. She also didn't see Emar's face pale as he read the words in the letter Mao handed him.

But the news would soon spread through court like fire: Baikalan, the feared Jade of Mengkhis Lai, had escaped the Well of Ice.

Thanks for reading! If you enjoyed this, why not join my reader list? You'll be first to know what happens next in the *Riders of Jade and Fire* series, plus you'll receive:

* *The Queen and the Dagger,* the prequel to my other series, *Book of Theo;*

* exclusive previews and bonus stories. JOIN NOW at www.melanieansley.com

If you enjoyed *Dragon Class*, please consider leaving a review on Amazon and Goodreads. You'll ensure many more of Jin's stories follow.

ACKNOWLEDGMENTS

Thanks to Sam, as always, for being an inspiration in finding one's own path. Thanks also to my kids, who were very patient with their mother's writing sessions.

Thanks to my beta readers, particularly Hannah Greer and also to my editor Mary Therese Hussey. A huge thank you to Heather Grierson and Austin Mitchell, who made sure I was on the right track with Aadan's background and culture.

I'm also extremely grateful to my Advance Reader Copy team. Without you all I wouldn't have a great group to champion the release and spread the word. Thank you for taking time to read this story before everyone else.

Last but not least, thanks to all the readers and subscribers who have come along with me on this journey. I appreciate each one of you!

Q&A

Why Tang China?

I've always been fascinated by Tang China, as it was considered a "golden age". Many of China's most famous stories and historical figures come from this period–including the Empress Wu. It was a time of relative openness and booming trade, where women were able to hold office, wear men's clothes, travel, and play polo on horseback. All of these things were forbidden before, and banned again afterwards. It was also a time when the capital had a large population of foreigners, and so became a melting pot for religions, fashion, food, and the arts.

How much of the history in this is true?

Much of the story is inspired by fact, but I've taken great liberties as well. The Empress Wu did exist, and ruled in her own right (not just through her husband or son) from 690 to 705. The capital city, Changan, was the biggest in the world at the time, with a population of 1 million people–many of them huren like Jin, Emar, and Aadan.

Aadan is loosely modeled on a real Iranian prince, Narsieh, who fled to China in the mid 650s with his father Peroz when his kingdom was invaded by the Arabs. He was in China during Empress Wu's ascent to the throne, so it's possible they knew each other.

Sanjin is a fictional character, but based on the very real secret police force Empress Wu kept–and which I've renamed the Royal Veil for the ROJAF series. Many of the department officials were notoriously ruthless.

Here are some other things in the book that really existed:

- A weighted wine drinking fountain from the spring ball: texts exist describing an elaborate machine in the shape of a mountain at an imperial banquet table, where wine cups could be filled from spouts in the mountain. The spouts would open when goblets were placed underneath, then stop pouring when the goblet was full.
- Nail polish: Tang dynasty women invented

nail polish, using crushed flower petals and beeswax.

- Official seals: in China, every official document had to be inked by the royal seal. Therefore, possession of the seals meant wielding great power.

What language did they speak in Tang China?

The Chinese of the Tang Court was known as Middle Chinese, and was the precursor to languages like Cantonese and Hakka. I took great liberties mixing and matching Mandarin and Cantonese pronunciation for names and places. I did this because Chinese is a tonal language, and therefore a lot of words sound exactly the same on the page when translated into English. For ease of distinguishing names, I decided it was best to not strictly follow one dialect or another, and thereby allow a greater breadth of name choices.

Rayshan and all the other dragons seem like "western" dragons. Why not use "Chinese" dragons?

I had a long debate about this! In Chinese culture, dragons are not traditionally seen as fighters. They are mystical, wise, and connected to nature, traditionally found living in seas or lakes. In imagining the world of Dragon Class, the dragons seemed more of the air and of war, more like the aggressive fire breathing dragons of western folklore. So I went with what Rayshan and the story was trying to tell me, rather than bending the

Chinese concept of a dragon to fit Jin's story. But who knows, perhaps I will write a story with Chinese style dragons in future.

Where did the idea of dragons loving oranges come from?

My childhood dog, Lady, loved oranges and mandarins, to the point where you couldn't break the skin of one without immediately hearing her race from the other end of the house to come find her favorite treat. I thought even meat loving dragons must have soft spots for unusual things.

Does Rayshan's name mean anything?

Rayshan's name was inspired by the Chinese word "rui", which means sharp, and "shan", meaning "compassion". The idea of a dragon who is both dangerous and compassionate appealed to me, and so this name seemed appropriate.

ABOUT THE AUTHOR

Melanie was born in Canada but raised in China, and now lives in Ballarat, Australia with her husband and two children. She loves to read, write, and laugh. She also makes movies.

ALSO BY MELANIE ANSLEY

The *Book of Theo* series:

Theo and the Forbidden Language

Theo and the Secret of Elshon

Theo and the Stolen Library

The *Riders of Jade & Fire* series:

Night of the Black Dragon

Dragon Class

www.ingramcontent.com/pod-product-compliance
Lightning Source LLC
Chambersburg PA
CBHW010315100726
47906CB00006B/1004